Mrs Peix

Henry Harland

Alpha Editions

This edition published in 2023

ISBN : 9789357951449

Design and Setting By
Alpha Editions
www.alphaedis.com
Email - info@alphaedis.com

Contents

CHAPTER I
A CASE IS STATED.

ON more than one account the 25th of April will always be a notable anniversary in the calendar of Mr. Arthur Ripley. To begin with, on that day he pocketed his first serious retainer as a lawyer.

He got down-town a little late that morning. The weather was superb—blue sky and summer temperature. Central Park was within easy walking distance. His own engagements, alas, were not pressing. So he had treated himself to an afterbreakfast ramble across the common.

On entering his office, toward eleven o'clock, he was surprised to find the usually empty chairs already tenanted. Mr. Mendel, the brewer, was established there, in company with two other gentlemen whom Arthur did not recognize. The sight of these visitors caused the young man a palpitation. Could it be—? He dared not complete the thought. That a client had at last sought him out, was too agreeable an hypothesis to be entertained.

Mr. Mendel greeted him with the effusiveness for which he is distinguished, and introduced his companions respectively as Mr. Peixada and Mr. Rimo. Of old time, when Arthur's father was still alive, and when Arthur himself had trotted about in knee-breeches and short jackets, Mr. Mendel had been their next door neighbor. Now he made the lawyer feel undignified by asking a string of personal questions: "Vail, how iss mamma?" and "Not married yet, eh?" and "*Lieber Gott!* You must be five-and-twenty—so tall, and with dot long mustache—yes?" And so forth; smiling the while with such benevolence that Arthur could not help answering politely, though he did hope that a desire for family statistics was not the sole motive of the brewer's visit.

But by and by Mendel cleared his throat, and assumed a look of importance. His voice modulated into a graver key, as he announced, "The fact is that we—or rather, my friends, Mr. Peixada and Mr. Rimo—want to consult you about a little matter of business." He leaned back in his chair, drawing a deep breath, as though the speech had exhausted him; mopped his brow with his handkerchief, and flourished his thumb toward Peixada.

"Ah," replied Arthur, bowing to the latter, "I am happy to be at your service, sir."

"Yes," said Peixada, in a voice several sizes larger than the situation required, "Mr. Mendel recommends you to us as a young man who is smart, and who, at the same time, is not so busy but that he can bestow upon our affairs the attention we wish them to have."

Notwithstanding Arthur's delight at the prospect of something to do, Peixada's tone, a mixture as it was of condescension and imperiousness, jarred a little. Arthur did not like the gratuitous assumption that he was "not so busy," etc., true though it might be; nor did he like the critical way in which Peixada eyed him. "Indeed," he said, speaking of it afterward, "it gave me very much such a sensation as a fellow must experience when put up for sale in the Turkish slave market—a feeling that my 'points' were being noted, and my money value computed. I half expected him to continue, 'Open your mouth, show your teeth!'.rdquo; Peixada was a tall, portly individual of fifty-odd, with a swarthy skin, brown, beady eyes, a black coat upon his back, and a fat gold ring around his middle finger. The top of his head was as bald as a Capuchin's, and shone like a disk of varnished box-wood. It was surrounded by a circlet of crisp, dark, curly hair. He had a solemn manner that proclaimed him to be a person of consequence. It turned out that he was president of a one-horse insurance company. Mr. Rimo appeared to be but slightly in advance of Arthur's own age—a tiny strip of a body, wearing a resplendent cravat, a dotted waistcoat, pointed patent-leather gaiters, and finger-nails trimmed talon-shape—a thoroughbred New York dandy, of the least effeminate type.

"I suppose the name, Peixada," the elder of the pair went on, "is not wholly unfamiliar to you."

"Oh, no—by no means," Arthur assented, wondering whether he had ever heard it before.

"I suppose the circumstances of my brother's death are still fresh in your mind."

Arthur put on an intelligent expression, and inwardly deplored his ignorance. Yet—Peixada?

Peixada? the name did have a familiar ring, of a truth. But where and in what connection had he heard it?

"Let me see," he ventured, "that was in—?"

"In July, 'seventy-nine—recollect?"

Ah, yes; to be sure; he recollected. So this man was a brother of the Peixada who, rather less than half a dozen years ago, had been murdered, and whose murder had set New York agog. In a general way Arthur recalled the glaring accounts of the matter that had appeared in the newspapers at the time. "Yes," he said, feeling that it behooved him to say something, "it was very sad."

"Fearful!" put in Mr. Mendel.

"Of course," Peixada resumed, in his pompous style, "of course you followed the trial as it was reported in the public prints; but perhaps you have forgotten the particulars. Had I better refresh your memory?"

"That would be a good idea," said Arthur.—To what was the way being paved?

With the air of performing a ceremony, Peixada rose, unbuttoned his coat, extracted a bulky envelope from the inner pocket, re-seated himself, and handed the envelope to Arthur. It proved to contain newspaper clippings. "Please glance them through," said Peixada.

The Peixada murder had been a sensational and peculiarly revolting affair. One July night, 1879, Mr. Bernard Peixada, "a retired Jewish merchant," had died at the hands of his wife. Edward Bolen, coachman, in the attempt to protect his employer, had sustained a death-wound for himself. Mrs. Peixada, "the perpetrator of these atrocities," as Arthur gathered from the records now beneath his eye, "was a young and handsome woman, of a respectable Hebrew family, who must have been actuated by a depraved desire to possess herself of her husband's wealth." They had "surprised her all but red-handed in the commission of the crime," though "too late to avert its dire results." Eventually she was tried in the Court of General Sessions, and acquitted on the plea of insanity. Arthur remembered—as, perhaps, the reader does—that her acquittal had been the subject of much popular indignation. "She is no more insane than you or I," every body had said; "she is simply lacking in the moral sense. Another evidence that you can't get a jury to be impartial when a pretty woman is concerned."

"She was bad," continued Peixada, as Arthur returned the papers, "bad through and through. I warned my brother against her before his marriage.

"'What,' said I, 'what do you suppose she would marry an old man like you for, except your money?' He said, 'Never mind.' She was young and showy, and Bernard lost his head."

"She was doocedly handsome, a sooperb creature to look at, you know," cried Mr. Rimo, with the accent of a connoisseur.

"Hainsome is as hainsome does," quoth Mr. Mendel, sententiously.

"She was as cold as ice, as hard as alabaster," said Peixada, perhaps meaning adamant. "The point is that after her release from prison she took out letters of administration upon my brother's estate."

"Why, I thought she was insane," said Arthur. "A mad woman would not be a competent administratrix."

"Exactly. I interposed objections on that ground. But she answered that she had recovered; that although insane a few months before—at the time of the murder—she was all right again now. The surrogate decided in her favor. A convenient form of insanity, eh?"

"Were there children?" Arthur inquired.

"No—none. My nephew, Mr. Rimo, son of my sister who is dead, and I myself, were the only next of kin. She paid us our shares right away." Then what could he be driving at now? Arthur waited for enlightenment.

"But now," Peixada presently went on, "now I have discovered that my brother left a will."

"Ah, I understand. You wish to have it admitted to probate?"

"Precisely. But first I wish to find Mrs. Peixada. The will isn't worth the paper it's written on, unless we can get hold of her. You see, she has about half the property in her possession."

"There was no real estate?"

"Not an acre; but the personalty amounted to a good many thousands of dollars."

"And you don't know where she is?"

"I haven't an idea."

"Have you made any efforts to find out?"

"Well, I should say I had—made every effort in my power. That's what brings me here. I want you to carry on the search."

"I shouldn't imagine it would be hard work. A woman—a widow—of wealth is always a conspicuous object—trebly so, when she is handsome too, and has been tried for murder. But tell me, what, have you done?"

"You'll be surprised when you hear. I myself supposed it would be plain sailing. But listen." Peixada donned a pair of gold-rimmed spectacles, opened a red leather memorandum-book, and read aloud from its pages. The substance of what he read was this. He had begun by visiting Mrs. Peixada's attorneys, Messrs. Short and Sondheim, the firm that had defended her at her trial. With them he got his labor for his pains. They had held no communication with the lady in question since early in January, 1881, at which date they had settled her accounts before the surrogate. She was then traveling from place to place in Europe. Her last letter, postmarked Vienna, had said that for the next two months her address would be *poste restante* at the same city. From the office of Short and Sondheim Mr. Peixada went to the office of his sister-in-law's surety, the Eagle and Phoenix Trust

Company, No.—Broadway. There he was referred to the secretary, Mr. Oxford. Mr. Oxford told him that the Company had never had any personal dealings with the administratrix, she having acted throughout by her attorneys. The Company had required the entire assets of the estate to be deposited in its vaults, and had honored drafts only on the advice of counsel. Thus protected, the Company had had no object in keeping the administratrix in view. Our inquirer next bethought him of Mrs. Peixada's personal friends—people who would be likely still to maintain relations with her—and saw such of these as he could get at. One and all professed ignorance of her whereabouts—had not heard of her or from her since the winter of '80—'81. Finally it occurred to him that as his brother's estate had consisted solely of stocks and bonds, he could by properly directed investigations learn to what corner of the world Mrs. Peixada's dividends were sent. But this last resort also proved a failure. The stocks and bonds, specified in the surrogate's inventory, had been sold out. He could find no clew to the reinvestments made of the money realized.

Peixada closed his note-book with a snap.

"You see," he said, "I've been pretty thorough and pretty unsuccessful. Can you think of any stone that I have left unturned?"

"How about relatives? Have you questioned her relatives?" asked Arthur.

"Of relatives—in America, at least—Mrs. P. has none. Her father died shortly after her marriage. Her mother died during the trial."

"But uncles, aunts, sister, brothers?"

"None to my knowledge. She was an only child."

"Her maiden-name was—?"

"Karon—Judith Karon. Her father, Michael Karon, used to keep a jewelry store on Second Avenue."

"About what is her age?"

"She was twenty-one at the time of the murder. That would make her twenty-five or six now."

"So young, indeed? Have you a photograph of her?"

"A photograph? No. I don't know that she ever sat for one. But I have these."

Peixada produced a couple of rough wood-engravings, apparently cuttings from illustrated papers, and submitted them for examination.

"They don't look any thing like each other," said Arthur. "Does either of them look like her?"

"Not much," Peixada answered. "In fact, the resemblance is so slight that they wouldn't assist at all in identifying her. On the contrary, I think they'd lead you quite astray."

Said Mr. Rimo, "Bah! They give you no more idea of her than they do of Queen Victoria. They'd answer for any other woman just as well."

Arthur said, "That's too bad. But I suppose you have brought a copy of the will?"

"Oh, yes, here's the original. It is in my brother's handwriting, dated a month before his death, and witnessed by two gentlemen of high standing. I have spoken to each of them. They acknowledge their signatures, and remember the circumstances. I made a search for a will right after Bernard died, but could find none. This I unearthed most unexpectedly. I was turning over the leaves of my poor brother's prayer-book, when, there it was, lying between the pages."

The will was brief and vigorous. In the name of God, amen, (on a half-sheet of legal-cap), it devised and bequeathed all the property, real or personal, of which testator should die seized or possessed, to his dearly beloved brother, Benjamin Peixada, and his dearly beloved nephew, Maurice Rimo, for them to hold and enjoy the same, in fee simple, share and share alike, absolutely and forever, provided that they should pay annually to testator's widow, (until such time as she should re-marry, or depart this life), the sum of three hundred dollars. It was attested by a well-known Jewish physician and by a well-known Jewish banker.

"It would seem from this," said Arthur, "that your brother got bravely over his illusions concerning his wife. It's lucky he had no real estate. She would be entitled to her dower, you know, as a matter of course."

"Yes, I know; and I guess that was the reason why my brother converted all his real estate into personalty shortly after his marriage—so that he could dispose of it as he chose. The reference to real estate here in the will is doubtless an inadvertence. He was probably following a form. He couldn't trust his wife. She made his life wretched."

"Well," Arthur began—but Peixada interrupted.

"I want you," he said in his dictatorial way, "to name a sum for which you will undertake to continue this investigation and bring it to a successful issue; that is, find Mrs. P., have the will proved, and compel her to refund the property—upwards of one hundred thousand dollars, unless she has squandered it—that remains subject to her control."

"Oh, I can't name a lump sum off-hand," replied Arthur, "neither can I guarantee success. I would of course do my utmost to succeed, but there is always the chance of failure. The amount of my compensation would be determined by the time I should have to spend, and the difficulties I should have to encounter."

"That sounds reasonable. Then suppose I should agree to defray all expenses by the way, pay a fee, as you suggest, proportionate to your service at the end, and now at the outset give you a retainer of—say two hundred and fifty dollars; would you be satisfied?"

Arthur's heart leaped. But to exhibit his true emotions would be unprofessional. He constrained himself to answer quietly, "Yes, I should be satisfied." It was, however, with a glow of genuine enthusiasm for his client that he folded up a check for the tidy sum of two hundred and fifty dollars, and tucked it into his pocket.

Said Peixada, "I shall trust the entire management of this business to your discretion. Only one thing I shall suggest. I think an adroitly worded advertisement in the principal newspapers of this country and Europe—an advertisement that would lead the reader to suppose that we felt friendly toward Mrs. P.—would be a wise measure. For instance, a notice to the effect that she could learn something to her advantage by communicating with you."

"Oh, that would be scarcely honorable, would it?"

"Honorable? In dealing with a murderess—with a woman, moreover, who is enjoying wealth not rightly hers—talk about honorable! All means are fair by which to catch a thief."

"But even so, she would be too shrewd to take the bait. An advertisement would merely put her on her guard. Mustn't bell the cat, you know."

"That's one way of considering it. On the other hand—However, I simply offer the suggestion; you're the pilot and can take whatever course you please."

"Well, then, we'll reserve our advertisement till other expedients have failed. The first thing to do is—" But Arthur stopped himself. He did not clearly know what the first thing to do was. "I'll think about it," he added.

"Good," said Peixada, rising; "there's nothing further for me to detain you with to-day."

"Give my regards to mamma, when you write, Arthur," said Mr. Mendel.

"I leave you my memoranda," said Peixada, laying his note-book upon Arthur's desk.

"Take care of yourself," enjoined Mr. Rimo, smiling and waving his hand.

The three gentlemen filed out. Arthur remained seated in his arm-chair a long while after their departure, his eyes fixed upon the wall, his fingers busily twirling his mustache. For three years he had been enrolled among the members of the bar. This was the first case he had received that seemed really worthy of his talents.

CHAPTER II.
"A VOICE, A MYSTERY."

ARTHUR RIPLEY—good-natured, impressionable, unpractical Arthur Ripley, as his familiars called him—dwelt in Beekman Place. Beek-man Place, as the reader may not know, is a short, chocolate-colored, unpretentious thoroughfare, perched on the eastern brink of Manhattan Island, and commanding a fine view of the river, of the penitentiary, and of the oil factories at Hunter's Point. Arthur and a friend of his, Mr. Julian Hetzel, kept house in the two upper stories of No. 43, an old German woman named Josephine acting as their maid-of-all-work. They had a kitchen, a dining-room, a parlor, two airy dormitories, a light closet which did duty for a guest-chamber; and over and above all, they had the roof. Upon the roof Hetzel had swung a hammock, and in earthen pots round about had ranged an assortment of flowering shrubs; so that by courtesy the roof was commonly styled the *loggia.* Here, toward sundown on that summery April day mentioned in the last chapter, the chums were seated, sipping their after-dinner coffee and smoking their after-dinner cigarettes. They could not have wished for a pleasanter spot for their pleasant occupation. By fits and starts a sweet breeze puffed up from the south. Westward the sun was sinking into a crimson fury. Eastward the horizon glowed with a delicate pink light. Below them, on one side, stretched the river—tinted like mother-o'-pearl by the ruddy sky overhead—up which a procession of Sound steamboats was sweeping in stately single file. On the other side lay the street, clamorous with the voices of many children at sport. Around the corner, an itinerant band was playing selections from Trovatore. Blatant and faulty though the music was, softened by distance, it had a quite agreeable effect. Of course, the topic of conversation was Arthur's case.

Hetzel said, "It will be slow work, and tedious."

"On the contrary," retorted Arthur, "it seems to me to furnish an opportunity for brilliant strategy. I must get a clew, you know, and then clinch the business with a few quick strokes."

"Just so; after the manner of Monsieur Lecoq. Well, where do you propose to strike your clew?"

"Oh, I haven't started in yet. I suppose I shall hit upon one soon enough."

"I doubt it. In my opinion you're booked for a sequence of wearisome details. The quality you'll require most of, is patience. Besides, if the lady should sniff danger, she'll be able to elude you at every turn. You want to make it a still hunt."

"I am aware of that."

"What's the first step you mean to take?"

"I haven't made up my mind. I need time for deliberation."

"There's only a single thing to do, and that's not the least Lecoq-like. Write to the place where she was last known to be—Vienna, did you say?—to the consul or postmaster or prefect of police, or better yet all three, and ask whither she went when she left there. Then, provided you get an answer, write to the next place, and so on down. This will take about a hundred years. So, practically, you see, Peixada has supplied you with permanent employment. The likelihood that it will ultimately succeed is extremely slim. There is danger of a slip-up at every point. However, far be it from me to discourage you."

"What do you think of Peixada's plan—an advertisement?"

"Gammon! You don't fancy she would march with open eyes into a palpable trap like that, do you? I suspect the matter will end by your making a trip to Europe. If Peixada knows what's what, he'll bundle you off next week. You could trace her much more effectively in person than by letters."

"Wouldn't that be jolly? Only it would involve my neglecting the other business that might turn up if I should stick here."

"What of it? What other business? What ground have you for believing that any other business will turn up? Has the past been so prolific? Besides, isn't the summer coming? And isn't the summer a lawyer's dull season? You might lose a couple of two-penny district-court cases; but suppose you did. See of what advantage it would be to your reputation. Somebody calls at your office. 'Is Mr. Ripley in?' 'No,' replies your clerk, 'Mr. Ripley is abroad on important business.' 'Ah,' thinks the caller, 'this Ripley is a flourishing young practitioner.' And mark my words, nothing hastens success like a reputation for success."

"Such a picture sends the blood to my head. I mustn't look at it. It would make me discontented with the reality."

"If you're diplomatic," Hetzel went on, "you can get a liberal education out of this Peixada case. Just fancy jaunting from town to town in Europe, and having your expenses paid. In your moments of leisure you can study art and languages and the manners, costumes, and superstitions of the hoary east."

"And all the while, Mrs. Peixada may be living quietly here in New York! Isn't it exasperating to realize the difficulty of putting your finger upon a given human being, when antecedently it would seem so easy? Nevermind; up-hill work though it be, it's sure to get interesting. A woman, young, beautiful, totally depraved, a murderess at the age of twenty-one—I wonder what she is like."

"Oh, probably vulgar to the last degree. Don't form a sentimental conception of her. Keep your head cool, or else your imagination will get the better of your common sense."

"No fear of that. But I shall go at the case with all the more zest, because I am anxious to view this novel specimen of womankind."

"You'll find she's a loud, flashy vixen—snapping eyes, strident voice, bediamonded person. Women who resort to powder and shot to get rid of their husbands in this peaceable epoch of divorce, are scarcely worth a respectable man's curiosity."

"Hello!" cried Arthur, abruptly. "What's that?"

"Oh, that," answered Hetzel, "that's the corner house—No. 46."

Hetzel spoke metonymically. "That" was a descending musical scale—*fa, mi, re, do, si, la, sol, fa,*—which rang out all at once in a clear soprano voice, from someplace near at hand; a wonderfully powerful voice, with a superb bugle-like quality.

"*Fa, sol, la, si, do, re, mi, fa,*" continued the songstress. .

"By Jove," exclaimed Arthur, "that's something like." Then for a moment he was all ears, and did not speak. At last, "The corner house?" he queried. "Has some one moved in?"

"Yes," was Hetzel's answer; "they moved in yesterday. I had this all the morning."

"This singing?"

"Exactly, and a piano to boot. Scales and exercises till I was nearly mad."

"But this—this is magnificent. You were to be envied."

"Oh, yes, it's very fine. But when a man is trying to prepare an examination paper in the integral calculus, it distracts and interferes. She quite broke up my morning's work." Hetzel was a tutor of mathematics in a college not a hundred miles from New York.

"Have you seen her?" Arthur asked.

"No, they only took possession yesterday. A singular thing about it is that they appear to confine themselves to one floor. The blinds are closed every where except in the third story, and last night there was no light except in the third story windows. Queer, eh?"

Arthur approached the verge of the roof, and looked over at the corner house across the street. The third story windows were open wide, and out of them proceeded that beautiful soprano voice, now practicing intervals—*fa-*

si, sol-do, and so forth. "Well," he affirmed, "this is a regular romance. Of course a woman with such a voice is young and beautiful and every thing else that's lovely. And then, living cooped up on the third floor of that dismal corner house—she must be in needy circumstances; which adds another element of charm and mystery. I suppose she's in training to become a prima donna. But who are *they?* Who lives with her?"

"How should I know? I haven't seen any of them. I take it for granted that she doesn't live alone, that's all."

"Hush-sh!" cried Arthur, motioning with his hand.

The invisible musician had now abandoned her exercises, and was fairly launched upon a song, accompanying herself with a piano. Neither Arthur nor Hetzel recognized the tune, but they greatly enjoyed listening to it, because it was rendered with so much intelligence and delicacy of expression. They could not make out the words, either, but from the languid, sensuous swing of the melody, it was easy to infer that the theme was love. There were several verses; and after each of them, occurred a brilliant interlude upon the piano, in which the refrain was caught up and repeated with variations. Arthur thought he had never heard sweeter music in his life; and very likely he never had. "That woman," he declared, when silence was restored, "that woman, whoever she is, has a *soul*—a rare enough piece of property in this materialistic age. Such power of making music betokens a corresponding power of deep feeling, clear thinking, noble acting. I'd give my right hand for a glimpse of her. Why doesn't some mesmeric influence bring her to the window? Oh, for an Asmodeus to unroof her dwelling, and let me peep in at her—observe her, as she sits before her key-board, unconscious of observation!" Even Hetzel, who was not prone to enthusiasms, who, indeed, derived an expert's satisfaction from applying the wet blanket, admitted that she sang "like an angel."

Arthur went on, "Opera? Talk about opera? Why, this beats the opera all hollow. Can you conceive a more exquisite *mise en scene?* Twilight! Lingering in the west—over there behind the cathedral—a pale, rosy flush! Above, a star or two, twinkling diamond-like on the breast of the coming night! In our faces, the fragrance of the south wind! Below us, the darkling river, alive with multitudinous craft! Can your Opera House, can your Academy of Music boast any thing equal to it? And then, as the flower and perfection of this loveliness, sounding like a clarion from heaven, that glorious woman's voice. I tell you, man, it's poetry—it's Rossetti, Alfred de Musset, Heinrich Heine—it's—Hello! there she goes again."

This time her selection was the familiar but ever beautiful *Erl Konig*, which she sang with such dramatic spirit that Hetzel himself exclaimed, when she had finished, "It actually made my heart stand still."

"'*Du liebes Kind, komm geh mit mir!*'" hummed Arthur. "Ah, how persuasively she murmured it! And then, '*Mein Vater, mein Vater, und horest du nicht?*'.—wasn't it blood-curdling? Didn't it convey the entire horror of the situation? the agony of terror that bound the child's heart? Beekman Place has had an invaluable acquisition. I'll wager, she's as good and as beautiful as St. Cecilia, her patroness. What do you guess, is she dark or fair, big or little?"

"The odds are that she's old and ugly. Patti herself, you know, is upwards of forty. It isn't probable that with her marvelous musical accomplishments, this lady is endowed with youth and beauty also. I wouldn't cherish great expectations of her, if I were you; because then, if you should ever chance to see her, you'll be so much disappointed. Better make up your mind that her attractions begin and end with her voice. Complexion? Did you ask my opinion of her complexion? Oh, she's blonde—that goes without saying."

"Wrong again! She's a brunette of the first water; dusky skin, red mouth, black, lustrous eyes. You can tell that from the fire she puts into her music. As for her age, you're doubly mistaken. If you had the least faculty for adding two and two together—arithmetician that you are—you'd know at once that a voice of such freshness, such compass, and such volume, could not pertain to a woman far beyond twenty. On the other hand, no mere school-girl could sing with such intelligent expression. Wherefore, striking an average, I'll venture she's in the immediate vicinity of twenty-five. However, conjectures are neither here nor there. Where's Josephine? Let's have her up, and interrogate her."

With this speech, Arthur began to pound his heel upon the roof—the method which these young bachelors employed to make known to their domestic that her attendance was wanted. When the venerable Josephine had emerged waist-high from the scuttle-door, "Josephine," demanded Arthur, "who is the new tenant of the corner house?"

But Josephine could not tell. Indeed, she was not even aware that the corner house had been taken. Arthur set her right on this score, and, "Now," he continued, "I wish you would gossip with the divers and sundry servants of the neighborhood until you have found out the most you can about these new-comers, and then report to me. For this purpose, you are allowed an evening's outing. But as you prize my good-will, be both diligent and discreet."

As the twilight deepened into darkness, Arthur remained posted at the roof's edge, looking wistfully over toward the third-story windows of the corner house. By and by a light flashed up behind them; but the next instant an unseen hand drew the shades; and a few moments later the light was extinguished.

"They retire early," he grumbled.

"By the way, don't you think it's getting a little chilly up here?" asked Hetzel.

"Decidedly," he assented, shivering. "Shall we go below?"

They descended into their sitting-room—a cozy, book-lined apartment, with a permanent savor of tobacco smoke upon its breath—and chatted together till a late hour. The Peixada matter and the mysterious songstress of No. 46 pretty equally divided their attention.

Next morning Hetzel—whose bed-chamber, at the front of the house, overlooked the street; whereas Arthur's, at the rear, overlooked the river—Hetzel was awakened by a loud rap at his door.

"Eh—er—what? Who is it?" he cried, starting up in bed.

"Can I come in?" Arthur's voice demanded.

Without waiting for a reply, Arthur entered.

Hetzel's wits getting out of tangle, "What unheard-of event brings you abroad so early?" he inquired.

"Early? You don't call this early? It's halfpast seven."

"Well, that's a round half hour earlier than I ever knew you to rise before. 'Is any thing the matter? Are you ill?"

"Bosh! I'm always up at half-past seven," averred Arthur, with brazen indifference to the truth.

He crossed the floor, and sent the curtains screeching aloft; having done which, he established himself in a rocking-chair, facing the window, and rocked to and fro.

"Ah, I—I understand," said Hetzel.

"Understand what?"

"The motive that impelled you to rise with the lark."

"You're making much ado about nothing," said Arthur. But he blushed and fidgeted uncomfortably. "Any body would suppose I was an inveterate sluggard. Grant that I *am* up a little in advance of my usual hour—is that an occasion for so much talk?"

"The question is, rather," rejoined Hetzel, with apparent irrelevancy, "are you rewarded?"

For a moment Arthur tried to appear puzzled; but as his eyes met those of his comrade, the corners of his mouth twitched convulsively; and thereupon, with a shrug of the shoulders, he laughed outright.

"Well, I'm not ashamed, anyhow," he said.

"I'd give a good deal for a glimpse of her; and if I can catch one before I go down-town, why shouldn't I?"

"Of course," replied Hetzel, sympathetically.

"But don't be secretive. Let's have the results of your observation."

"Oh, as yet the results are scanty. The household seems to be asleep—blinds down, and every thing as still as a mouse.—No, there, the blinds are raised—but whoever raises them knows how to keep out of sight. Not even a hand comes in view.—Now, all's quiet again.—Ah, speaking of mice, they have a cat. A black cat sallies forth upon the stone ledge outside the window, and performs its ablutions with tongue and paw.—Another! Two cats. This one is of the tiger sort, striped black and gray. Isn't it odd—two cats? What on earth, do you suppose, possesses them to keep two cats?—One of them, the black one, returns indoors. Number two whets his claws upon the wood of the window frame—gazes hungrily at the sparrows flitting round about—yawns—curls himself up—prepares for a nap there on the stone in the sun.—Why doesn't *she* come to the window? She ought to want a breath of the morning air. This is exasperating."

The above monologue had been delivered piecemeal, at intervals of a minute or so in duration. At its finish, Hetzel got out of bed.

"Well," he cried, stretching himself, "maintain your vigil, while I go for a bath. Perhaps on my return you may have something more salient to communicate."

But when he came back, Arthur said, "Not a sign of life since you left, except that in response to a summons from within the tiger-cat has reentered the house; probably is discussing his breakfast at this moment. Hurry up—dress—and let us do likewise."

At the breakfast table, "Well, Josephine," said Arthur, "tell us of the night."

Josephine replied that she had subjected all the available maid-servants of the block to a pumping process, but that the most she had been able to extract from them was—what her employers already knew. On Thursday, the 24th, some person or persons to the deponents unknown, had moved into No. 46. But two cart-loads of furniture, besides a piano, had been delivered there; and the new occupants appeared to have taken only one floor: whence it was generally assumed that they were not people of very great consequence. Arthur directed her to keep her eyes and ears open, and to inform him from time to time of any further particulars that she might glean. This she promised to do. Then he lingered about the front of the house till Hetzel began to twit him, demanding sarcastically whether he wasn't going downtown at all that morning. "Oh, well, I suppose I must," he sighed, and reluctantly took himself off.

Down-town he stopped at the surrogate's office, and verified the statements Peixada had made about the administration of his brother's estate. Mrs. Peixada had taken the oath to her accounting before the United States consul at Vienna, January 11, 1881, Short and Sondheim appearing for her here. It was decidedly against the woman—added, if any thing could add, to the blackness of her offense—the fact that she was represented by such disreputable attorneys as Short and Sondheim.

From the court house, Arthur proceeded to Peixada's establishment in Reade Street near Broadway. He had concluded that the search for Mrs. Peixada would have to be very much such an inch by inch process as Hetzel had predicted. He could not rid his mind of a feeling that on general principles it ought to be no hard task to determine the whereabouts of a rich, handsome, and notorious widow: but when he came down to the circumstances of this particular case, he had to acknowledge that it was an undertaking fraught with difficulties and with uncertainties. He wanted to consult his client, and tell him the upshot of his own deliberations. The more he considered it, the more persuaded he became that he had better cross the ocean and follow in person the trail that Mrs. Peixada had doubtless left behind her. Probably the wish fostered the thought. As Hetzel had said, he would not run the risk of losing much by his absence. A summer in Europe had been the fondest dream of his youth. The very occupation of itself, moreover, was inviting. He would be a huntsman—his game, a beautiful woman! And then, to conduct the enterprise by letters would not merely consume an eternity of time, but ten chances to one, it would end in failure. It did not strike him that this was properly a detective's employment, rather than a lawyer's; and even had it done so, I don't know that it would have dampened his ardor.—Meanwhile, he had turned into Reade Street, and reached Peixada's place. He was surprised to find it closed, until he remembered that to-day was Saturday and that Peixada was an orthodox Jew. So he saw nothing for it but to remain inactive till Monday. He returned to his office, and spent the remainder of the day reading a small, canary-colored volume in the French language—presumably a treatise upon French jurisprudence.

He dined with a couple of professional brethren at a restaurant that evening, and did not get home till after dark. Ascending his stoop, he stopped to glance over at the corner house. A light shone at the edges of the curtains in the third story; but even as he stood there, looking toward it, and wishing that by some necromancy his gaze might be empowered to penetrate beyond, the light went out. Immediately afterward, however, he heard the shades fly clattering upward; and then, all at once, the silence was cloven by the same beautiful soprano voice that had interested him so much the night before. At first it was very low and soft, a mere liquid murmur; but gradually it waxed stronger and more resonant; and Arthur recognized the melody as that of Schubert's *Wohin*. The dreamy, plaintive phrases, tremulous with doubt and tense with yearning, gushed in a mellow stream from out the darkness. No wonder they set Arthur's curiosity on edge. The exquisite quality of the voice, and the perfect understanding with which the song was interpreted, were enough to prompt a myriad visions of feminine loveliness in any man's brain. That a woman could sing in this wise, and yet not be pure and bright and beautiful, seemed a self-contradictory proposition. Arthur seated himself comfortably upon the broad stone balustrade of his door-step, and made up his mind that he would retain that posture until the musical entertainment across the way should be concluded.

"I wonder," he soliloquized, "why she chooses to sing in the dark. I hope, for reasons of sentiment—because it is in darkness that the effect of music is strongest and most subtle. I wonder whether she is alone, or whether she is singing to somebody—perhaps her lover. I wonder—ah, with what precision she caught that high note! How firmly she held it! How daintily she executed the cadenza! A woman who can sing like this, how she could love! Or rather, how she must have loved already! For such a comprehension of passion as her music reveals, could never have come to be, except through love. I wonder whether I shall ever know her. Heaven help me, if she should turn out, as Hetzel suspects, old and ugly. But that's not possible. Whatever the style of her features may be, whatever the number of her years, a young and ardent spirit stirs within her. Isn't it from the spirit that true beauty springs? I mean by the spirit, the capability of inspiring and of experiencing noble emotions. This woman is human. Her music proves that. And just in so far as a woman is deeply, genuinely human, is she lovely and lovable."

In this platitudinous vein Arthur went on. Meanwhile the lady had wandered away from Schubert's *Wohin*, and after a brief excursion up and down the keyboard, had begun a magically sweet and thrilling melody, which her auditor presently identified as Chopin's *Berceuse*, so arranged that the performer could re-enforce certain periods with her voice. He listened, captivated, to the supple modulations of the music: and it was with a sensation very like a pang of physical pain that suddenly he heard it come to an abrupt termination-break sharply off in the middle of a bar, as though interrupted by some second person. "If it is her lover to whom she is singing," he said, "I don't blame him for stopping her. He could no longer hold himself back—resist the impulse to kiss the lips from which such beautiful sounds take wing." Then, immediately, he reproached himself for harboring such impertinent fancies. And then he waited on the alert, hoping that the music would recommence. But he waited and hoped in vain. At last, "Well, I suppose there'll be no more to-night," he muttered, and turned to enter the house. As he was inserting his latch-key into the lock, somebody below on the sidewalk pronounced a hoarse "G'd evening, Mr. Ripley."

"Ah, good evening, William," returned Arthur, affably, looking down at a burly figure at the bottom of the steps.—William was the night-watchman of Beekman Place.

"Oh, I say—by the way—William—" called Arthur, as the watchman was proceeding up the street.

"Yassir?" queried William, facing about.

Arthur ran down the stoop and joined his interlocutor at the foot.

"I say, William, I see No. 46 has found a tenant. You don't happen to know who it is?"

"Yes," responded William; "moved in Thursday—old party of the name of Hart."

"Old party? Indeed! Then I suppose he has a daughter—eh? It was the daughter who was singing a little while ago?"

"I dunno if she's got a darter. Party's a woman. I hain't seen no darter. Mebbe it was the lady herself."

"Oh, no; that's not possible.—Hart, do you say the name is?"

"Mrs. G. Hart."

"What does G. stand for?"

"I dunno. Might be John."

"Who is *Mr.* G. Hart?"

"I guess there ain't none. Folks say she's a I widder.—Well, Wiggins ought to thank his stars to have that house taken at last. It's going on four years now, it's lain there empty."

Mused Arthur, absently, "An old lady named Hart; and he doesn't know whether the musician is her daughter or not."

"Fact is," put in William, "I dunno much about 'em—only what I've heerd. But we'll know all about them before long. Every body knows every body in this neighborhood."

"Yes, that's so.—Well, good night."

"Good night, sir," said William, touching his cap.

Upstairs in the sitting-room, Arthur threw himself upon a sofa. Hetzel was away. By and by Arthur picked up a book from the table, and tried to read. He made no great headway, however: indeed, an hour elapsed, and he had not yet turned the page. His thoughts were busy with the fair one of the corner house. He had spun out quite a history for her before he had done. He devoutly trusted that ere long Fate would arrange a meeting between her and himself. He whistled over the melody of *Wohin*, imitating as nearly as he could the manner in which she had sung it. When his mind reverted to the Peixada business, as it did presently, lo! the prospective trip to Europe had lost half its charm. He felt that there was plenty to keep one interested here in New York.

All day Sunday, despite the fun at his expense in which Hetzel liberally indulged, Arthur haunted the front of the house. But when he went to bed Sunday night, he was no wiser respecting his musical neighbor than he had been four-and-twenty hours before.

CHAPTER III.
STATISTICAL.

MONDAY morning Arthur entered Peixada's warehouse promptly as the clock struck ten. Peixada had not yet got down.

Arthur was conducted by a dapper little salesman to an inclosure fenced off at the rear of the showroom, and bidden to "make himself at home." By and by, to kill time, he picked up a directory—the only literature in sight—and extracted what amusement he could from it, by hunting out the names of famous people—statesmen, financiers, etc. The celebrities exhausted, he turned to his own name and to those of his friends. Among others, he looked for Hart. Of Harts there were a multitude, but of G. Harts only three—a Gustav, a Gerson, and a George. George was written down a laborer, Gerson a peddler, Gustav a barber; none, it was obvious, could be the G. Hart of Beekman Place. In about half an hour Peixada arrived.

"Ah, good morning," he said briskly. "Well?"

"I am sorry to bother you so soon again, Mr. Peixada," said Arthur, stiffly; "but——"

"Oh, that's all right," Peixada interrupted. "Glad to see you. Sit down. Smoke a cigar."

"Then," pursued Arthur, his cigar afire, "having thought the matter well over——"

"You have concluded—?"

"That your view of the case was correct—that we're in for a long, expensive, and delicate piece of business."

"Not a doubt of it."

"You see, beforehand it would strike one as the simplest thing in the world to locate a woman like your sister-in-law. But this case is peculiar. It's going on four years that nobody has heard from her. Clear back in January, 1881, she was somewhere in Vienna. But since then she's had the leisure to travel around the world a dozen times. She may be in Australia, California, Brazil—or not a mile away from us, here in New York. She may have changed her name. She may have married again. She may have died.—The point I'm driving at is that you mustn't attribute it to a lack of diligence on my part, if we shouldn't obtain any satisfactory results for a long while."

"Oh, certainly not, certainly not," protested Peixada, making the words very large, and waving his hand deprecatingly. "I'm a man of common sense, a business man. I don't need to be told that it's going to be slow work. I knew that. Otherwise I shouldn't have hired you. I could have managed it by myself, except that I hadn't the time to spare."

"Well, then," said Arthur, undismayed by Peixada's frankness, "my idea of the tactics to be pursued is to begin with Vienna, January, '81, and proceed inch by inch down to the present time. There are two methods of doing this."

"Which are——?"

"One is to enlist the services of the United States consuls. I can write to Vienna, to our consul, and ask him to find out where Mrs. Peixada went when she left there; then *to* the consul at the next place—and so on to the end. But this method is cumbrous and uncertain. The trail is liable to be lost at any point. At the best, it would take a long, long time. Besides, the consuls would expect a large remuneration."

"Well, the other method?"

"I propose it reluctantly. It is one which, so far as my personal inclinations are concerned, I should prefer not to take. I—I might myself go to Vienna and conduct the investigation on the spot."

"Hum," reflected Peixada.—After a pause, "That would be still more expensive," he said.

"Perhaps."

"Sure.—It seems to me that there is a third method which you haven't thought of."

"Indeed? What is it?"

"Why not engage the services of an attorney in Vienna, instead of the consul's? You can easily get the name of some reliable attorney there. Then write on, stating the case, and offering a sum in consideration of which he is to furnish us with the information we want."

"Yes, I might do that," Arthur answered, with a mortifying sense that Peixada's plan was at once more practical and more promising than either of those which he had proposed.

"Better try it, anyhow," his client went on. "Attorney's fees, as I chance to know, are low in Austria. Fifty dollars ought to be ample for a starter. I'll give you a check for that amount now. You can exchange it for a draft, after you've decided on your man."

Peixada filled out a check. Arthur took up his hat.

"Oh, àpropos," said Peixada, without explaining what it was àpropos of, "I showed you some newspaper clippings about Mrs. P.'. trial the other day—recollect? Well, I've got a scrapbook full of them in my safe. Suppose you'd find it useful?"

"I don't know. It could do no harm for me to run it over."

Peixada touched a bell, gave the requisite orders to the underling who responded, and said to Arthur, "He'll fetch it."

Presently the man returned, bearing a large, square volume, bound in bluish black leather. Arthur bowed himself out, with the volume under his arm.

The remainder of the day he passed in procuring the name of a trustworthy Viennese attorney, drafting a letter to him in English, and having it translated into German. The attorney's name was Ulrich. Arthur inclosed the amount of Peixada's check in the form of an order upon an Americo-Austrian banking house. At last, weary, and with his zeal in Peixada's cause somewhat abated, he went home.

In the course of the evening he dropped into a concert garden on Fifty-eighth Street. He had not been seated there a great while before somebody greeted him with a familiar tap upon the shoulder and an easy "How are you?" Looking up, he saw Mr. Rimo.

"Ah," said Arthur, offering his hand, "how do you do? Sit down."

Mr. Rimo had an odoriferous jonquil in his buttonhole, and carried a silver-headed Malacca cane. He drew up to the table, lit a cigar with a wax match, and called for Vichy water.

"Well, Mr. Ripley," he questioned solicitously, "how are *you* getting on?"

"Oh, very well, thanks. I saw your uncle this morning."

"That so? Any news?"

"You mean about the case? Nothing decisive as yet. It's hardly time to expect anything."

"Oh, no; of course not. I'll tell you one thing. You've got a nice job before you."

"Yes, and an odd one."

"What I was thinking of especially was the lady. She's a specimen. Not many like her."

"It's to be hoped not. You of course knew her very well?"

“No, I can’t say as I did. I can’t say as I *knew* her very well. She wasn’t an easy woman to know. But I’d seen a great deal of her. It was a mere chance that I didn’t marry her myself. Lucky, wasn’t I?”

“Why, how was that?”

“Well, it was this way. You see, one evening while she was still Miss Karon, I called on her. Who should sail in five minutes later but Uncle Barney? She was right up to the top notch that evening—devilish handsome, with her black eyes and high color, and as sharp as an IXL blade. When we left—we left together, the old man and I—when we left, I was saying to myself, ’By gad, I couldn’t do better. I’ll propose for her to-morrow.’ Just then he pipes up. ’What is your opinion of that young lady?’ he asks. ’My opinion?’ says I. ’My opinion is that she’s a mighty fine gal.’ ’Well, you bet she is,’ says he; ’and I’m glad you think so, because she’s apt to be your auntie before a great while.’ ’The devil!’ says I. ’Yes, sir, says he. ’I’ve made up my mind to marry her. I’m going to speak to her father about it in the morning.’ Well, of course that settled my hash. I wasn’t going to gamble against my uncle. Narrow escape, hey?”

Having concluded this picturesque narrative, Mr. Rimo emptied a bumper of sparkling Vichy water, with the remark, “Well, here’s *to* you,” and applied a second wax match to his cigar, which had gone out while he was speaking.

“Who were her people?” asked Arthur. “What sort of a family did she come from?”

“Oh, her family was correct enough. Name was Karon, as you know already. Her old man was a watch-maker by trade, and kept a shop on Second Avenue. I guess he did a pretty comfortable business till he got struck on electricity. He invented some sort of an electric clock, and sent it to the Centennial at Philadelphia. It took the cake; and after that Michael Karon was a ruined man. Why? Because after that he neglected his business, and spent all his time and all the money he had saved, in fooling around and trying to improve what the Centennial judges had thought was good enough. He couldn’t let well alone. Result was he spoiled the clock, and went all to pieces. He was in a desperate bad way when Uncle Barney stepped up and married his daughter. Hang a man who’s got an itch for improvement. What I say is, lay on to a good thing, and then stick to it for all you’re worth.”

“He died shortly after the marriage, didn’t he?”

“Yes—handed in his checks that fall. She had had a tip-top education; used to give lessons in music, and this, that, and the other ’ology. She was the most knowing creature I ever saw—had no end of *chochmah*. Don’t know what *chochmah* is? Well, that means Jewish shrewdness; and she held a corner in it, too. But such a temper! Lord, when she got excited, her eyes were terrible. I can just imagine her downing the old man. I'll never forget the way she looked at me one time."

"Tell me about it."

"Oh, there ain't much to tell—only this. Of course, you know, it's the fashion to kiss the bride at her wedding. But I happened to be on the road at the date of their wedding, and couldn't get back in time. I didn't mean to lose that kiss, just the same. So when I called on them, after my return, 'Aunt Judith,' says I, 'when are you going to liquidate that little debt you owe me?' 'Owe you?' says she, looking surprised. 'I didn't know I owed you any thing.' 'Why, certainly,' says I; 'you owe me a kiss:' She laughed and shied off and tried to change the subject. 'Come,' says I, 'stepup to the captain's office and settle.' 'Yes,' says Uncle Barney, 'kiss your nephew, Judith.' 'But I don't want to kiss him,' says she, beginning to look dark. 'You kiss him,' says Uncle Barney, looking darker. And she—she kissed me. But, gad, the way she glared! Her eyes were just swimming in fire. I swear, it frightened me; and I'm pretty tough. I don't want any more kisses of that sort, thank you. It stung my lips like a hornet." Mr. Rimo drew a deep breath, and caressed the knob of his cane with the apple of his chin. "It was an awful moment," as they say on the stage, he added.

"Who was that—what was his name?—the second of her victims," inquired Arthur.

"Oh, Bolen—Edward Bolen. He was Uncle Barney's coachman. After the old boy got married and retired from business, he set up a team, and undertook to be aristocratic. The theory was that when he and she began rowing that night, Bolen attempted to step in between them, and that she just reminded him of his proper place with an ounce of lead. She never was tried for his murder. I suppose her acquittal in the case of Uncle Barney made the authorities think it wouldn't pay to try her again. Every body said it was an infernal outrage for her to go free; but between you and me—and mum's the word—I was real glad of it. Not that she hadn't ought to have been punished for shooting her husband. But to have locked up her confoundedly pretty face out of sight in a prison—that would have been an infernal outrage, and no mistake. As for hanging her, they'd never have hanged her, anyhow—not even if the jury had convicted. But I don't mean to say that she was innocent. Sane? Well, you never saw a saner woman. She knew what she was about better than you and I do now."

"How do you account for the murder? What motive do you assign?"

"Most everybody said 'money'—claimed that she went deliberately to work and killed the old man for his money. Some few thought there must be another man at the bottom of it—that she had a paramour who put her up to it. But they didn't know her. She had a hot temper; but as far as men were concerned, she was as cool as a Roman punch. My own notion is that she did it in a fit of passion. He irritated her somehow, and she got mad, and let fire. You see, I recollect the way she glared at me that time. Savage was no word for it. If she'd had a gun in her hand, my life wouldn't have been worth that"—and Mr. Rimo snapped his fingers.

"I must say, you have contrived to interest me in her. I shall be glad when I have an opportunity of seeing her with my own eyes."

"Well, you take my advice. When you've found out her whereabouts, don't go too close, as they tell the boys at the menagerie. She's as vicious as they make them, I don't deny it. But she's got a wonderful fascination about her, notwithstanding, and if she thought it worth her while, she could wind you around her finger like a hair, and never know she'd done it. I wish you the best possible luck."

Mr. Rimo rose, shook hands, moved off.

Arthur's dreams that night were haunted by a wild, fierce, Medusa-like woman's face.

At his office, next morning, the first object that caught his eye was the black, leather-bound scrapbook that Peixada had given him yesterday. It lay where he had left it, on his desk. Beginning by listlessly turning the pages, he gradually became interested in their contents. I shall have to beg the reader's attention to an abstract of Mrs. Peix-ada's trial, before my story can be completed; and I may as well do so now.

The prosecution set out logically by establishing the fact of death. A surgeon testified to all that was essential in this regard. The second witness was one 'Patrick Martin. I copy his testimony word for word from the columns of the *New York Daily Gazette*.

"Mr. Martin," began the district-attorney, "what is your business?"

"I am a merchant, sir."

"And the commodities in which you deal are?

"Ales, wines, and liquors, your honor.

"At retail or wholesale?"

"Both, sir; but mostly retail."

"Where is your store situated, Mr. Martin?"

"On the southwest corner of Eighty-fifth Street and Ninth Avenue."

"Was the residence of the deceased, Mr. Bernard Peixada, near to your place of business?"

"It was, sir—on the next block."

"What block? How is the block bounded?"

"The block, sir, is bounded by Eighty-fifth and Eighty-sixth Streets, and Ninth and Tenth Avenues, your honor."

"Many houses on that block?

"None, your honor; only the house of the deceased. That stands on the top of a hill, back from the street, with big grounds around it."

"Had Mr. Peixada lived there long?

"Since the 1st of May, this year."

"Now, Mr. Martin, do you remember the night of July 30th?"

"Faith, I do, sir; and I'll not soon forget it."

"Good. Will you, then, as clearly and as fully as you can, tell the court and jury all the circumstances that combine to fix the night of July 30th in your memory? Take your time, speak up loudly, and look straight at the twelfth juryman."

"Well, sir, on that night, toward two o'clock the next morning—"

(Laughter among the auditors; speedily repressed by the court attendants.)

"Don't be disconcerted, Mr. Martin. On the morning of July 31st?"

"The same, sir. On that morning, at about two o'clock, I was outside in the street, putting the shutters over the windows of my store. While I was doing it, your honor, it seemed to me that I heard a noise—very weak and far away—like as if some one—a woman, or it might be a child—was crying out. I stopped for a moment, sir, and listened. Sure enough, I heard a voice—so faint you'd never have known it from the wind, except by sharpening your ears—I heard a voice, coming down the hill from the Jew's house over the way. I couldn't make out no words, but it was that thin and screechy that, 'Certain,' says I to myself, 'that old felley there is up to some mischief, or my name's not Patsy Martin.' Well, after I had got done with the shutters, I went into the house by the family entrance, and says I to my wife, 'There's a woman yelling in the house on the hill,' says I. 'What of that?' says she. 'Maybe I'd better go up,' says I. 'You'd better be after coming to bed and minding your business,' says she. 'It's most likely a way them heathen have of amusing themselves,' says she. But, 'No,' says I. 'Some one's in distress,' says I; 'and I guess the best thing I can do will be to light a lantern and go along up,' says I. So my wife, your honor, she lights the lantern for me, and, 'Damminus take 'em,' says she, to wish me good luck; and off I started, across the street, through the gate, and up the wagon-road that leads to Peixada's house. Meanwhile, your honor, the screaming had stopped. Never a whisper more did I hear; and thinks I to myself, 'It was only my imagination,' thinks I—when whist! All of a sudden, not two feet away from me, there in the road, a voice calls out 'Help, help.' The devil take me, I thought I'd jump out of my skin for fright, it came so unexpected. But I raised my lantern all the same, and cast a look around; and there before me on the ground, I seen an object which, as true as gospel, I took to be a ghost until I recognized it for Mrs. Peixada—the lady that's sitting behind you, sir—the Jew's wife, herself. There she lay, kneeling in front of me and when she seen who I was, 'Help, for God's sake, help,' says she, for all the world like a Christian. I knew right away that something wrong had happened, from her scared face and big, staring eyes; and besides, her bare feet and the white rag she wore in the place of a decent dress—"

At this point considerable sensation was created among the audience by the prosecuting attorney, who, interrupting the witness and addressing the court, remarked, "Your honor will observe that the prisoner has covered her face with a veil. This is a piece of theatricalism against which I must emphatically protest. It is, moreover, the jury's prerogative to watch the prisoner's physiognomy, as the story of her crime is told."

Recorder Hewitt ordered the prisoner to remove her veil.

"Go on, Mr. Martin," said the prosecutor to the witness.

"Well, sir, as I was saying, there I seen Mrs. Peix-ada, half crouching and half sitting there in the road. And when I got over the start she gave me, 'Excuse me, ma'am,' says I, 'but didn't I hear you hollering out for help?' 'Faith, you did,' says she. 'Well, here I am, ma'am,' says I; 'and now, will you be kind enough to inform me what's the trouble?' says I. 'The trouble?' says she. 'The trouble is that there's two men kilt up at the house, that's what's the trouble,' says she. 'Kilt?' says I. 'Yes, shot,' says she. 'And who shot them?' says I. 'Myself,' says she. 'Mother o' God!' says I. 'Well,' says she, 'wont you be after going up to the house and trying to help the poor wretches?' says she. 'I don't know but I will,' says I. And on up the road to the house I went. The front door, your honor, was open wide, and the gas blazing at full head within. I ran up the steps and through the vestibil, and there in the hall I seen that what Mrs. Peixada had said was the truest word she ever spoke in her life. Old Peixada, he lay there on one side, as dead as sour beer, with blood all around him; and on the other side lay Mr. Bolen—whom I knew well, for he was a good customer of my own, your honor—more dead than the Jew, if one might say so. I, sir, I just remained long enough to cross myself and whisper, 'God have mercy on them and then off I went to call an officer. On the way down the hill, I passed Mrs. Peixada again; and this time she was laying out stiff in the road, with her eyes closed and her mouth open, like she was in a fit. She had nothing on but that white gown I spoke of before; and very elegant she looked, your honor, flat there, like a corpse."

Again the district-attorney stopped the witness.

"Your honor," he said, "I must again direct your attention to the irregular conduct of the prisoner. She has now turned her back to the jury, and covered her face with her hands. This is merely a method of evading the injunction which your honor saw fit to impose upon her with respect to her veil. I must insist upon her displaying her full face to the jury."

Mr. Sondheim, of counsel for the defendant: "If the Court please, it strikes me that my learned brother is really a trifle too exacting. I can certainly see no objection to my client's holding her hands to her face. Considering the painfulness of her situation, it is no more than natural that she should desire to shield her face. I must beg the Court to remember that this prisoner is no ordinary criminal, but a lady of refined and sensitive instincts. A little indulgence, it seems to me, is due to her on account of her sex."

The district-attorney: "The prisoner had better understand once for all that her sex isn't going to protect her in this prosecution. The law is no respecter of sex. As for her refined and sensitive instincts, if she has any, I advise her to put them into her pocket. This jury has too much good sense to be affected by any exhibition that she may make for their benefit. I submit the matter to the Court's good judgment."

The recorder: "Madam, you will turn your chair toward the jury, and keep your face uncovered."

The district-attorney: "Well, Mr. Martin, what next?"

The witness: "Weil, sir, I hurried along down as fast as ever I could, and stopped at my own place just long enough to tell my wife what had happened, and to send her up to Mrs. Peixada with a bottle of spirits to bring her around. Then I went to the station-house, and informed the gentleman at the desk of the state of affairs. Him and a couple of officers came back with me; and they, your honor, took charge of the premises, and—and that's all I know about it."

Martin was not cross-examined. Police Sergeant Riley, succeeding him, gave an account of the prisoner's arrest and of her subsequent demeanor at the station-house. "The lady," said he, "appeared to be unable to walk—leastwise, she limped all the way with great difficulty. We thought she was shamming, and treated her accordingly. But afterwards it turned out that she had a sprained ankle." She had answered the formal questions—name? age? residence?—in full; and to the inquiry whether she desired to make any statement or remark relative to the charge preferred against her, had replied, "Nothing, except that I shot them both—Bernard Peixada and Edward Bolen." They had locked her up in the captain's private room for the rest of the night; and the following morning she had been transferred to the Tombs.

The next witness was Miss Ann Doyle.

"Miss Doyle, what is your occupation?" asked the district-attorney.

"I am a cook, sir."

"Have you a situation, at present?"

"I have not, sir."

"How long have you been idle?"

"Since the 31st of July, sir."

"Prior to that date where were you employed?"

"In the family of Mr. Peixada, sir."

"Were you present at Mr. Peixada's house on the night of July 30th?"

"I was not, sir."

"Tell us, please, how you came to be absent?"

"Well, sir, just after dinner, along about seven o'clock, Mrs. Peixada, who was laying abed with a sore foot, she called me to her, sir, and, 'Ann,' says she, 'you can have the evening out, and you needn't come home till to-morrow morning,' sir, says she."

"And you availed yourself of this privilege?"

"Sure, I did, sir. I came home the next morning, sir, in time to get breakfast, having passed the night at my sister's; and when I got there, sir—"

"Never mind about that, Miss Doyle. Now, tell us, was it a customary thing for Mrs. Peixada to let you go away for the entire night?"

"She never did it before, sir. Of course I had my regular Thursday and Sunday, but I was always expected to be in the house by ten o'clock, sir."

"That will do, Miss Doyle. Miss Katharine Mahoney, take the stand."

Miss Mahoney described herself as an "upstairs girl," and said that she, too, until the date of the murder, had been employed in Mr. Peixada's household. To her also, on the evening of July 30th, Mrs. Peixada had accorded leave of absence for the night.

"So that," reasoned the district-attorney, "all the servants were away, by the prisoner's prearrangement, at the hour of the perpetration of the crime?"

"Yes, sir; since me and Ann were the only servants they kept. Mr. Bolen staid behind, to his sorrow."

In the case of each of these witnesses, the prisoner's counsel waived cross-examination, saying, "If the court please, we shall not take issue on the allegations of fact."

The prosecution rested, reserving, however, the right to call witnesses in rebuttal, if need should be. The defense started with a physician, Dr. Leopold Jetz, of Lexington Avenue, near Fifty-ninth Street.

"Dr. Jetz, how long have you known Mrs. Peix-ada, the prisoner at the bar?"

"Ever since she was born. I helped to bring her into the world."

"When did you last attend her professionally?"

"I paid her my last professional visit on the 1st of August, 1878; eight days before she was married."

"What was her trouble at that time?"

"General depression of the nervous system. To speak technically, cerebral anemia, or insufficient nourishment of the brain, complicated by sacral neuralgia—neuralgia at the base of the spine."

"Were these ailments of long standing?"

"I was called in on the 29th of May. I treated her consecutively till August 1st. That would make two months. But she had been suffering for some time before I was summoned. The troubles had crept upon her gradually. On the 8th of August she was married. She had just completed her nineteenth year."

"Now, doctor, was the condition of Mrs. Peixada's health, at the time your treatment was discontinued, such as to predispose her to insanity?" (Question objected to, on the ground that the witness had not been produced as an expert, and that his competence to give expert testimony was not established. Objection overruled.)

"In my opinion," said Dr. Jetz, "at the time I last saw her professionally, Mrs. Peixada was in an exceedingly critical condition. Although evincing no symptoms of insanity proper, her brain was highly irritated, and her whole nervous system deranged; so that an additional strain of any kind put upon her, might easily have precipitated acute mania. I told her father that she was in no wise fit to get married; but he chose to disregard my advice. I think I may answer your question affirmatively, and say that her health was such as to predispose her to insanity."

By the district attorney: "Doctor, are your sentiments—your personal sentiments—for the prisoner of a friendly or an unfriendly nature?"

"Decidedly, sir, of a friendly nature."

"You would be sorry to see her hanged?"

The doctor replied by a gesture.

"Or sent to State Prison?"

"I could not bear to think of it."

"You would do your utmost—would you not?—to save her from such a fate?"

"Eagerly, sir, eagerly."

"That's sufficient, doctor."

An alienist of some distinction followed Dr. Jetz. He said that he had listened attentively to the evidence so far adduced in court, had read the depositions taken before the magistrate and the coroner, had conferred at length with the preceding witness, and finally had made a diagnosis of Mrs. Peixada's case in her cell at the Tombs. He believed that, though perfectly sane and responsible at present, she had "within a brief period suffered from a disturbance of cerebral function." There were "indications which led him to infer that at the time of the homicide she was organically a lunatic." The district-attorney took him in hand.

"Doctor, are you the author of a work entitled, 'Pathology of Mind Popularly Expounded'—published, as I see by the title page, in 1873?"

"I am, sir, yes."

"Does that book express with tolerable accuracy your views on the subject of insanity?'

"It does—certainly."

"Very well. Now, doctor, I will read aloud from Chapter III., page 75. Be good enough to follow.—'It is then a fact that there exists a borderland between pronounced dementia, or mania, and sound mental health, in which it is impossible to apply the terms, sane and insane, with any approach to scientific nicety. Nor is it to be disputed that a person may have entered this borderland may have departed from the realm of unimpaired intelligence, and not yet have attained the pandemonium of complete madness—and withal, retain the faculty of distinguishing between right and wrong, together with the control of will necessary to the selection and employment of either. This borderland is a sort of twilight region in which, though blurred in outline, objects have not become invisible. Crimes committed by subject? in the state thus described, can not philosophically be extenuated on the ground of mental aberration.'—I suppose, doctor, you acknowledge the authorship of this passage?"

"Yes, sir."

"And subscribe to its correctness?"

"It expresses the opinion which prevails among the authorities."

"Well and good. Now, to return to the case at bar, are you willing to swear that on the night of July 30th, the 'disturbance of cerebral function' which, you have told us, Mrs. Peixada was perhaps suffering from—are you willing to swear that it had progressed beyond this borderland which you have so clearly elucidated in your book?"

"I am not willing to swear positively. It is my opinion that it had."

"You are not willing to swear positively. Then, you are not willing to swear positively, I take it, that Mrs. Peixada's crime did not belong to that category which 'can not philosophically be extenuated on the ground of mental aberration?'.rdquo;

"Not positively—no, sir."

"It is your opinion?"

"It is my opinion."

"How firm?"

"Very firm."

"So firm, doctor, that if you were on this jury, you would feel bound, under any and all circumstances, to acquit the prisoner?"

"So firm that I should feel bound to acquit her, unless evidence of a highly damaging character was forthcoming."

"Well, suppose that evidence of a highly damaging character was forthcoming, would you convict?"

"I might."

"Thanks, doctor. You can go."

Having thus sought to prove the prisoner's irresponsibility, the defense endeavored to establish her fair name. Half-a-dozen ladies and two or three gentleman attested that they had known her for many years, and had always found her to be of a peculiarly sweet and gentle temperament. Not one of them would believe her capable of an act of violence, unless, at the time of committing it, she was out of her right mind. As the last of these persons left the stand, Mr. Sondheim said, "Your honor, our case is in."

"And a pretty lame case it is," commented the district-attorney. "I beg leave to remind the court that it is Friday, and to move for an adjournment until Monday, in order that the People may have an opportunity to produce witnesses in rebuttal." The motion was granted.

On Monday a second alienist, one whose renown quite equaled that of the first, declared it as his opinion, based upon a personal examination of the accused, that she was not and never had been in the slightest degree insane.

"Is Dr. Julius Gunther in court?" called out the district-attorney.

Dr. Gunther elbowed his way to the front, and was sworn.

"Dr. Gunther," the prosecutor inquired, "you are a physician in general practice—yes?"

"Yes, sir, I am."

"You were also, I believe, up to the time of his death, physician to the family of Mr. Bernard Peixada?"

The doctor nodded affirmatively.

"Did you ever attend the decedent's wife—Mrs. Peixada—this woman here—the prisoner at the bar?"

"On the 20th of July last I began to treat her for a sprained ankle. I called on her every day or two, up to the 30th."

"You were treating her for a sprained ankle. Did you make any observation of her general health?"

"Naturally."

"And you found it?"

"Excellent."

"How about her mental faculties? Any symptoms of derangement?"

"Not one. I have seldom known a smarter woman. She had an exceptionally well-balanced mind."

"That'll do, doctor," said the district-attorney. To the other side, "Want to cross-examine?"

"Is a well-balanced mind, doctor," asked Mr. Sondheim, "proof positive of sanity? Is it not possible for one to be perfectly rational on ordinary topics, and yet liable to attacks of mama when irritated by some special circumstances?"

"Oh, speaking broadly, I suppose so. But in this particular instance, no. That woman is no more crazy than you are."

"Now," said the prosecutor, "now, as to my lady's alleged good character?"

A score of witnesses proceeded to demolish it. Miss Emily Millard had acted as music teacher to the prisoner when she was a little girl. Miss Millard related a dozen anecdotes illustrative of the prisoner's ungovernable temper. Misses Sophie Dedold, Florentine Worch, and Esther Steinbaum had gone to school with the prisoner. If their accounts were to be believed, she was a "flirt," and a "doubleface." At length, Mrs. George Washington Shapiro took the stand.

"Mrs. Shapiro, were you acquainted with Mr. Bernard Peixada, the decedent?"

"Well acquainted with him—an old friend of his family."

"And with his wife, the prisoner?

"I made her acquaintance shortly before Mr. Peixada married her. After that I saw her as often as once a week."

"Will you please give us your estimate of her character?"

"Bad, very bad. She is false, she is treacherous, but above all, she is spiteful and ill-humored."

"For example?"

"Oh, I could give twenty examples."

"Give one, please."

"Well, one day I called upon her and found her in tears. 'My dear,' said I, 'what are you crying about?' 'Oh,' she answered, 'I wish Bernard Peixada'—she always spoke of her husband as Bernard Peixada—'I wish Bernard Peixada was dead.' 'What!' I remonstrated. 'You wish your husband was dead? You ought not to say such a thing. What can you mean?' 'I mean that I hate him,' she replied. 'But if you hate him,' said I, 'if you are unhappy with him, why don't you wish that you yourself were dead, instead of wishing it of him?' 'Oh,' she explained, 'I am young. I have much to live for. He is an old, bad man. It would a good thing all around, if he were dead.'.rdquo;

"Can you give us the date of this extraordinary conversation?"

"It was some time, I think, in last June; a little more than a month before she murdered him."

The efforts of the prisoner's counsel to break down Mrs. Shapiro's testimony were unavailing.

"Mr. Short," says the *Gazette*, "now summed up in his most effective style, dwelling at length upon the prisoner's youth and previous good character, and arguing that she could never have committed the crime in question, except under the sway of an uncontrollable impulse induced by mental disease. He wept copiously, and succeeded in bringing tears to the eyes of several jurymen. He was followed by Assistant-district-attorney Sardick, for the People, who carefully analyzed the evidence, and showed that it placed the guilt of the accused beyond the reach of a reasonable doubt. Recorder Hewitt charged dead against the fair defendant, consuming an hour and a quarter. The jury thereupon retired; but at the expiration of seventeen minutes they returned to the court-room, and, much to the surprise of every one present, announced that they had agreed upon a verdict. The prisoner was directed to stand up. She was deathly pale; her teeth chattered; her hands clutched at the railing in front of the clerk's desk. The formal questions were put in their due order and with becoming solemnity. A profound sensation was created among the spectators when the foreman pronounced the two decisive words, 'Not guilty.' A vivid crimson suffused the prisoner's throat and cheeks, but otherwise her appearance did not alter. Recorder Hewitt seemed for a moment to discredit his senses. Then, suddenly straightening up and scowling at the jury-box, 'You have rendered an outrageous verdict; a verdict grossly at variance with the evidence,' he said. 'You are one and all excused from further service in this tribunal.' Turning to Mrs. Peixada, 'As for you, madam,' he continued, 'you have been unrighteously acquitted of as heinous a crime as ever woman was guilty of. Your defense was a sham and a perjury. The ends of justice have been defeated, because, forsooth, you have a pretty face. You can go free. But let me counsel you to beware, in the future, how you tamper with the lives of human beings, better and worthier in every respect than yourself. I had hoped that it would be my duty and my privilege to sentence you to a life of hard labor in the prison at Sing Sing, if not to expiation of your sin upon the gallows. Unfortunately for the public welfare, and much to my personal regret, I have no alternative but to commit you to the keeping of your own guilty conscience, trusting that in time you may, by its action, and by the just horror with which your fellow-beings will shun your touch, be chastised and chastened. You are discharged.' Mrs. Peixada bowed to the court, and left the room on the arm of her counsel."

Undramatic and matter-of-fact though it was, Arthur got deeply absorbed in the perusal of this newspaper report of Mrs. Peixada's trial. When the jury returned from their deliberations, it was with breathless interest that he learned the result; he had forgotten that he already knew it. As the words "Not guilty" took shape before him, he drew a genuine sigh of relief. Then, at once recollecting himself, "Bah!" he cried. "I was actually rejoicing at a miscarriage of justice. I am weak-minded." By and by he added, "I wish, though, that I could get at the true inwardness of the matter—the secret motives that nobody but the murderess herself could reveal." For the sake of local color, he put on his hat and went over to the General Sessions court-room—now empty and in charge of a single melancholy officer—and tried to reconstruct the scene, with the aid of his imagination. The recorder had sat there, on the bench; the jury there; the prisoner there, at the counsel table. The atmosphere of the court-room was depressing. The four walls, that had listened to so many tales of sin and unhappiness, seemed to exude a deadly miasma. This room was reserved for the trial of criminal causes. How many hearts had here stood still for suspense! How many wretched secrets had here been uncovered! How many mothers and wives had wept here! How many guilt-burdened souls had here seen their last ray of light go out, and the shadows of the prison settle over them! The very tick-tack of the clock opposite the door sounded strangely ominous. Looking around him, Arthur felt his own heart grow cold, as if it had been touched with ice.

CHAPTER IV.
"THAT NOT IMPOSSIBLE SHE."

AT home that evening, on the *loggia*, Hetzel said, "I have news for you."

"Ah?" queried Arthur.

"Yes—about your mystery across the way."

"Well?"

"She's no longer a mystery. The ambiguity surrounding her has been dispelled."

"Well, go on."

"To start with, after you went down-town this morning, carts laden with furniture began to rattle into the street, and the furniture was carried into No. 46. It appears that they *have* taken the whole house, after all. They were merely camping out in the third story, while waiting for the advent of their goods and chattels. So we were jumping to a conclusion, when we put them down as poverty-stricken. The furniture was quite comfortable looking. It included, by the way, a second piano. Confess that you are disappointed."

"Why should I be disappointed? The divine voice remains, doesn't it? Go ahead."

"Well, I have learned their names.—The lady of the house is an elderly widow—Mrs. Gabrielle Hart. She has been living till recently in an apartment-house on Fifty-ninth Street, facing Central Park—'The Modena'."

"But the songstress?"

"The songstress is Mrs. Hart's companion. She is also a Mrs.—Mrs. Lehmyl—L-e-h-m-y-l—picturesque name, isn't it?"

"And Mr. Lehmyl—who is he?"

"Perhaps Mrs. Lehmyl is a widow, too. She dresses in black."

"Ah, you have seen her? Describe her to me."

"No, I haven't seen her. But Josephine has. It is to Josephine that I owe the information so far communicated."

"What does Josephine say she looks like?"

"Josephine doesn't say. She caught but a meteoric glimpse of her, as she stood for a moment this afternoon at her front door. Like the woman she is, she paid more attention to her costume than she did to her features."

"Well, any thing further?"

"Nothing."

"Has she sung for you since I left?"

"Not a bar. Probably she has been busy, helping to put the house to rights."

"Let us hope she will sing for us to-night."

"Let us hope so."

But bed-time stole upon them, and their hopes had not yet been rewarded.

The week wound away. Nothing new transpired concerning the occupants of No. 46. Mrs. Lehmyl sang almost every evening. But neither Arthur nor Hetzel nor Josephine succeeded in getting sight of her; which, of course, merely aggravated our hero's curiosity. Sunday afternoon he stood at the front window, gazing toward the corner house. The two cats, heretofore mentioned, were disporting themselves upon the window-ledge.

Hetzel, who was seated in the back part of the room, noticed that Arthur's attitude changed all at once from that of languid interest to that of sharp attention. His backbone became rigid, his neck craned forward; it was evident that something had happened. Presently he turned around, and remarked, with ill-disguised excitement, "If—if you're anxious to make the acquaintance of that Mrs. Lehmyl, here's your chance."

It struck Hetzel that this was pretty good. "If I am anxious to make her acquaintance!" he said to himself. Aloud, "Why, how is that?" he asked.

"Oh," said Arthur, "two ladies—she and Mrs. Hart, I suppose—have just left the corner house, and crossed the street, and entered our front door—to call on Mrs. Berle, doubtless."

Mrs. Berle was the down-stairs neighbor of our friends—a middle-aged Jewish lady, whose husband, a commercial traveler, was commonly away from home.

"Well?" questioned Hetzel.

"Well, you ought to call on Mrs. Berle, anyway, you know. She has been so polite and kind, and has asked you to so often, that really it's no more than right that you should show her some little attention. Why not improve this occasion?"

"Oh," said Hetzel, yawning, "I'm tired. I prefer to stay home this afternoon."

"Nonsense. You're simply lazy. It's—it's positively a matter of duty, Hetz."

"Well, you have so frequently asserted that I have no sense of duty, I'm trying to live up to your conception of me."

After a minute of silence, "The fact of the matter is," ventured Arthur, "that I too owe Mrs. Berle a visit, and—and won't you go down with me, as a favor?"

"Oh, if you put it on that ground, it's another question. As a favor to you, I consent to be dragged out."

"Hurrah!" cried Arthur, casting off the mask of indifference that he had thus far clumsily worn. "I'll go change my coat, and come back in an instant. Wasn't I lucky to be posted there by the window at the moment of their exit? At last we shall see her with our own eyes."

Ere a great while, Mrs. Berle's maid-servant ushered them into Mrs. Berle's drawing-room.

Mrs. Lehmyl was at the piano—playing, not singing. Arthur enjoyed a fine view of her back. My meaning is literal, when I say "enjoyed." Impatient though he was to see her face, he took an indescribable pleasure in watching her back sway to and fro, as her fingers raced up and down the keyboard. Its contour was refined and symmetrical. Its undulations lent stress to the music, and denoted fervor on the part of the executant. Arthur can't tell what she was playing. It was something of Rubenstein's, the title of which escapes him—something, he says, as vigorous as a whirlwind—a bewitching melody sounding above a tempest of harmony—it was the restless, tumultuous, barbaric Rubenstein at his best.

At its termination, the audience applauded vehemently, and demanded more. The result was a *Scherzo* by Chopin. Afterward, Mrs. Lehmyl rose from the piano and fanned herself. Every body began simultaneously to talk.

Mrs. Berle presented Hetzel and Arthur in turn to the two ladies. Of the latter she was kind enough to remark, "Dot is a young lawyer down-town, and such a *goot* young man"—which made him blush profusely and wish his hostess a dozen apoplexies.

Mrs. Hart was tall and spare, a severe looking woman of sixty, or thereabouts. She wore a gray poplin dress, and had stiff gray hair, and a network of gray veins across the backs of her hands. A penumbra upon her upper lip proved, when inspected, to be due to the presence of an incipient mustache. Her eyes were blue and good-natured.

Mrs. Lehmyl's manner was at once dignified and gracious. Arthur made bold to declare, "Your playing is equal to your singing, Mrs. Lehmyl—which is saying a vast deal."

"It is saying what is kind and pleasant," she answered, "but I fear, not strictly accurate. My playing is very faulty, I have so little time to practice."

"If it is faulty, a premium ought to be placed upon such faults," he gushed.

Mrs. Lehmyl laughed, but vouchsafed no reply. "And as for your singing," he continued, "I hope you won't mind my telling you how much I have enjoyed it. You can't conceive the pleasure it has given me, when I have come home, fagged out, from a day down-town, to hear you sing."

"I am very glad if it is so. I was afraid my musical pursuits might be a nuisance to the neighbors. I take for granted that you are a neighbor?"

"Oh, yes. Hetzel and I inhabit the upper portion of this house."

"Ah, then you are the young men whom we have noticed on the roof. It is a brilliant idea, your roof. You dine up there, do you not?"

"Let's go into the back room," cried Mrs. Berle; and she led the way.

In the back room wine and cakes were distributed by a German *Madchen* in a French cap. The gentlemen—there were two or three present besides Arthur and Hetzel—lit their cigars. The ladies, of whom there were an equal number, with the exception of Mrs. Lehmyl, gathered in a knot around the center-table. Mrs. Lehmyl went to the bay-window and admired the view. It was, indeed, admirable. A crystalline atmosphere permitted one to see as far down the river as the Brooklyn Navy Yard; and leagues to the eastward, on Long Island, the marble of I know not what burying-ground glittered in the sun. An occasional schooner slipped past almost within stone's throw. On the wharf under the terrace, fifty odd yards away, an aged man placidly supported a fishing pole, and watched a cork that floated immobile upon the surface of the water. Over all bent the sky, intensely blue, and softened by a few white, fleecy clouds. But Arthur's faculties for admiration were engrossed by Mrs. Lehmyl's face.

I think the first impression created by her face was one of power, rather than one of beauty. Not that it was in the slightest degree masculine, not that it was too strong to be intensely womanly. But at first sight, especially if it chanced then to be in repose, it seemed to embody the pride and the solemnity of womanhood, rather than its gentleness and flexibility. It was the face of a woman who could purpose and perform, who could suffer and be silent, who could command and be inexorable. The brow, crowned by black, waving hair, was low and broad, and as white as marble. The nose and chin were modeled on the pattern of the Ludovici Juno's. Your first notion was: "This woman is calm, reserved, thoughtful, persistent. Her emotions are subordinated to her intellect. She has a tremendous will. She was cut out to be an empress." But the next instant you noticed her eyes and her mouth:

and your conception had accordingly to be reframed. Her eyes, in color dark, translucent brown, were of the sort that your gaze can delve deep into, and discern a light shimmering at the bottom: eyes that send an electric spark into the heart of the man who looks upon them; eyes that are eloquent of pathos and passion and mystery. Her lips were full and ruddy, and indicated equal capacities for womanly tenderness and for girlish mirth. It was easy to fancy them curling in derisive laughter: it was quite as easy to fancy them quivering with intense emotion, or becoming compressed in pain. Insensibly, you added: "No—not an empress: a heroine, a martyr to some noble human cause. It was like this that the Mother of Sorrows must have looked."

She was beautiful: on that score there could be no difference of opinion. Her appearance justified the expectations that her voice aroused. She was beautiful not in a pronounced, aggressive way, but in a quiet, subtle, and all the more potent way. Her beauty was of the sort that grows upon one, the longer one studies it; rather than of the sort that, bullet-like, produces its greatest effect at once. Join to this that she was manifestly young, at the utmost five-and-twenty, and the reader will not wonder that Arthur's antecedent interest in her had mounted several degrees. I must not forget to mention her hands. These were a trifle larger than it is the fashion for a lady's hands to be; but they were shaped and colored to perfection, and they had an unconscious habit of toying with each other, as their owner talked or listened, that made it a charm to watch them. They were suggestive hands. Arthur felt that, had he understood the language of hands, he could, by observing these, have divined a number of Mrs. Lehmyl's secrets; and he bethought him of an old treatise on palmistry that lay gathering dust in his book-case up-stairs. Around her wrist she wore a bracelet of amber beads. She was dressed entirely in black, and had a sprig of mignonette pinned in her button-hole.

As has been said, she admired the view. "I am so glad we have come to live in Beekman Place," she added; "it is such a contrast to the rest of dusty, noisy, hot New York."

"To hear this woman utter small talk," says Arthur, "was like seeing a giant lift straws. I half wished that she would not speak at all, unless to proclaim mighty truths in hexameters. Still, had she kept silence, I am sure I should have been disappointed."

She was much amused by the old fisherman down on the wharf; wondered whether he had met with any luck; and thought that such patient devotion as he displayed, merited recognition on the part of the fishes. She was curious to know what the granite buildings were on Blackwell's Island. Arthur undertook the office of cicerone.

"Prison and hospital and graveyard constantly in sight," was her comment; "I should think they would make one gloomy."

"*A memento mori*, as one's eyes feast on sky and water. On moonlight nights in summer, it is superb here—quite Venetian. Every now and then some dark, mysterious craft, slowly drifting by, reminds one of Elaine's barge."

"It must be very beautiful," she said, simply.

At this juncture an excursion steamboat made its appearance upon the river, and conversation was suspended till it had passed. It was gay with bunting and black with humanity. It strove its best to render day hideous by dispensing a staccato version of "Home, Sweet Home" from the blatant throat of a *Calliope*—an instrument consisting of a series of steam whistles graduated in chromatic scale.

"How uncomfortable those poor people must be," said Mrs. Lehmyl. "Is—is this one of the dark, mysterious craft?"

"It is a product of our glorious American civilization. None but an alchemist with true American instincts, would ever have thought of transmuting steam to music."

"Music?" queried Mrs. Lehmyl, dubiously.

Arthur was about to qualify his use of the term when the door opened and admitted a procession of Mrs. Berle's daughters and sons-in-law. An uproar of greetings and presentations followed. The men exchanged remarks about the weather and the state of trade; the women, kisses and inquiries concerning health. Bits of news were circulated. "Lester Bar is engaged to Emma Frankenstiel," "Mrs. Seitel's baby was born yesterday—another girl," "*Du lieber Gott!*" "*Ist's moglich?*" and so on; a breezy mingling of German with English, of statement with expletive; the whole emphasized by an endless swaying of heads and lifting of eyebrows. The wine and cakes made a second tour of the room. Fresh cigars were lighted. The ladies fell to comparing notes about their respective offspring. One of the gentlemen volunteered a circumstantial account of a Wagner concert he had attended the night previous. It was a long while before any thing resembling quiet was restored. Arthur seized the first opportunity that presented itself to edge back to Mrs. Lehmyl's side.

"All this talk about music," he said, "has whetted my appetite. You are going to sing for us, aren't you?"

"Oh, I shouldn't dare to, in this assemblage of Wagnerites. The sort of music that I can sing would seem heresy from their point of view. I can't sing Wagner, and I shouldn't venture upon any thing so retrograde as Schumann or Schubert. Besides, I'm rather tired to-day, and—so please don't introduce the subject. Mrs. Berle might follow it up; and if she asked me, I couldn't very well refuse."

Mrs. Lehmyl's tone showed that she meant what she said.

"This is a great disappointment," Arthur rejoined.

"You don't know how anxious I am to hear you sing at close quarters. But as for your music being retrograde, why, only the other night I was admiring your fine taste in making selections. *Wohin*, for instance. Isn't *Wohin* abreast of the times?"

"The Wagnerites wouldn't think so. It is melody. Therefore it is—good enough for the uninitiated, perhaps—but not to be put up with by people of serious musical cultivation. The only passages in Wagner's own work that his disciples take exception to, are those where, in a fit of artistic obliquity, he has become truly melodious. Here, they think, he has been guilty of backsliding. His melodies were the short-comings of genius—pardonable, in consideration of their infrequency, but in no wise to be commended. The further he gets away from the old standards of excellence—the more perplexing, complicated, artificial, soporific, he becomes—the better are his enthusiasts pleased. The other day I was talking with one of them, and in the desire to say something pleasant, I spoke of how supremely beautiful the Pilgrim's Chorus is in Tannhâuser. A look of sadness fell upon my friend's face, and I saw that I had blundered. 'Ah,' she cried, 'don't speak of that. It makes my heart ache to think that the master could have let himself down to any thing so trivial.' That's their pet word—trivial. Whenever a theme is comprehensible, they dispose of it as trivial."

Arthur laughed and said, "It is evident to what school you belong. For my part, I always suspect that when a composer disdains to write melodies, it is a case of sour grapes."

"Yes, he lacks the inventive faculty, and then affects to despise it," said Mrs. Lehmyl. "My taste is very old-fashioned. Of course every body must recognize Wagner's greatness, and must appreciate him in his best moods. But when he cuts loose from all the established laws of composition—well, I heard my sentiments neatly expressed once by Signor Zacchinelli, the maestro. 'It is ze music of ze future?' he inquired. 'Zen I am glad I shall be dead.' Smiting his breast he went on, 'I want somezing to make me feel good *here*.' That's the trouble. Except when Wagner abides by the old traditions, he never makes one feel good *here*. The pleasure he affords is intellectual rather than emotional. He amazes you by the intricate harmonies he constructs, but he doesn't touch your heart. Now and then he forgets himself—is borne away from his theories on the wings of an inspiration—and then he is superb."

"I wonder," Arthur asked, by and by, "whether you can tell me what it was that you sang the evening I first heard you. It was more than a week ago—a week ago Friday. At about sunset time, we were out on our roof, and you sang something that I had never heard before,—something soft and plaintive, with a refrain that went like this——" humming a bar or two of the refrain. "Oh, that? Did you like that?"

"I did, indeed. I thought it was exquisite."

"I am glad, because it is a favorite of my own. It's an old French folk-song, arranged by Bizet. The title is *Le Voile d'une Religieuse.*"

"I wish I could hear it again. I can't tell you how charming it was to sit there in the open air, and watch the sunset, and listen to that song. Only, it was so exasperating not to be able to see the songstress. Won't you be persuaded to sing it now? I'm sure you are not too tired to sing that."

"What? Here? I should never be absolved. The auditors—I dare not fancy what the effect upon them might be. That song, of all things! Why, it is worse than Schubert.—But seriously," she added, gravely, "I could not bear to expose any thing so dear to me as my music is, to the ridicule it would provoke from the Wagnerites. It hurts me keenly to hear a song that I love, picked to pieces, and made light of, and tossed to the winds. It hurts me just as keenly to hear it praised insincerely—merely for politeness' sake. Music—true music—is like prayer. It is too sacred to—you know what I mean—to be laid bare to the contempt of unbelievers."

"Yes, indeed, like prayer. It is the most perfect vehicle of expression for one's deepest, most solemn feelings—that and——"

"And poetry."

"How did you guess that I was going to say poetry?"

"It was obvious. The two go together."

"So they do. Do you know, Mrs. Lehmyl, if I were to try my hand at guesswork, I think I could name your favorite poet."

"Indeed; who is he?"

"Robert Browning."

Mrs. Lehmyl cast a half surprised, half startled glance at Arthur. "Are you a mind-reader? Or was it simply a chance hit?" she asked.

"Then I was right?"

"Yes, you were right, though I ought not to tell you so. You ought not to know your power, if power it was, and not mere random' guesswork. One with that faculty of penetrating another's mind must be a dangerous associate. But tell me, what hint did I let fall, that made you suspect I should be fond of Browning?"

"If I should answer that question, I am afraid you might deem me presumptuous. I could not do so, without paying you a compliment."

"Then, leave it unanswered," she said, coldly.

At this moment Mrs. Hart rose and bade good-by to Mrs. Berle; then called across to Mrs. Lehmyl, "Come, Ruth;" and the latter wished Arthur good afternoon.

He and Hetzel left soon after. Mrs. Berle said, "If you young gentlemen have no other engagement, won't you take tea here a week from to-night?"

"You are very kind," Hetzel answered; "and we shall do so with great pleasure."

Upstairs, "Well, how did you like her?" inquired Arthur.

"Like whom? Mrs. Berle?"

"No—Mrs. Lehmyl, of course, stupid."

"That's a pretty question for you to ask; as though you'd given me a chance to find out. How did *you* like her?"

"Oh, she's above the average."

"Is that all? Then you were disappointed? She didn't come up to your anticipations?"

"Oh, I don't say that. Yes, she's# a fine woman."

"But her friend, Mrs. Hart, is a trump."

"So? Nobody would suspect it from her looks. Her austere coloring inspires a certain kind of awe."

"She's no longer young. But she's very agreeable, all the same. We talked a good deal together. She asked me to call. You weren't a bit clever."

"No?"

"No, sir. If you had been, you would have devoted yourself to Mrs. Hart. Then she would have invited you to call, too. So you could have cultivated Mrs. Lehmyl at your leisure."

"But you and I are one. You can take me to call with you, can't you?"

"I don't know about that. She asked me to drop in informally any afternoon. You're never home in the afternoon. Besides, you're old enough to receive an invitation for yourself."

"Nonsense! You can arrange it easily enough. Ask permission to bring your Fidus Achates."

"I'll see about it. If you behave yourself for the next week or two, perhaps I'll exert my influence. By the way, how did you like Mrs. Lehmyl's playing?"

"She played uncommonly well—didn't you think so?"

"Indeed, I did. Execution and expression were both fine. She has studied in Europe, Mrs. Hart says."

"Did you learn who her husband is?"

"I learned that he isn't. I was right in my conjecture. She is a widow."

"That's a relief. I am glad she is not-encumbered with a husband."

"Fie upon you, man! You ought to be ashamed to say it. He has been dead quite a number of years."

"Quite a number of years? Why, she can't be more than twenty-four or five years old—and besides, she's still in mourning."

"I guess that's about her age. But the mourning doesn't signify, because it's becoming to her; and so she would naturally keep it up as long as possible."

"That introduces the point of chief importance. What did you think of her appearance?"

"Oh, she has magnificent eyes, and looks refined and interesting—looks as though she knew what sorrow meant, too—only, perhaps the least bit cold. No, cold isn't the word. Say dignified, serious, a woman with whom one could never be familiar—in whose presence one would always feel a little—a little constrained. That isn't exactly what I mean, either. You understand—one would always have to be on one's guard not to say any thing flippant or trivial."

"You mean she looks as though she were deficient in levity?"

"Well, as though she wouldn't tolerate any thing petty—a dialogue such as ours now, for example."

"I don't know whether you have formed a correct notion of her, or not. Cold she certainly isn't. She's an enthusiast on the subject of music. And when we were talking about Wagner, she—wasn't exactly flippant—but she showed that she could be jocose. There's something about her that's exceedingly impressive, I don't know what it is. But I know that she made me feel, somehow, very small. She made me feel that underneath her quiet manner—hidden away somewhere in her frail woman's body—there was the capability of immense power. She reminded me of the women in Robert Browning's poetry—of the heroine of the 'Inn Album' especially. Yet she said nothing remarkable—nothing to justify such an estimate."

"You were affected by her personal magnetism. A woman with eyes like hers—and mighty scarce they are—always gives you the idea of power. Young as she is, I suspect she's been through a good deal. She has had her experiences. That seems to be written on her face. Yet she didn't strike me as having the peach-bloom rubbed off—though, of course, I had no chance to examine her closely."

"Oh, no; the peach-bloom is there in abundance. Well, at all events, she's a problem which it will be interesting to solve. By the way, what possessed you to accept Mrs. Berle's invitation to tea?"

"What possessed me? Why should I have done otherwise?"

"It will be an insufferable bore."

"Who was it that somewhat earlier in the afternoon preached me a sermon on the duties we owe that identical Mrs. Berle?"

Arthur spent the evening reading. Hetzel, peeping over his shoulder, saw that the book of his choice was "The Inn Album" by Robert Browning.

CHAPTER V.
"A NOTHING STARTS THE SPRING."

ANOTHER week slipped away. The weather changed. There was rain almost every day, and a persistent wind blew from the north-east. So the *loggia* of No. 43 Beekman Place was not much patronized. Nevertheless, Arthur heard Mrs. Lehmyl sing from time to time. When he would reach home at night, he generally ensconced himself near to a window at the front of the house; and now and then his vigilance was encouraged by the sound of her voice.

Hetzel, of course, ran him a good deal. He took the running very philosophically. "I admit," he said, "that she piques my curiosity, and I don't know any reason why she shouldn't. Such a voice, joined to such beauty and intelligence, is it not enough to interest any body with the least spark of imagination? When are you going to call upon them?" But Hetzel was busy. "Examinations are now in full blast," he pleaded. "I have no leisure for calling on any one."

"'It sometimes make a body sour to see how things are shared,'.rdquo; complained Arthur. "To him who appreciates it not, the privilege is given; whereas, from him who would appreciate it to its full, the privilege is withheld. I only wish I had your opportunity."

Hetzel smiled complacently.

"And then," Arthur went on, "not even an occasional encounter in the street. Every day, coming and going, I cherish the hope that we may meet each other, she and I. Living so close together, it would be but natural if we should. But I'm down in my luck. We might as well dwell at the antipodes, for all we gain by being near neighbors. Concede that Fate is deucedly unkind."

"I don't know about that," said Hetzel, reflectively. "Perhaps Fate is acting for the best. My private opinion is that the less you see of that woman, the better for you. You're a pretty susceptible young man; and those eyes of hers might play sad havoc with your affections."

"That's just the way with you worldly, practical, materialistic fellows. You can't conceive that a man may be interested in a woman, without making a fool of himself, and getting spoony over her. You haven't enough spiritualism in your composition to realize that a woman may appeal to a man purely on abstract principles."

Hetzel laughed.

"You're a cynic," Arthur informed him.

"I don't believe in playing with fire," he retorted.

Thereafter their conversation drifted to other themes.

Well, the week glided by, and it was Sunday again; and with Sunday there occurred another change in the weather. The mercury shot up among the eighties, and the sky grew to an immense dome of blue. Sunday morning Hetzel said, "I suppose you haven't forgotten that we are engaged to sup with Mrs. Berle this evening?" To which Arthur responded, yawning, "Oh, no; it has weighed upon my consciousness ever since you accepted her invitation."

"I wouldn't let it distress me so much, if I were you. And, by the way, don't you think it would be well for us to take some flowers?"

"I suppose it would be a polite thing to do."

"Then why don't you make an excursion over to the florist's on Third Avenue, and lay in an assortment?"

"You're the horticulturist of this establishment. Go yourself."

"No. Your taste is superior to mine. Go along. Get a goodly number of cut flowers, and then two or three nosegays for the ladies."

"Ladies? What ladies?" demanded Arthur, brightening up. "Who is to be there, besides us and Mrs. Berle?"

"Oh, I don't say that any body is. I thought perhaps one of her daughters, or a friend, or—"

"Well, maybe I'll go over this afternoon. For the present—"

"This afternoon will be too late. The shops close early, you know, on Sunday."

Arthur issued forth upon his quest for flowers.

What was it that prompted him, after the main purchase had been made, to ask the tradesman, "Now, have you something especially nice, something unique, that would do for a lady's corsage?" The shopkeeper replied, "Yes, sir, I have something very rare in the line of jasmine. Only a handful in the market. This way, sir."—Arthur was conducted to the conservatory behind the shop; and there he devoted a full quarter hour of his valuable time to the construction of a very pretty and fragrant bunch of jasmine. What was it that induced this action?

When he got back home and displayed his spoils to Hetzel, the latter said, "And this jasmine—I suppose you intend it for Mrs. Berle to wear, yes?" To which Arthur vouchsafed no response.

They went down stairs at six o'clock. Mrs. Berle was alone in her parlor. They had scarcely more than made their obeisance, however, when the door-bell rang; and presently the rustle of ladies' gowns became audible in the hallway. Next moment the door opened—and Arthur's heart began to beat at break-neck speed. Entered, Mrs. Hart and Mrs. Lehmyl.

"I surmised as much, and you knew it all the while," Arthur gasped in a whisper to Hetzel.

His friend shrugged his shoulders.

The first clamor of greetings being over with, Arthur, his bunch of jasmine held fast in his hand, began, "Mrs. Lehmyl, may I beg of you to accept these little——"

"Oh, aren't they delicious!" she cried, impulsively.

Her eyes brightened, and she bent over the flowers to breathe in their incense.

"But I mustn't keep them all for myself," she added.

"Oh, we are equally well treated," said Mrs. Hart, flourishing a knot of Jacqueminot roses.

"Yes, indeed," Mrs. Berle joined in, pointing to a table, the marble top of which was hidden beneath a wealth of variegated blossoms.

"Nevertheless," said Mrs. Lehmyl. And she went on picking her bouquet to pieces. Mrs. Hart and Mrs. Berle received their shares; Hetzel his; and then, turning to Arthur, "*Maintenant, monsieur*" she said, with a touch of coquetry, "*maintenant à votre tour.*" She fastened a spray of jasmine to the lappel of his coat. In doing so, a delicate whiff of perfume was wafted upward from her hair. Whether it possessed some peculiar elixir-like quality, or not, I can not tell; but at that instant Arthur felt a thrill pierce to the very innermost of his heart.

"It is so warm," said Mrs. Berle, "I thought it would be pleasant to take supper out of doors. If you are agreeable, we will go down to the backyard."

In the back-yard the table was set beneath a blossoming peach-tree. The grass plot made an unexceptionable carpet. Honeysuckle vines clambered over the fence. The river glowed warmly in the light of the declining sun. The country beyond on Long Island lay smiling at the first persuasive touch of summer—of the summer that, ere long waxing fiercely ardent, was to scorch and consume it.

Mrs. Lehmyl looked around, with child-like happiness shining in her eyes. Arthur looked at her.

"Permit me to make you acquainted with my brother, Mr. Lipman," said the hostess.

Mr. Lipman had a head that the Wandering Jew might have been proud of; snow-white hair and beard, olive skin, regular features of the finest Oriental type, and deep-set, coal-black eyes, with an expression in them—an anxious, eager, hopelessly hopeful expression—that told the whole story of the travail and sorrow of his race. He kissed the hands of the ladies and shook those of the gentlemen.

"Now, to the table!" cried Mrs. Berle.

The table was of appetizing aspect; an immaculate cloth, garnished by divers German dishes, and beautified by the flowers our friends had brought. Arthur's chair was placed at the right of Mrs. Lehmyl's. Conversation, however, was general from first to last. Hetzel contributed an anecdote in the Irish dialect, at which he was an adept. Arthur told of a comic incident that had happened in court the other day. Mrs. Lehmyl said she could not fancy any thing being comic in a courtroom—the atmosphere of a court-room sent such a chill to the heart, she should think it would operate as an anaesthetic upon the humorous side of a person. Mr. Lipman gave a few reminiscences of the Hungarian revolt of '49, in which he had been a participant, wielding a brace of empty seltzer bottles, so he said, in default of nobler weapons. This led the talk up to the superiority of America over the effete monarchies of Europe. After a good deal of patriotism had asserted itself, a little criticism began to crop out. By and by the Goddess of Liberty had had her character thoroughly dissected. With the coffee, Mrs. Berle, who had heretofore shone chiefly as a listener, said, "Now, you young gentlemen may smoke, just as if you were three flights higher up." So they lit their cigars—in which pastime Mr. Lipman joined them—and sat smoking and chatting over the table till it had grown quite dark. At last it was moved that the party should adjourn to the parlor and have some music. There being no Wagnerites present, Mrs. Lehmyl sang Jensen's *Lehn deine Wang*, with so much fervor that two big tears gathered in Mr. Lipman's eyes and rolled down his cheeks. Then, to restore gayety, she sang *La Paloma*, in the merriest way imaginable; and finally, to bring the pendulum of emotion back to its mean position, *Voi chi Sapete* from the "Marriage of Figaro." After this there was an interim during which every body found occasion to say his say; and then Mrs. Berle announced, "My brother plays the 'cello. Now he must also play a little, yes?"

Mrs. Lehmyl was delighted by the prospect of hearing the 'cello played; and Mr. Lipman performed a courtly old bow, and said it would be a veritable inspiration to play to her accompaniment. Thereupon they consulted together until they had agreed upon a selection. It proved to be nothing less antiquated than Boccherini's minuet. The quaint and graceful measures, wrung out from the deep-voiced 'cello, brought smiles of enjoyment to every face. "But," says Arthur, "what pleased me quite as much as the music was to keep my eyes fixed on the picture that the two musicians presented; that old man's wonderful countenance, peering out from behind the neck of his instrument, intent, almost fierce in its earnestness; and hers, pale, luminous, passionate, varying with every modulation of the tune. And all the while the scent of the jasmine bud haunted my nostrils, and recalled vividly the moment she had pinned it into my buttonhole."—In deference to the demand for an encore, they played Handel's *Largo*. Then Mrs. Berle's maid appeared, bearing the inevitable wine and cakes. By and by Mrs. Hart began to make her adieux. At this, Arthur slipped quietly out of the room. When he returned, half a minute later, he had his hat in his hand. Mrs. Hart protested that it was quite unnecessary for him to trouble himself to see them home. "Why, it is only straight across the street," she submitted. But Arthur was obstinate.

On her door-step, Mrs. Hart said, "We should be pleased to have you call upon us, Mr. Ripley."

He and Hetzel sat up till past midnight, talking. The latter volunteered a good many favorable observations anent Mrs. Lehmyl. Arthur could have listened to him till daybreak.—In bed he had difficulty getting to sleep. Among other things, he kept thinking how fortunate it was that Peixada had disapproved of the trip to Europe. "Why, New York," he soliloquized, "is by all means the most interesting city in the world."

He took advantage of Mrs. Hart's permission to call, as soon as he reasonably could. While he was waiting for somebody to appear, he admired the decorations of Mrs. Hart's parlor. Neat gauze curtains at the windows, a rosy-hued paper on the wall, a soft carpet under foot, pretty pictures, pleasant chairs and tables, lamps and porcelains, and a book-case filled with interesting looking books, combined to lend the room an attractive, homelike aspect; for all of which, without cause, Arthur assumed that Mrs. Lehmyl was answerable. An upright piano occupied a corner; a sheet of music lay open on the rack. He was bending over it, to spell out the composer's name, when he heard a rustling of silk, and, turning around, he made his bow to—Mrs. Hart.

Mrs. Hart was accompanied by her cats.

Arthur's spirits sank.

"Ah, how do you do?" said Mrs. Hart. "I'm so glad to see you."

She shook his hand cordially and bade him be seated. He sat down and looked at the ceiling.

"Why didn't you bring your comrade, Mr. Hetzel?" she asked.

"Oh, Hetzel, he's got an examination on his hands, you know, and has perforce become a recluse—obliged to spend his evenings wading through the students' papers," explained Arthur, in a tone of sepulchral melancholy.

Mrs. Hart tried to manufacture conversation. Arthur responded absent-mindedly. Neither alluded to Mrs. Lehmyl. Arthur, fearing to appear discourteous, endeavored to behave as though it was to profit by Mrs. Hart's society alone that he had called. His voice, notwithstanding, kept acquiring a more and more lugubrious quality. But, by and by, when the flame of hope had dwindled to a spark, a second rustling of silk became audible. With a heart-leap that for a moment rendered him dumb, he heard a sweet voice say, "Good evening, Mr. Ripley." He lifted his eyes, and saw Mrs. Lehmyl standing before him, smiling and proffering her hand. Silently cursing his embarrassment, he possessed himself of the hand, and stammered out some sort of a greeting. There was a magic about that hand of hers. As he touched it, an electric tingle shot up his arm.

All three found chairs. Mrs. Hart produced a bag of knitting. One of the cats established himself in Mrs. Lehmyl's lap, and went to sleep. The other rubbed up against Arthur's knee, purring confidentially. Arthur cudgeled his wits for an apt theme. At last he got bravely started.

"What a fine-looking old fellow that Mr. Lipman was," he said. "It isn't often that one sees a face like his in America."

"No—not among the Americans of English blood; they haven't enough temperamental richness," acquiesced Mrs. Lehmyl.

"Yes, that's so. The most interesting faces one encounters here belong to foreigners—especially to the Jews. Mr. Lipman, you know, is a Jew."

"Naturally, being Mrs. Berle's brother."

"It's rather odd, Mrs. Lehmyl, but the more I see of the Jews, the better I like them. Aside from the interest they possess as a phenomenon in history, they're very agreeable to me as individuals. I can't at all comprehend the prejudice that some people harbor against them."

"How very liberal," If there was a shade of irony in her tone, it failed of its effect upon Arthur, who, inspired by his subject, went gallantly on:

"Their past, you know, is so poetic. They have the warmth of old wine in their blood. I've seen a great deal of them. This neighborhood is a regular ghetto. Then down-town I rub elbows with them constantly. Indeed, my best client is a Jew. And my friend, Hetzel, he's of Jewish extraction, though he doesn't keep up with the religion. On the average, I think the Jews are the kindest-hearted and clearest-minded people one meets hereabouts. That Mr. Lipman was a specimen of the highest type. It was delightful to watch his face, when you and he were playing—so fervent, so unselfconscious."

"And he played capitally, too—caught the true spirit of the music."

"So it seemed to me, though of course, I'm not competent to criticise. Speaking of faces, Mrs. Lehmyl, I hope you won't mind me saying that your face does not look to me like and American—I mean English-American."

"There is no reason why it should. I'm not' English-American."

"Ah, I felt sure of it. I felt sure you had Italian blood in your veins."

"No—nor Italian either."

"Well, Spanish, then?"

"Why, I supposed you knew. I—I am a Jewess."

"Mercy!" gasped Arthur, blushing to the roots of his hair. "I hope—I hope you—" He broke off, and squirmed uncomfortably in his chair.

"Why, is it possible you didn't know it?" asked Mrs. Lehmyl.

"Indeed, I did not. If I had, I assure you, I shouldn't have put my foot in it as I did—shouldn't have made bold to patronize your race as I was doing. I meant every word I spoke, though. The Jews are a noble and beautiful people, with a record that we Gentiles might well envy."

"You said nothing that was not perfectly proper. Don't imagine for an instant that you touched a sensitive spot. I am a Jewess by birth, though, like your friend, Mr. Hetzel, I don't go to the temple. Modern ceremonial Judaism is not to me especially satisfying as a religion."

"You are not orthodox?"

"I am quite otherwise."

"I am glad to hear it. I am glad that there is this tendency amoung the better educated Jews to cast loose from their Judaism. I want to see them intermarry with the Christians—amalgamate, and help to form the American people of the future. That of course is their destiny."

"I suppose it is."

"You speak as though you regretted it."

"No; I don't regret it. I am too good an American to regret it. But it is a little melancholy, to say the least, to see one of the most cherished of Jewish ideals being abandoned before the first step is made toward realizing it."

"What ideal is that?"

"Why, the hope that cheered the Jews through the many centuries of their persecution—the hope that a time would come when they could compel recognition from their persecutors, when, as a united people, they could stand forth before the world, pure and strong and upright, and exact credit for their due. The Jew has been for so long a time the despised and rejected of men, that now, when he has the opportunity, it seems as though he ought to improve it—show the stuff he is made of, prove that Shylock is a libel upon him, justify his past, achieve great results, demonstrate that he only needed light and liberty to develop into a leader of progress. The Jew has eternally been complaining—crying, 'You think I am such an inferior style of personage; give me a chance, and I will convince you of your error.' Now that the chance is given him, it seems a pity for him quietly to efface himself, become indistinguishable in the mass of mankind. I should like him to retain the name of Jew until it has grown to be a term of honor, instead of one of reproach. However, his destiny is otherwise; and he must make the best of it. It is the destiny of the dew-drop to slip into the shining sea.' Probably it is better that it should be so."

"But how many Jews are there who would subscribe to your view of the case—who would admit that amalgamation is inevitable?"

"Doubtless, very few. Most of them have no views at all on the subject. The majority of the wealthier Jews here in America are epicureans. Eat, drink, be merry, and lay up a competence for the rainy day, is about their philosophy. But among the older people the prejudice against intermarriage is wonderfully strong. We shall have to wait for a generation or two, before it can become common. But it is a prejudice pure and simple, the offspring of superstition, and not the result of allegiance to that ideal I was speaking of. The average Jew of a certain age may not care a fig for his religion, but if he hears of an instance of intermarriage, he will hold up his hands in horror, and wag his head, and predict some dire calamity for the bride and bridegroom. The same man will not enter a synagogue from year's end to year's end, and should you happen to discuss theology with him, you'd put him down for an out-and-out rationalist at once. But then, plenty of people who pride themselves on being freethinkers, are profoundly superstitious—Gentiles as well as Jews."

"No doubt about that. In fact, I think that every body has a trace of superstition in his makeup, no matter how emancipated he may fancy himself. Now I, for example, can't help attributing some uncanny potency to the number seven. There are more things in heaven and earth than are dreamed of by modern science; and perhaps superstition is a crude way of acknowledging this truth. It is the reaction of the imagination, when confronted with the unknowable."

"It seems to me that much which passes for superstition in the world, ought not to be so called. It is, rather, a super-sense. There is a subtle something that broods over human life—as the aroma broods over a goblet of old wine—a something of such fine, impalpable texture, that many men and women are never able to perceive it, but which others of more sensitive organization, feel all the time—are forever conscious of. This is the material which the imagination seizes hold of, and out of which it spins those fantastic, cobweb shapes that practical persons scoff at as superstitions. I can't understand, however, how any body can specialize it to the extent of linking it to arithmetic, as you do, and as those do who are afraid of thirteen."

"What you have reference to falls, rather, under the head of mysticism, does it not? And mysticism is one form of poetry. You come rightfully by your ideas on this subject. A strain of mysticism is your birthright, a portion of your inheritance as a Jewess. It's one of the benefits you derive from being something more than an American."

"Oh, but I am an American, besides. It is a privilege to be one."

"I meant American of English ancestry. We are all Americans—or more precisely, we are all immigrants or the descendants of immigrants. But those of us that have an infusion of warmer blood than the English in our veins, are to be congratulated."

"It seems to me that Ripley is an English name."

"So it is. But my father's mother was a Frenchwoman."

"A ruddy drop of Gallic blood outweighs a world of gold," parodied Mrs. Lehmyl.

"Oh, you may make fun of me, if you like," cried Arthur; "but my comfort in thinking of that French grandmother of mine will remain undiminished. I wonder," he added, more gravely, "I wonder whether you have ever suffered from any of the indignities that your people are sometimes put to, Mrs. Lehmyl. I declare I have been tempted to wring the necks of my fellow Gentiles, now and then."

"Suffered? I have occasionally been amused. I should not have much self-respect, if any thing like that could cause me suffering. Last summer, for instance, Mrs. Hart and I were in the mountains, at a hotel. Every body, to begin with, was disposed to be very sociable. Then, innocently enough, one day I said we were Jewesses. After that we were left severely alone. I remember, we got into an omnibus one afternoon to drive to the village. A young man and a couple of young ladies—guests at the same house—were already in it. They glared at us quite savagely, and whispered, *'Jews!'* and signaled the driver to stop and let them out. So we had the conveyance to ourselves, for which we were not sorry."

"I wish I had been there!" cried Arthur, with astonishing energy.

"Why?" asked Mrs. Lehmyl.

"Oh, that young man and I would have had an interview alone," he answered, in a blood-curdling key.

"He means that he would have given that young man a piece of his mind," put in Mrs. Hart.

The sound of her voice occasioned Arthur a veritable start. He had forgotten that she was present.

"I hope not," said Mrs. Lehmyl. "To resent such conduct would lend undue importance to it."

"All the same it makes my blood boil—the thought that those young animals dared to be rude to you."

The pronoun "you" was spoken with a significant emphasis. A student of human nature could have inferred volumes from it. Mrs. Hart straightway proceeded to demolish her own claims to be called a student of human nature, if she had any, by construing the syllable in the plural number.

"I'm sure we appreciate your sympathy," she said. "Ruth, play a little for Mr. Ripley."

Was this intended as a reward of merit? Contrariwise to the gentleman in *Punch*, Arthur would so much rather have heard her talk than play.

"Shall I?" she asked.

"Oh, I should be delighted," he assented.

She played the Pathetic Sonata. Before she had got beyond the first dozen bars, Arthur had been caught up and borne away on the strong current of the music. She played with wonderful execution and perfect feeling. I suppose Arthur had heard the Pathetic Sonata a score of times before. He had never begun to appreciate it till now. It seemed to him that in a language of superhuman clearness and directness, the subtlest and most sacred mysteries of the soul were being explained to him. Every emotion, every passion, that the heart can feel, he seemed to hear expressed by the miraculous voice that Mrs. Lehmyl was calling into being; and his own heart vibrated in unison. Deep melancholy, breathless terror, keen, quivering anguish, blank despair; flashes of short-lived joy, instants of hope speedily ingulfed in an eternity of despond; tremulous desire, the delirium of enjoyment, the bitter awakening to a sense of satiety and self-deception; intervals of quiet reflection, broken in upon by the turbulent cries of a hundred malicious spirits; weird glimpses into a world of phantom shapes, exaltation into the seventh heaven of delight, descent into the bottom pit of darkness; these were a few of the strange and vague, but none the less intense, emotional experiences through which Mrs. Lehmyl led him. When she returned to her chair, opposite his own, he could only look upon her face and wonder; he could not speak. A delicate flush had overspread her cheeks, and her eyes shone even more brightly than their wont. She evidently misunderstood his silence.

"Ah," she said, with frank disappointment, "it did not please you."

"Please me?" he cried. "No, indeed, it did not please me. It was like Dante's journey through the three realms of the dead. It was like seeing a miracle performed. It overpowered me. I suppose I am too susceptible—weak, if you will, and womanish. But such music as that—I could no more have withstood its spell, than I could withstand the influence of strong wine."

"Speaking of strong wine," said Mrs. Hart, "what if you should try a little mild wine?" And she pointed to a servant who had crossed the threshold in the midst of Arthur's rhapsody, and who bore a tray with glasses and a decanter.

"In spite of this anti-climax," he said, sipping his wine, "what I said was the truth."

"It is the fault, no doubt, of your French blood, Monsieur," said Mrs. Lehmyl. "But I confess that, perhaps in a moderated degree, music has much the same effect upon me. When I first heard *La Damnation de Faust*, I had to hold on to the arms of my chair, to keep from being carried bodily away. You remember that dreadful ride into perdition—toward the end? I really felt that if I let go my anchorage, I should be swept off along with Faust and Mephistopheles."

"I remember. But that did not affect me so. I never was so affected till I heard you play just now."

"I don't know whether I ought to feel complimented, or the reverse."

"What is the feeling we naturally have at perceiving our power over another human being?" Mrs. Lehmyl changed the subject.

"That was an exceedingly clever guess you made the other day," she said, "that I was a lover of Browning. I can't understand what suggested it."

"I told you then that I dared not enlighten you, lest I might be deemed presumptuous. If you will promise me absolution, beforehand—"

"But you, too, I take for granted, share my sentiments."

"What I have read is unsurpassed. 'The Inn Album,' for example."

"And 'The Ring and the Book.'.rdquo;

"I haven't read 'The Ring and the Book.'.rdquo;

"Oh, then you must read it at once. Then you don't half know Browning. Will you read it, if I lend it to you?"

"You are very kind. I should like nothing better."

Mrs. Lehmyl begged to be excused and left the room. Arthur followed the sound of her light, quick footsteps up the stairs.

"Browning is her patron saint," volunteered Mrs. Hart. "She spends her time about equally between him and her piano."

Mrs. Lehmyl came back.

"There," she said, giving him the volume, and smiling, "there is my *vade mecum*. I love it almost as dearly as I could if it were a human being. You must be sure to like it."

"I am sure you honor me very highly by entrusting it to me," he replied.

At home he opened it, thinking to read for an hour or two before going to bed. What interested him, however, even more than the strong, virile, sympathetic poetry, and, indeed, ere long, quite absorbed his attention, were the traces of Mrs. Lehmyl's ownership that he came across every here and there—a corner dog-eared, a passage inclosed by pencil lines, a fragment of rose-petal stuck between the pages. It gave him a delicious sense of intimacy with her to hold this book in his hands. Had not her hand warmed it? her hair shadowed it? her very breath touched it? Had it not been her companion in solitary moments? a witness to the life she led when no human eye was upon her? What precious secrets it might have whispered, if it had had a tongue! There was a slight discoloration of the paper, where Pompilia tells of her miseries as Guido's bride. Who could say but that it had been caused by Mrs. Lehmyl's tears? That she had loaned him the book seemed somehow like a mark of confidence. On the flyleaf something had been written in ink, and subsequently scratched out—probably her name. He wondered why she had erased it. Toward the close of Caponsacchi's version, one of the pages had been torn clear across, and then neatly pasted together with tissue paper braces. He wondered what the circumstances were under which the mischief had been done, and whether the repair was her handiwork. A faint, sweet perfume clung to the pages. It had the power of calling her up vividly before him, and sending an exquisite tremor into his heart. And, withal, had any body suggested that he was at the verge of falling in love with her, he would have denied it stoutly—so little was he disposed to self-analysis.

But ere a great while, the scales fell from his eyes.

By dint of much self-discipline, he managed to let a week and a day elapse before paying his second call. While he stood in the vestibule, waiting for the opening of the door, sundry bursts of sound escaping from within, informed him that a duet was being played upon the piano. Intuitively he concluded that the treble part was Mrs. Lehmyl's; instinctively he asked, "But who is carrying the bass?" On entering the parlor, it was with a sharp and significant pang that he beheld, seated at Mrs. Lehmyl's left, no less redoubtable a creature than a Man. He took a chair, and sat down, and suffered untold wretchedness until that duet was finished. He could not see the man's face, but the back of his head indicated youth. The vicissitudes of the composition they were playing brought the two performers painfully close together. This was bad enough; but to poor Arthur's jealous mind it seemed as if from time to time, even when the music furnished no excuse, they voluntarily approached each other. Every now and then they hurriedly exchanged a whispered sentence. He felt that he would eagerly have bartered his ten fingers for the right to know what it was they said. How much satisfaction would he have obtained if he had been stationed near enough to overhear? All they said was, "One, two, three, four, five, six." Perhaps in his suspicious mood he would have magnified this innocent remark into a confidence conveyed by means of a secret code.

When the musicians rose Arthur experienced a slight relief. Mrs. Lehmyl greeted him with marked kindness, and shook hands warmly. She introduced her co-executant as Mr. Spencer. And Mr. Spencer was tall, lean, gawky and bilious-looking.

But Arthur's relief was of short duration. Mr. Spencer forthwith proceeded to exhibit great familiarity with both of the ladies—a familiarity which they did not appear to resent. Mrs. Hart, indeed, reciprocated to the extent of addressing him as Dick. His conversation made it manifest that he had traveled with them in Europe. He was constantly referring to people and places and events about which Arthur was altogether ignorant. His every other sentence began: "Do you remember?" Arthur was excessively uneasy; but he had determined to sit Mr. Spencer out, though he should, peradventure, remain until sunrise.

Mr. Spencer did indeed remain till the night had got on its last legs. It lacked but a quarter of midnight when, finally, he accomplished his exit.

Said Mrs. Hart, after he had gone: "A Boston man."

"We met him," said Mrs. Lehmyl, "at Aix-les-Bains. He's a remarkably well-informed musician—writes criticisms for one of the Boston papers."

"He came this evening," went on Mrs. Hart, "to tell us of the happy termination of a love affair in which he was involved when we last saw him. He's going to be married."

At these words Arthur's spirits shot up far above their customary level. So! There was no occasion for jealousy in the quarter of Mr. Spencer, at any rate. The reaction was so great that had Mr. Spencer still been present, I think our hero would have felt like hugging him.

"A very fine fellow, I should judge," he said. "I have outstaid him because I wanted to tell you that Hetzel and I have devised a jolly little plan for Sunday, in which we are anxious to have you join us. Our idea is to spend the afternoon in the Metropolitan Art Museum. You know, the pictures are well worth an inspection; and on Sunday there is no crowd. Hetz has procured a Sunday ticket through the courtesy of the director. Then, afterward, you are to come back with us and take dinner—if the weather permits, out on our roof. Mrs. Berle will be at the dinner, though she doesn't care to go with us to see the pictures. We may count upon you, may we not?"

"Oh, certainly; that will be delightful," said Mrs. Hart.

"Then we will call for you at about three o'clock?"

"Yes."

"Good-night."

His hand was hot and trembling as it clasped Mrs. Lehmyl's; a state of things which she, however, did not appear to notice. She gazed calmly into his eyes, and returned a quiet good-night. He stood a long while in the doorway of his house, looking across at No. 46. He saw the light quenched in the parlor, and other lights break out in the floors above. Then these in their turn were extinguished; and he knew that the occupants were on their way to the land of Nod. "Good angels guard her slumbers," he said, half aloud, and climbed the stairs that led to his own bedchamber. There he lay awake hour after hour. He could hear the waters of the river lapping the shore, and discern the street lamps gleaming like stars along the opposite embankment. Now and again a tug-boat puffed importantly up stream—a steam whistle shrieked—a schooner glided mysteriously past. I don't know how many times he confessed to his pillow, "I love her—I love her—I love her!"

The next day—Saturday—he passed in a fever of impatience. It seemed as though to-morrow never would arrive. At night he scarcely slept two hours. And on Sunday morning he was up by six o'clock. Then, how the hours and minutes did prolong themselves, until the hands of his watch marked three!

"What's the matter with you?" Hetzel asked more than once. "Why are you so restless? You roam around like a cat who has lost her kittens. Any thing worrying you? Feeling unwell? Or what?"

"Oh, I'm a little nervous—guess I drank more coffee for breakfast than was good for me," he replied.

He tried to read. The print blurred before his eyes. He tried to write a letter. He proceeded famously thus far: "New York, May 24, 1884.—My dearest mother.—" But at this point his pen stuck. Strive as he might, he could get no further.

He tore the paper up, in a pet. He smoked thrice his usual allowance of tobacco. Every other minute he had out his watch. He half believed that Time had slackened its pace for the especial purpose of adding fuel to the fires that were burning in his breast. Such is the preposterous egotism of a man in love.

When at length the clock struck half after two, his pulse quickened. This last half hour was as long as the entire forepart of the day had been. With each moment, his agitation increased. Finally he and Hetzel crossed the street. He had to bite his lips and press his finger-nails deep into the flesh of his hands, in order to command a tolerably self-possessed exterior.

Arthur says that he remembers the rest of that Sunday as one remembers a bewildering dream. He remembers, to begin with, how Mrs. Lehmyl met him in Mrs. Hart's drawing-room, and gave him a warm, soft hand, and spoke a few pleasant words of welcome. He remembers how his heart fluttered, and how he had to catch for breath, as he gazed into her unfathomable eyes, and inhaled that daintiest of perfumes which clung to her apparel. He remembers how he marched at her side through Fiftieth Street to Madison Avenue, in a state of delirious intoxication, and how they mounted a celestial chariot—Hetzel says it was a Madison Avenue horse car—in which he sat next to her, and heard her voice mingle with the tinkling of silver bells, like a strain of heavenly music. He remembers how they sauntered through the galleries, chatting together about—oddly enough, he can not remember what. Oddly enough, also, he can not remember the pictures that they looked at. He can remember only "the angelic radiance of her face and the wonderful witchery of her presence." Then he remembers how they walked home together through the Park, green and fragrant in the gentle May weather, and took places side by side at the table on the roof. "What is strangest," he says, "is this, that I do not remember any thing at all about the other people who were present—Hetzel and Mrs. Berle and Mrs. Hart. As I look back, it seems as though she and I had been alone with each other the whole time." "But we were there, nevertheless," Hetzel assures me; "and one of us enjoyed hugely witnessing his young friend's infatuation. It was delightful to see the big, stalwart, imperious Arthur Ripley, helpless as a baby in the power of that little woman. One not well acquainted with him might not have perceived his condition; but to me it was as plain as the nose on his face."—"There was a full moon that evening," Arthur continues, "and I wish you could have seen her eyes in the moonlight. I kept thinking of the old song,

'In thy dark eyes splendor,

Where the warm light loves to dwell.'.rdquo;

"I dare say you'll think me sentimental, but I can't help it. The fact is that those eyes of hers glowed with all the tenderness and pathos and mystery of a martyr's. Pale, ethereal fires burned deep down in them, and showed where her soul dwelt. They haunted me for days afterward. Days? No—months. They haunt me now. My heart thrills at this moment, thinking of them, just as it did then, when I was looking into them. I tell you it hurt here"—thumping his chest—"when I had to part with her. It was like—yes, sir; you needn't smile—it was like having my heart wrenched out. My senses were in confusion. I walked up and down my floor pretty much all night. You never saw such a wretched fellow. At least I fancied I was wretched. The thought of how hopeless my case was—of how unlikely it was that she would ever care a farthing for me—drove me about frantic. All the same, I wouldn't have exchanged that wretchedness for all the other treasures of the world." In this exaggerated vein, he would gladly babble on for the next twenty pages; but to what profit, since it is already clear that he was head-over-ears in love?

Of course Arthur had no idea of making a declaration. That she should cherish for him a feeling at all of the nature of his for her, seemed the most improbable of contingencies. So long as he could retain the privilege of seeing her frequently, he would be contented; he would not run the risk of having it withdrawn by revealing to her a condition of affairs which, very likely, she would not sanction. His supremest aspiration, he derived a certain dismal satisfaction from fancying, would be realized if he could in some way become useful and helpful to her, no matter after how lowly a fashion. Henceforward he spent at least one evening a week in her company. 'She never received him alone; but Mrs. Hart's presence was not objectionable, because she had the sensible custom of knitting in silence, and leaving the two younger folks to do the talking. Their talk was generally about music and literature and other edifying themes; rarely about matters personal. Arthur got pretty well acquainted with Mrs. Lehmyl's views and tastes and habits of thought; but when he stopped to reckon up how much he had gathered concerning herself, her family connections, her life in the past, he acknowledged that it could all be represented by a solitary nought. Not that she was conspicuously reserved with him. She made it unmistakably evident that she liked him cordially. Only, the pronouns, I and thou, played a decidedly minor part in her ordinary conversation.

He experienced all the pains and pleasures of first love, and all the strange hallucinations that it produces. The man who looks at the world through a lover's eyes, is as badly off as he who looks at it through a distorting lens—objects are thrown out of their proper relations; proportion and perspective go mad; big things become little, and *vice versa.* Especially is it remarkable how completely his notions of time will get perverted. For instance, the hours flew by with a rapidity positively astounding when Arthur was in Mrs. Lehmyl's presence. He would sit down opposite her at eight o clock; they would converse for a few moments; she would sing a song or two; and then, to his unutterable stupefaction, the clock would strike eleven! On the other hand, when he was away from her, time lagged in an equally perplexing manner. He and Hetzel, to illustrate, would finish their dinner at half past seven—only a half hour before he would be at liberty to cross the street. But that half hour! It stretched out like an eternity, beyond the reach of Arthur's imagination. Life had changed to a dream or to a delirium—it would be hard to say which. The laws of cause and effect had ceased to operate. The universe had lost its equilibrium. Arthur's heart would swing from hot to cold, from cold to hot, without a pretense of physiological rhyme or reason. He became moody and capricious. A fiber in his composition, the existence of which he had never hitherto suspected, acquired an alarming prominence. That was an almost womanish sensitiveness. It was as if he had been stripped of his armor. Small things, trifling events, that had in the past left him entirely unimpressed, now smote his consciousness like sharpened arrows. Sights of distress in the streets, stories of suffering in the newspapers, moved him keenly and profoundly. He had been reading *Wilhelm Meisler.* He could not finish it. The emotions it occasioned him were poignant enough to border upon physical pain. The long and short of it is that Love had turned his rose-tinted calcium light upon the world in which Arthur moved, and so made visible a myriad beauties and blemishes that had lain hidden in the darkness heretofore. Among other things that Arthur remarked as curious, was the frequency with which he saw her name, Lehmyl, or other names resembling it, Lemyhl, Lehmil, etc., on sign-boards, as he was being whirled through the streets on the elevated railway. He was sure that he had never seen it or heard it till she had come to dwell in Beekman Place. Now he was seeing it all the time. He was disposed to be somewhat superstitious anent this circumstance, to regard it as an omen of some sort—but whether for good or evil, he could not tell. Of course its explanation was simple enough. With the name uppermost in his mind, it was natural that his attention should be caught by it wherever it occurred; whereas formerly, before he had known her, it was one of a hundred names that he had passed unnoticed every day. And yet, emerging from a brown study of which she had been the subject, it was a little startling to look out of the window, and find Lehmyl staring him in the face.

Now and then, if the weather was fine, he would go up-town early and accompany her for a walk in Central Park. Occasionally he would tuck a book into his pocket, so that when they sat down to rest he could read aloud to her. One day the book of his selection chanced to be a volume of Nathaniel Hawthorne's shorter tales. They had appropriated unto themselves a bench in a secluded alley; and now Arthur opened to "The Snow Image."

But before he had proceeded beyond the second sentence, Mrs. Lehmyl stopped him. "Oh, please—please don't read that," she cried, in a sharp, startled tone.

Arthur looked up. He saw that her face had turned deathly pale, that her lips were quivering, and that her eyes had moistened. Thrusting the book into his pocket, he stammered out a few hasty words of anxiety. She was not ill?

"Oh, no," she said, "not ill. Only, when you began to read that story—when I realized what it was that you were reading—I—it—it recalled disagreeable memories. But—shall we walk on?" She was silent or monosyllabic, and her face wore a grave expression, all the rest of their time together. At the door of her house she gave him her hand, and looked straight into his eyes, and said, "You must forgive me if I have spoiled your afternoon. I could not help it. You know how it is' when one is happy—very happy—to be reminded suddenly of things one would like to forget."

Arthur's heart went out to her in a mighty bound. "When one is happy—very happy!" The phrase echoed like a peal of gala bells in his ears. He had a hard struggle to keep from flinging himself at her feet there in the open street. But all his love burned in the glance he gave her—an intense, radiant glance, which she met with one that threw his soul into a transport. She knew now that he loved her! There could be no doubt about that. And, since her eyes did not quail before his—since she had sustained unflinchingly the gaze which, more eloquently than any words, told her of the passion that was consuming him—might he not conclude—? Ah, no; he would trust himself to conclude nothing till he had spoken with her by word of mouth.

"Good-by," she said.

"May—may I call upon you to-morrow?"

"Yes."

He relinquished her hand, which he had been clinging to all this time, and went his way.

"When one is happy—very happy," he repeated again and again. "So she was happy—very happy!—until I opened that ill-fated book. What can the associations be that darkened her mood so abruptly? But *to-morrow!*"

CHAPTER VI.
"THE WOMAN WHO HESITATES."

RIPLEY, attorney, New York:

"Draft accepted. Begin immediately.

"Ulrich."

Such was the cable dispatch that Arthur got a fortnight after he had mailed his letter to Counselor Ulrich of Vienna. A fortnight later still, the post brought him an epistle to the same effect. Then ensued four weeks of silence. During these four weeks one question had received a good share of his attention. The substance and the solution of it, may be gathered from the following conversation held between him and Peixada.

Arthur said, "Suppose the residence of your sister-in-law to be discovered: what next? Suppose we find that she is living in Europe: how can we induce her to return hither and render herself liable to the jurisdiction of our courts? Or suppose even that she should turn out to be established here in New York: what's to prevent her from packing her trunks and taking French leave the day after citations to attend the probate of her husband's will are served upon her? In other words, how are we to compel her to stand and deliver? Ignorant as we are of the nature and location of her properties, we can't attach them in the regular way."

Peixada said, "Hum! That's so. I hadn't thought of that. That's a pretty serious question."

"At first," said Arthur, "it struck me as more than serious—as fatal. But there's a way out of it—the neatest and simplest way you can imagine."

"Ah," sighed Peixada, with manifest relief.

"Now see," continued Arthur. "Mrs. Peixada shot her husband—was indicted—tried—acquitted'—yes?"

"To be sure."

"But at the same time she also took the life of a man named Edward Bolen, her husband's coachman—eh?"

"She did—certainly."

"Was she indicted for his murder as well as for the other?"

"She was indicted, yes, but——"

"But never arraigned for trial. Then the indictment is still in force against her?"

"I suppose it is—unless the statute of limitations——"

"The statute of limitations does not apply after an indictment has once been found."

"Oh."

"Well, I was thinking the matter over the other day—confronting that difficulty I have mentioned, and wondering how the mischief it was to be surmounted—when it occurred to me that it might be possible to interest the authorities in our behalf, and so get Mrs. Peixada under lock and key."

"Splendid!"

"I went over to the district-attorney's office, and saw Mr. Romer, the senior assistant, who happens to be a good friend of mine, and told him the sum and substance of our case. Then I asked him whether for the sake of justice he wouldn't lend us the machinery of the law—that is, upon our finding out her whereabouts, cause her extradition and imprisonment under the indictment *in re* Bolen. I promised that you would assume the entire expense."

"And he replied?"

"That it was a rather irregular proposition, but that he would think it over and let me know his conclusion."

"Well, have you heard from him since?"

"Yes—yesterday morning I received a note, asking me to call at his office. When I got there, this is what he said. He said that he had read the indictment, and consulted his chief, Mr. Orson, and pondered the matter pretty thoroughly. Extraordinary as the proceeding would be, he had decided to do as I wished. 'Because,' he added, 'there's a mighty strong case against the woman, and I shouldn't wonder if it would be worth our while to try her. At any rate, if you can set us on her track, we'll arrest her and take our chances. We've made quite a point, you know, of unearthing indictments that our predecessors had pigeonholed; and more than once we've secured a conviction. It doesn't follow that because the jury in the Peixada case stultified themselves, another jury will. So, you go ahead with your inquiries; and when she's firmly pinned down, we'll take her in custody. Then, after you've recovered your money, we can step in and do our best to send her up to Sing Sing.'—I declare, I was half sorry to have prepared new troubles for the poor creature; but, you see, our interests are now perfectly protected."

"A brilliant stroke!" cried Peixada. "Then we shall not merely rescue my brother's property, but, indirectly at least, we shall avenge his death! I am delighted. Now we must redouble our efforts to ferret her out."

"Precisely. And that brings me to another point. I have had a long letter—sixteen solid pages—from Ulrich, the Austrian lawyer. He has traced her from Vienna to Paris, from Paris to London. He's in London now, working up his clew. The last news of her dates back to May, 1882. On the 23d of that month she left the hotel she had been stopping at in London, and went—Ulrich is trying to discover where. I think our best course now will be to retain an English solicitor, and let him carry the matter on from the point Ulrich has reached. With your approval, I shall cable Ulrich to put the affair into the hands of Mr. Reginald Graham, a London attorney in whom I have the utmost confidence. What do you think?"

"Oh, you're right. No doubt about that. Meantime, here."—Peixada handed his legal adviser a check for one hundred dollars. "This is to keep up your spirits," he said.

The above conference had taken place on the forenoon of Wednesday, the 25th of June. It was on that afternoon that Arthur started to read "The Snow Image" to Mrs. Lehmyl.

Next day, after an eternity of impatience, he rang her bell.

"Mrs. Lehmyl," said the servant, "is sick in her room with a headache."

"What?" cried Arthur, and stood still, gaping for dismay.

"Yes," repeated Bridget; "sick in her room."

"Oh, but she will receive me. I call by appointment. Please tell her that I am here."

"She said that she could receive no one; but if you'll step into the parlor, I'll speak to Mrs. Hart."

Mrs. Hart appeared and corroborated the maid's statement. A big lump gathered in Arthur's throat. He had looked forward so eagerly to this moment—had hoped so much from it—and it had been such a long time coming—that now to have it slip away unused, like this—the disappointment was bitter. He felt utterly miserable and dejected. As he dragged himself down the stoop—he had sprung up it, two steps at a stride, a moment since—he noticed a group of urchins, standing on the curbstone and grinning from ear to ear. He fancied that they had guessed his secret, and were laughing at his discomfiture; if he had obeyed his impulse, he would have wrung their necks on the spot. He crossed the street, locked himself in his room, and surrendered unresistingly to the blue devils.

These vivacious sprites played fast and loose with the poor boy's imagination. They conjured up before him a multitude of unlikely catastrophes. They persuaded him that his case was worse than hopeless.

Mrs. Lehmyl cared not a fig for him. Why, forsooth, should she? Probably he had a successful rival. That a woman such as she should love an insignificant young fellow like himself—the bare idea was preposterous. He was to blame for having allowed the flower of hope to take root in his bosom. He laughed bitterly, and wondered how he had contrived to deceive himself even for a moment.

It was trebly absurd that she should love him after so brief and so superficial an acquaintance. Life wasn't worth living; and, but for his mother and Hetzel, he would put an end to himself forthwith. Yet, the next instant he was recalling the "Yes" that she had spoken yesterday, in response to his "May I call to-morrow?" and the fearless glance with which she had met his eyes. "Ah," he cries, "it set my blood afire. It dazzled me with visions of impossible joy. I could almost hear her murmur—oh, so softly—'I love you, Arthur!' You may guess the effect that fancy had upon me." It is significant that not once did he pity her for her headache. He took for granted that it was merely a subterfuge for refusing' to receive him. But her motive for refusing to see him— There was the rub! If he could only have divined it—known it to a certainty—then his suspense would have been less of an agony, then his mind could have borrowed some repose, though perhaps the repose of despair.

Well, he got through the night after a fashion. A streak of cold, gray light lay along the eastern horizon, and the river had put off the color of ink for the color of lead, before he fell asleep. His sleep was troubled. A nightmare played frightful antics upon his breast. It was broad day when he awoke. The river sparkled gayly in the sunlight, the sky shimmered with warmth, the sparrows outside quarreled vociferously. A brief glow of cheerfulness was the result. But memory speedily asserted itself. Heartsick and weary he began his toilet. "What had I to look forward to?" he demands. He climbed the staircase, and entered the breakfast room. Hetzel sat near the window, reading a newspaper. Hetzel grunted forth a gruff good-morning, without looking up. I doubt however, whether Arthur knew that Hetzel was there at all. For, as he crossed the threshold, his eye was caught by something white lying upon his plate. He can't tell why—but he guessed at once that it was a note from Mrs. Lehmyl. His lover's instinct scented the truth from afar.

He snatched the letter up eagerly. But he delayed about opening it. He scrutinized the direction—written in a frank, firm, woman's hand. The paper exhaled never so faint a perfume. Still he did not open it. He was afraid. He would wait till his agitation had subsided a little. He could hear his heart going thump, thump, thump, like a hammer against his side. He had difficulty with his breath. Then a dreadful possibility loomed up before him! What—what if it should not be from her after all! This thought endowed him with the courage of desperation. He tore the missive open.

He was standing there, one hand grasping the back of his chair, the other holding the letter to his eyes, when Hetzel, throwing his newspaper aside, got up, turned about the room, then abruptly came to a halt, facing Arthur.

"Mercy upon me, man," cried Hetzel, "what has happened? Cheeks burning, fingers trembling! No bad news? Speak—quickly."

But Arthur did not speak.

Hetzel went on: "I've noticed lately, there's been something wrong with you. You're nervous, restless, out of kilter. Is there a woman in the case? Is your feeling for our neighbor something more than a passing fancy? Are you taking her seriously? Or, are you simply run down-+-in need of rest and change? Why not make a trip up to Oldbridge, and see your mother?"

By the time Hetzel had finished speaking, Arthur had folded his letter and stowed it away in his pocket.

"Eh? What were you saying?" he inquired, with a blank look.

"Oh, I was saying that breakfast is getting cold; coffee spoiling, biscuit drying up—whatever you choose. Letter from home?"

"Home? No; not from home," said Arthur.

"Well, draw up, anyhow. Is—is—By Jove, what is the matter with you? Where are you now? Why don't you pay attention when I speak? What has come over you the last week or two? You're worrying me to death. Out with it! No secrets from the head of the house."

"I have no secrets," Arthur answered, meekly; "only—only, if you must know it, I'm—" No doubt he was on the point of making a full confession. He restrained himself, however; added, "There! I won't talk about it;" applied himself to his knife and fork, and preserved a dismal silence till the end of the meal. He went away as soon as ordinary courtesy would warrant.

No sooner had he closed the door behind him, than his hand made a dive into his pocket, and brought out Mrs. Lehmyl's letter. He read it through for perhaps the twentieth time. It ran thus:

"46 Beekman Place,

"Thursday evening.

"Dear Mr. Ripley After a sleepless night, my head is aching cruelly. That is why I was unable to receive you. But, since you had told me that you were coming, I feel that I must write this note to explain and to apologize. I should have sent you word not to come, except that until now I have been too ill to use my eyes. The only help for me when I have a headache like this, is solitary confinement in a darkened room. I have braved the gaslight for an instant, to write you this note, and already I am suffering the consequences. But I felt that I really owed you my excuses. You will accept them in a lenient spirit, will you not?

"Sincerely yours,

"Ruth Lehmyl."

I think Arthur's first sentiment on reading this communication, had been one of disappointment. It was just such an apology as she might have written to anybody else under similar circumstances. He had nerved himself, he thought, for the worst before breaking the seal—for a decree forbidding him future admittance to her presence, for an announcement of her betrothal to another man—for what not. But a quite colorless, polite, and amiable "I beg your pardon," he had not contemplated. It produced the effect of a wet blanket. From the high and mighty heroic mood in which he had torn it open, to the unimpassioned sentences in which it was couched, was too rapid a transition, too abrupt a plunge from hot to cold, an anti-climax equally unexpected and depressing.

But after a second perusal—and a second perusal followed immediately upon the first—his pulse quickened. With a lover's swift faculty for seizing hold of and interpreting trifles light as air, he discerned what he believed to be encouraging tokens. Under what obligation had Mrs. Lehmyl been to write to him so promptly? At the cost of severe pain, she had hastened to make her excuses for a thing that there was not really the least hurry about. If she were quite indifferent to him, would she not have deferred writing until her headache had passed off? To be sure, it was just such a note as she might have written to Brown, Jones, or Robinson; but would she have "braved the gaslight" and "suffered the consequences" for Brown, Jones, or Robinson? Obviously, she had felt a strong desire to set herself right with him; the recognition of which fact afforded Arthur no end of pleasure.

By the time he had committed Mrs. Lehmyl's note to memory, he was in a fair way to recover his wonted buoyancy of spirits.

Of course he rang her door-bell in the afternoon.

"How is Mrs. Lehmyl to-day?" he inquired of the maid. "I hope her headache is better."

"Oh, she's all well again to-day—just the same as ever," was the reply.

An idea occurred to him. He had intended merely to inform himself concerning her health, leave the bunch of flowers he held in his right hand, and go his way. But if she was up and about, why not ask to see her?

"Is—is she in?" he questioned.

"Oh, yes; she's in."

"Will you please give her my card, then?"

He walked into the parlor.

The parlor was darkened—blinds closed to exclude the heat—and intensely still. The ticking of the clock on the mantel-piece was the only interruption of the silence, save when at intervals the distant roar of a train on the elevated railway became audible for a moment.

Mrs. Lehmyl entered, and gave him her hand, and looked up smiling at him, all without a word. She wore a white gown, and an amber necklace and bracelet; and my informant says that she had "a halo of sweetness and purity all around her." For a trice Arthur was tongue-tied.

At length, "I have brought you a few flowers," he began.

She took the flowers, and buried her nose in them, and thanked their donor, and pinned one of the roses at her breast.

"I hope you are quite well again," he pursued.

"Oh, yes," she said, "quite well."

"It was very thoughtful of you to write me that letter—when you were in such pain."

"I owed it to you. I had promised to receive you. It would have been unfair, if I had not written."

"I—I was quite alarmed about you. I was afraid your headache might—" He faltered.

"There was no occasion for alarm. I am used to such headaches. I expect one every now and then."

"But—do you know?—at first I did not believe in it—not until your letter confirmed what Mrs. Hart and the servant had said."

"Why?"

"I thought perhaps—perhaps you did not care to see me, and had pleaded a headache for politeness' sake."

"You did me an injustice."—A pause.—"I did care to see you."

A longer pause. Arthur's heart was beating madly. Well it might. She had pronounced the last sentence with an emphasis calculated to move a man less deeply in love than he.

"Do you mean what you have just said?" he asked presently. His voice quivered.

"Yes."

"I suppose you knew—I—I suppose you knew what it was I wanted to say to you—what it was I would have said, if I had been admitted."

"Yes, I knew," she answered, in almost a whisper, and bowed her head.

Arthur sprang toward her and grasped her hand. "You knew—then, you know that—that I love you—*Ruth!*"

She withdrew her hand, but did not raise her head. He waited for a moment, breathless; then, "Ah, speak to me—won't you speak to me?" he begged, piteously.

She raised her head now, and gazed into his eyes; but her gaze was not one of gladness.

"Yes, alas, alas, I know it," she said, very slowly.

Arthur started back.

"Alas, alas?" he repeated after her.

"Oh, yes," she said, in the same slow, grave way; "it is very, very sad."

"Sad?" His eyes were full of mystification.

"I mean that it is sad that you should care for me. If I had only foreseen it—but I did not. You knew so little of me, how could I foresee? But on Wednesday—the way you looked at me—oh, forgive me. I—I never meant to make you care for me."

"I do not understand," said Arthur, shaking his head.

"That is why I wanted to see you. After what passed on Wednesday, I felt that it was best for us both that I should see you and tell you what a mistake you had made. I wanted to tell you that you must try hard to forget about it. It would be useless and cruel for me to pretend not to have understood, when you looked at me so. It was best that we should meet again, and that I should explain it to you."

"But your explanation puts me in the dark."

"You would not want to love a woman unless there was hope that some day you might marry her. Would not that be a great unhappiness?"

"It is not a question of *want.* I should love you under any and all conditions."

"But you never, never can marry me."

"I will not believe it until—"

"Wait. Do not say things that you may wish to unsay a moment hence. You never can marry me, for one sufficient reason—because—" She hesitated.

"Because?" There was panic in Arthur's heart. Was she not a widow, after all?

She drew a deep breath, and bit her lip. Her cheek had been pale. Now a hot blush suffused it. With an air of summoning her utmost strength, she went on, "You never can marry me, because you never would marry me—never, unless I should tell you—something—something about my life—my life in the past—which I can never tell—not even to you."

"Oh!" cried Arthur, with manifest relief. "Is that all?"

"It is enough—it is final, fatal."

"Oh, I thought it might be worse."

There befell a silence. Arthur was mustering his forces, to get them under control.. He dared not speak till he had done this. At last, struggling hard to be calm, he said, "Do you suppose I care any thing about your past life? Do you suppose that my love for you is so mean and so small as that? I know all that it is needful for me to know about your past. I know *you*, do I not? I know, then, that every act, every thought, every breath of your life, has been as pure and as beautiful as you are yourself. But what I know best, and what it is most essential for me to know, is this, Ruth, that I love you. I *love you!* I can not see that what you have spoken of is a bar to our marriage."

"Ah, but I—I would not let you enter blindfold into a union which some time you might repent. Should I be worthy of your love, if I would? But, what is worse, were I—were I to tell you this thing—which I can not tell you—then you—you would not ask me to marry you. Then you would not love me. The truth—the truth which, if I should become your wife, I could never share with you—which would remain forever a secret kept by me from my husband—it is—you would abhor me if you should find it out. If you should find it out after we were married—if somebody should come to you and tell you—oh, you would hate me. It is far more dreadful than you can fancy."

"No—no; for I will fancy the worst, and still beg of you to become my wife. If I loved you less—if I did not know you so well—the hints you utter might prompt some horrible suspicion in my mind. Will you take it as a proof of my love, that I dare assert positively, confidently, this?—Whatever the past may have been, so far as you were concerned in shaping it, it was good beyond reproach. Whatever your secret may be, it is not a secret that could show you to be one jot or tittle less noble than I know you to be. Whatever the truth you speak of is, it is a truth which, if it were understood in its entirety, would only serve to shed new luster upon the whiteness of your soul. And should I—should I by accident ever find it out—and should its form seem, as you have said, dreadful to me—why, I should say to myself, 'You have not pierced its substance? You do not understand it. However it may appear to you, you know that your wife's part in it was the part of a good angel from first to last 1'—Now do you think I love you?"

"But if—if you should find out that I had been guilty of sin—do you mean to say that—that you would care for me in spite of that?"

"I mean to say that I love you. I mean to say that no power under heaven can destroy my love of you. I mean to say that no power under heaven can prevent my marrying you, if you love me. I mean to say that my heart and soul—the \ inmost life of me—are already married to you, and that they will remain inseparably bound to you—*to you!*—until I die. More than this I mean to say. You speak of sin. You sin, forsooth! Well, talk of sin, if you like. Tell me that you have been guilty of—of what you will—of the blackest crimes in the calendar. I will not believe it. I will not believe that you were answerable for it. I will tell you that it was not your fault. I will tell you that if your hand has ever done any human being wrong, it was some other will than your own that compelled it. For this I know—I know it as I know that fire burns, that light illuminates—I know that you, the true, intrinsic you, have always been as sweet and undefiled as—as the breath that escapes now from your lips. There are some things that can not be—that no man could believe, though he beheld them with his open eyes. Can a circle be square? Can black be white? No man, knowing you as I know you, could believe that you in your soul were capable of sin."

He had spoken with immense fervor, consuming her the while with his eyes, and wrenching the hand he held until it must have ached in every bone. She, again as pale as death, had trembled under his fierce, hot utterance, like a reed in the wind. But now that he had done, she seemed to recover herself. She withdrew her hand from his, and moved her chair away.

"Mr. Ripley," she began, "you must not speak to me like this. It was not to hear you speak like this that I wished to see you to-day. You make it very hard for me to say what I have to say—what it was hard enough to say, at the best. But I must say it, and you must listen and understand. You have not understood yet. Now, please try to."

She pressed her hand to her throat, and swallowed convulsively. It was evident that she was nerving herself to the performance of a most painful task. Finally she went on, "I have told you frankly that I understood the other day—understood what you meant when you looked at me that way. After you were gone, I thought it all over—all that I had learned. I thought at first that the only thing for me to do would be never to see you again—to refuse to receive you when you called—to avoid you as much as I possibly could. That, I thought, would be the best thing to do. But then I thought further about it, and then it seemed that that would not be right. To break off in that sudden way with you, and not to explain it, would be wrong and cruel. So I put aside that first thought, and said, 'No, I will not refuse to receive him. I will receive him just as before. Only I will act in such a manner toward him that he will not say any thing about caring for me. I will act so as to prevent him from saying any thing about that. Then we will go on and be friends the same as ever.' But by and by that did not seem right either. It would be as cruel as the other, because, if you really did care for me, it would be a long suspense, a long agony for you; and perhaps, if nothing were said about it, you might get to caring still more for me, and might allow yourself to cherish false hopes, hopes that could never come true. So I decided that this course was as far from right as the first one. And, besides, I distrusted my own power—my power to keep you from speaking. It would be a long, long battle. I doubted whether I should have the strength to carry it through—always to be on my guard, and prevent you from speaking. 'No,' I said, 'it is bound to come. Sooner or later, if we go on seeing each other, he will surely speak. Is it not better that I should let him know at once—what waiting will make harder for him to hear and for me to tell him—that I can never become his wife? Then, when he knows that he has made a mistake in caring for me, then he will go away, and think of other things, and see other women, and perhaps, by and by, get over it, and forget about me.' I knew that if I told you that it was impossible for us to get married, and why it was impossible, I knew that you would give up hoping; and I thought that this course was the best of all. It was very hard. I shrank from the idea of speaking to you as I have done. Your good opinion is very precious to me. It was hard to persuade myself to say things to you that would, perhaps, make you think differently of me. But I felt that it was best. I had no right to procrastinate—to let you go on caring for me, and hoping for what could never be. Then I decided that I would see you and tell you about it right away."

She paused and breathed deeply; but before Arthur had had time to put in a word, she resumed: "I do not believe that you have meant to make it more difficult for me to-day than it had to be; but it has pained me very much to hear you speak as you have spoken. You have not understood; but now you understand—must understand. I never can be your wife. You must try to get over caring for me. You must go away, now that I have explained, and never come any more."

She had said all this in a low tone, though each syllable had been fraught with earnestness, and had manifestly cost an effort. Arthur, during the last few sentences, had been pacing up and down the room. Now he came to a standstill before her.

"And do you mean to say," he demanded, "that that is your last word, your ultimatum? Do you mean to say that you will send me away—banish me from your presence—forbid me the happiness of seeing you and hearing you—all for a mere paltry nothing? If there were a real impediment to our marriage, I should be the first to acknowledge it, to bow before it. But this thing that you have mentioned—this—well, call it a secret, if you will—is this empty memory to rise up as a barrier between your life and mine? Oh, no, no! You have spoken of cruelty—you have wished not to be cruel. And yet this utmost cruelty you seem willing to perpetrate in cold blood. Stop, think, reflect upon what you are doing! Have you not seen how much I love you? how my whole life is in my love of you? Do you not know that what you propose to do—to send me away, all on account of this miserable secret—is to break my life forever? is to put out the light forever from my sky, and turn my world to a waste of dust and ashes? Can you—you who recoil from cruelty—be as wantonly cruel as this? Have I not told you that I care nothing for your secret, that I shall never think of your secret, if you will only speak one word? Oh, it is not possible that you can deliberately break my heart, for a mere dead thing like that! If it were something actual, something substantial, something existing now and here, it would be different. Then I, too, should recognize the size and the weight of it. I should accept the inevitable, and resign myself as best I could. But a bygone, a thing that is past and done with, how can you let that stand between us? I can never resign myself to that. Can't you imagine the torture of my position? To want a thing with all my soul, to know that there is no earthly reason why I should not have it, and yet to know that I can not have it—why, it is like being defeated by a soap bubble, a vapor. Of what use is all this talk? We are merely confusing each other, merely beating about the bush. I have told you what you did not expect to hear. You thought that I would be swerved from my purpose when you said that you had a secret. You thought I would go away, satisfied that it was best for us not to marry. But, you see, you did yourself an injustice. You did not guess the real depth of the love you had inspired. You see, I love you too much to care about the past. Confess that you did not consider this, when, you made up your mind to send me away. But this talk is of no use. All the talk in the world can not alter the way we stand. Here are the simple facts: I love you. *I love you!* I ask you to be my wife. I kneel down before you, and take your hand in mine, and beg of you not to spurn my love—not to be guided by a blind, deluded conscience—not to think of the past—but to think only of the present and the future—to think only of how much I love you—of how all the happiness of my life is now at stake, for you to make or to destroy. I ask you to be merciful. I ask you to look into your heart, and let that prompt you how to act. If there is one atom of love for me in it—you—"

He broke off sharply; drew a quick, hard breath. Something—a sudden, furtive gleam far down in her eyes—a swift coming and going of color to and from her cheek—caused his heart to throb with an exultant thrill, that for an instant deprived him of the power of speech. Then, all at once, "Oh, my God! You do love me. *You do love me!*" he cried. He caught her in his arms, and strained her rapturously to his breast.

For a moment she did not resist. Her face lay for a moment buried upon his shoulder. It was a supreme moment of silence. Then she broke away. There were tears in her eyes. She sobbed out, "It is wrong, all wrong."

But Arthur knew that he had gained the day. Her first sign of weakness was his assurance of success. Protest now as she might, she could no longer hide her love from him. And if she loved him, what had he to fear? There was much further talk between them. She tried to regain the ground she had lost. Failing in this, she wept, and spoke of the wrong she had done him, and said that she had forfeited her self-respect. But Arthur summoned all his eloquence to induce her to look at the matter through his eyes, and in the end—Somewhat later an eavesdropper outside the parlor door might have caught the following dialogue passing within:

Ruth's voice: "It is strange, Arthur, but a little while ago it seemed to me that I could never tell that—that thing—I spoke about, to any living soul; yet now—now I feel quite otherwise. I feel as though I could tell it to you. I want to tell it to you. It is only right that I should tell you every thing about my life. It is a long story; shall I begin?"

Arthur's voice: "No, Ruth. Shall I let the happiness of this hour be marred for you and me, by your thinking and speaking of what would pain you? Besides, I prefer that you should keep this—this thing—this secret—as an evidence of my unwavering confidence in you. Why should we trouble ourselves about the past at all, when the present is at hand, and the future is waiting for us? You and I—we have only just been born. The past is dead. Our life dates from this moment. Oh, it is to the future that we must look!"

"But it seems as though you ought to know—ought to know your wife—ought to know who she is, and what she has done."

"But I do know her. I do know who she is and what she has done. I know it all by instinct. I want her to have this constant proof of my love—that I can trust her without, learning her secrets."

"But you will not forget—never forget—that I have offered to tell you, will you? You will remember that I am always willing to tell you—that whenever you wish to know it, you will only have to ask me."

"Yes, I will remember it; and it will make me happy to remember it. But if you wish to tell me something now that I should like to hear, tell me on what day we shall be married?"

"Oh, it is too soon to fix that—we can wait about fixing that."

"No, no. It must be fixed before I take leave of you to-day. Every thing must be finally settled. When?"

"Whenever you wish."

"To-morrow."

"Of course I did not mean that."

"As soon, then, as possible."

"Not sooner than—"

"Not longer at the utmost than a month."

"A month? It is a very short time, a month."

"But it is a month too long. Make it a month, or less."

"Well, a month, then: this day month."

"This day month—to-day being Friday—falls on Sunday. Say, rather this day four weeks, the 25th of July."

"How shall I get ready in that interval?"

"How shall I live through that interval?"

"What interval? Talking about music, as usual?" said Mrs. Hart, entering at this moment. "Mr. Ripley, how do you do?"

"I am the happiest man in the world," he answered.

"I congratulate you. Have you won a case?"

"No; I have won a wife."

"I congratulate you doubly. Who is the lady?"

"Let me present her to you," he laughed, taking Ruth by the hand.

Mrs. Hart dropped every thing she held—scissors, spectacles, knitting-bag—struck an astonished attitude, and uttered a sharp cry of surprise. Ruth blushed and smiled. For an instant the two ladies stood off and eyed each other. Then simultaneously they rushed toward each other, and fell into each other's arms; and then there were tears and kisses and incoherent sounds.

Finally, "I congratulate you trebly," said Mrs. Hart, turning to Arthur.

For a while every body was very happy and very sentimental.

When, toward midnight, Arthur returned to his own abode, Hetzel asked him where he had spent the evening.

"In heaven," he replied.

"And with what particular divinity?"

"With Mrs. Lehmyl."

"So?"

"Yes, sir. And—and what do you suppose? She and I are going to be married."

"What?" cried Hetzel.

"Yes; we are engaged, betrothed. We are going to be married."

"Engaged? Betrothed? Married? You? Nonsense!"

"Nothing of the kind. Our wedding day is fixed for the 25th of next month."

"Oh, come, be rational."

"I am rational. Why should I jest about it?"

"Have you suddenly fallen heir to a fortune?"

"Of course not; why?"

"Why? Why, what are you going to get married on?"

"How do you mean?"

"I mean who's to foot the bills?"

"I have my income, have I not?"

"Oh, your income. Oh, to be sure. Let's see—how many thousands did it amount to last year?"

"It amounted to fifteen hundred."

"Fifteen hundred what?"

"Hundred dollars."

"Is that all?"

"It is enough."

"Do you seriously intend to marry on that?"

"Why not?"

"Why, it won't keep your wife in pocket handkerchiefs, let alone feeding and clothing her."

"I hadn't thought about it, but I'm sure we can get along on fifteen hundred—added to what I can earn."

"What was her opinion?"

"I didn't mention the subject."

"You asked her to marry you without exhibiting your bank account. Shame!"

"We love each other."

"When poverty comes in at the door, what is it love's habit to do?"

"Such love as ours waxes greater."

"And—and your mother. What will she say?"

"I'm going to write to her to-night—now."

"Has your mother much respect for my judgment?"

"You know she has."

"Well, then, tell her from me that you've just done a most sensible thing; that your bride's an angel, yourself a trump, and each of you to be envied above all man and woman kind."

CHAPTER VII.
ENTER MRS. PEIXADA.

THE four weeks had wound away. I shall not detain the reader with a history of them. The log-book of a prosperous voyage is apt to be dull literature. They were four weeks of delightful progress toward a much-desired goal—four weeks of unmitigated happiness. The course of true love ran smooth. Time flew. Looking forward, to be sure, Arthur thought the hoped-for day would never come. But looking backward from the eve of it, he was compelled to wonder whither the time had sped.

On Thursday, the 24th of July, in the office of Assistant-district-attorney Romer, were seated Arthur, Peixada, and Mr. Romer himself. Arthur held an open letter in his hand. The letter, written in a heavy, English chirography, was signed with considerable flourish, "Reginald Graham." Arthur had just finished reading it aloud. Said he, folding it up and putting it into his pocket, "So all trace of her is lost. We are back at the point we started from."

Said Peixada, "Well, we shall simply be obliged to adopt the plan that I suggested in the first place—advertise."

Assented Romer, "Yes, an advertisement is our last hope."

"A forlorn one. She would never answer it," croaked Arthur.

"That depends," said Romer.

"Upon what?"

"Upon the adroitness with which the advertisement is framed."

"Well, for instance? Give us a sample."

"Let me think," said Romer. After a moment's reflection, "How would this answer?" And he applied pen to paper. Presently he submitted the paper for inspection to his companions. Its contents were as follows:

"Peixada.—If Mrs. Judith Peixada, née *Karon, widow of Bernard Peixada, Esquire, late of the city of New York, deceased, and formerly administratrix of the goods, chattels, and credits of said decedent, will communicate either personally or by letter with her brother-in-law, Benjamin Peixada, No.———-Reade Street, New York, she will learn something affecting the interests of her estate greatly to her advantage."*

"That, I think," said Romer, "ought to be inserted in the principal newspapers of America, England, France, and Germany."

"That's what I call first-rate," was Peixada's comment.

Arthur held his peace.

"Well," demanded Romer, "how does it strike *you?*"

Arthur deliberated; at length said, "Candidly, Romer, do you regard that as altogether square and above-board?"

"Why not? It's a decoy. The use of decoys in dealing with criminals—this woman is a criminal, mind you; a murderess and practically a thief as well—the use of decoys in such cases is justified by a hundred precedents."

"What's the matter with you?" asked Peixada. "Nothing's the matter with me," retorted Arthur, a bit sharply; "but I must say, I think such a proceeding as this is pretty low."

"Oh, come; no, you don't," urged Romer.

"I do. And what's more, I won't lend myself to it. If that advertisement appears in the papers, Mr. Peixada will have to retain another man in my place."

"But, goodness alive, it's our last resort. Would you rather have the whole business fall through? Be reasonable. Why, it's a ruse the daintiest men at the bar wouldn't stick at."

"Perhaps they wouldn't; but I do."

"Well, what else is there to be done?"

"And besides," said Arthur, not heeding Romer's question, "you make a great mistake in fancying that she would be deceived by it. If that woman is any thing, she's shrewd. She's far too shrewd to bite when the hook's in sight."

"How do you mean?"

"I mean she'd sniff danger at once—divine that it is—what you have called it—a decoy. What under the sun could her brother-in-law have to communicate that would be to her advantage?"

"All right," said Romer, shrugging his shoulders; "suggest a more promising move, and I'll be with you."

"I'll tell you what," said Arthur, "I'm not too squeamish. I won't connive at downright falsehood; but I'm willing to compromise. It's a bitter pill to swallow—it goes against the grain—but I'll consent to something like this. Let me take your pen."

Arthur scratched off a line or two.

"Here," he said.

"*Peixada.—If Mrs. Judith Peixada,* née *Karon, widow of Bernard Peixada, Esquire, deceased, will communicate with her brother-in-law, Benjamin Peixada, No.—— Reade Street, New York, she will confer a favor,*" was what Arthur had written.

"This," he added verbally, "will be quite as likely to fetch her as the other. Its very frankness will disarm suspicion. Besides, it's not such an out-and-out piece of treachery."

"What do you think, Mr. Peixada?" inquired Romer.

"Oh, I think she'd sooner cut her thumbs off than do me a favor. But I leave the decision with you lawyers."

"I may as well repeat," volunteered Arthur, "that in the event of your employing the form Mr. Romer drew, I shall withdraw from the case."

"Well," said Romer, "I'm not sure Ripley isn't right. At any rate, no harm giving his way a trial. If it should fail to attract our game, we can use sweeter bait later on. Who'll see to its insertion?"

"I shall have to beg you to do that," said Arthur, "because to-morrow I'm going out of town—to stay about a fortnight. I shall be on deck again two weeks from Monday—August 11th. Meanwhile, here's my country address. Telegraph me, if any thing turns up."

Telling the story of his morning's work to Hetzel, he concluded thus, "I suppose it was a legitimate enough stratagem—one that few lawyers would stop at—but, all the same, I feel like a sneak. I should like to kick myself."

Hetzel responded, cheeringly, "You've made your own bed, and now you've got to lie in it. You ought to have observed these little drawbacks to the beauty of Themis, before you dedicated yourself to her service."

Next day in Mrs. Hart's parlor, Arthur Ripley and Ruth Lehmyl were married. Besides themselves and the clergyman who tied the knot, the only persons present were Arthur's mother, Mrs. Hart, Julian Hetzel, and a certain Mr. Arthur Flint.

This last named gentleman was Arthur's godfather, and had been a classmate of Arthur's father at Yale college. He was blessed with a wife, a couple of married daughters, and a swarm of grandchildren of both sexes; despite which, he had always taken a more than godfatherly interest in his namesake. For whatever business Arthur had to do, prior to his connection with Peixada, he was indebted to Mr. Flint. It was but natural, therefore, that he should have apprised Mr. Flint of his matrimonial projects as soon as they were distinctly formed. He had visited him one day at his office, and asked him to attend the wedding.

"The 25th of July?" cried Mr. Flint. "At such short notice? And my wife and Sue and Nellie away in Europe! It's a pity I can't call them home by the next steamer, to wish you joy. It'll break their hearts not to be present at your marriage. However—however, where are you going on your wedding-journey?"

"I haven't made up my mind. We were thinking of some place on the New Jersey coast."

"The New Jersey coast is all sand and glare. It would spoil your bride's complexion. I'll tell you what you'd better do. You'd better go and pass your honeymoon at my cottage in New Hampshire—Beacon Rock. It's shut up and doing no one any good—consequence of my wife's trip to Europe. Say the word, and I'll wire Perkins—my general factotum there—to open and air the house, start fires, and be ready to welcome you with a warm dinner on the 26th."

"You're too kind. I don't know what to say,"

"Then say nothing. I'll take yes for granted. You'll find Beacon Rock just the place for a month's billing and cooing. Eastward, the multitudinous sea; westward, the hardy New England landscape; and all around you, the sweetest air it will ever be your luck to breathe. Look here."

Mr. Flint opened a drawer of his desk and extracted a pile of photographs.

"Here's Beacon Rock taken from every available point of view. Here are some glimpses of the interior," he said.

Divided between delight and gratitude, Arthur could only stammer forth broken phrases.

"Oh, by the way, what's her address?" demanded Mr. Flint, as Arthur was on the point of bidding him good-by.

"I thought I had told you. You'll be sure to call soon, won't you? No. 46 Beekman Place."

"Now, mum's the word," proceeded Mr. Flint.

"I don't want you to breathe a syllable of this business to your sweetheart. Lead her to suppose that you're going to some Purgatorial summer hotel; and then enjoy her surprise when she spies Beacon Rock. Oh, yes, I'll call and pay her my respects—likely enough some night this week. Good-by. God bless you."

Mr. Flint called, pursuant to his promise. On the stoop, as he was leaving, he clapped Arthur upon the shoulder, and cried, "By George, my boy, your Jewess is a jewel!"

Three days later came a paper parcel, addressed to Mrs. Lehmyl. It contained a small purple velvet box. To the outside of the box was attached a card, bearing the laconic device, "Sparks from a Flint." Inside, upon a cushion of lavender silk lay a gold breastpin, from the center of which a cluster of wondrous diamonds shot prismatic rays. It was the sole bit of jewelry that adorned Ruth's wedding-gown.

"Immediately after the ceremony," says Hetzel, in a letter written at the time, "they got into a hack, and were driven to the Fall River boat. We, who were left behind, crossed the street and assembled upon the *loggia*. There we waited till the Bristol hove in sight down the river. Then, until it had disappeared behind Blackwell's Island, there was much waving of handkerchiefs between the travelers—whom we could make out quite clearly, leaning against the rail—and us poor stay-at-homes. Afterward, Mrs. Ripley and Mrs. Hart adapted their handkerchiefs to other purposes."

A week elapsed before the bride and groom were heard from. Eventually Hetzel got a voluminous missive. Portions of it read thus:

"In Boston, as our train didn't leave till noon, we sought the Decorative Art Rooms, and spent an hour or so coveting the pretty things that they are full of. At the depot I had a slight unpleasantness with the potentate from whom I bought our tickets—(confound the insolence of these railroad officials! Why doesn't some ingenious Yankee contrive an automaton by which they may be superseded?)—but despite it, we got started comfortably enough, and were set down at Portsmouth promptly at three o'clock. She enjoyed the drive in an open carriage through the quaint old New England town immensely; but when we had reached the open country, and were being whisked over bridges, down leafy lanes, across rugged pasture lands, on our way to New Castle, her pleasure knew no bounds. There is something peculiarly refreshing in this keen New Hampshire air, compounded as it is of pine odors and the smell of the sea, and something equally refreshing in this homely New Hampshire landscape, with its thorns and thistles growing alongside daisies and wild roses.

'The locust dinned amid the trees;

The fields were high with corn,'

as we spun onward behind the horses' hoofs. Now and then, much to her consternation, a brilliant striped snake darted from the foot-path into the bushes.... I had given her to believe, you know, that our destination was the * * * hotel, a monstrous barracks of an establishment, perched on the top of a hill in this neighborhood; and when we clattered past it without stopping, she was altogether mystified. I parried her questions successfully, however; and at the end of another half mile Beacon Rock rose before us.... For a while we did—could do-nothing but race around the outside of the house, and attempt by eloquent attitudes, frantic gestures, ecstatic monosyllables, to express something of the admiration which it inspired. Mr. Flint had shown me photographs of the cottage before I left New York; but he had shown me no photographs of the earth, sea, and sky by which it is surrounded—and that is its superlative merit. It falls in perfectly with the nature round about. It is indigenous—as thoroughly so as the seaweed, the stone walls, the apple trees. It looks as though it might have grown out of the soil: or as if the waters, in a mood of titanic playfulness, had cast it up and left it where it stands upon the shore. Fancy a square tower, built of untrimmed stone, fifty feet in height and twenty in diameter, springing straight up from a bare granite ledge— which, in its turn, sprouts from a grassy lawn, which, in its turn, slopes gradually down to the rocks at the sea's edge. This solemn, sturdy tower is pierced at its base by divers sinister looking portholes, which suggest cannon and ambushed warriors, but which, in point of fact, perform no more bellicose a function than that of admitting daylight into the cellar. Above these there are deep-set windows, through which the sun pours merrily all day long. I am seated at one of them, writing, now. . . . The tower faces the sea, and defies it. Behind the tower, and sheltered by it, nestles the cottage proper, a most picturesque, gabled, rambling structure of wood, painted terra cotta red... . . I don't know how long we stood around outside. Finally, Mr. Perkins, a native who, aided by his wife, cooks and 'chores' for us, suggested the propriety of entering. We entered; and if the exterior had charmed us, the interior simply carried us away. I shall not attempt an itemized description of it, because probably I shouldn't be able to make the picture vivid enough to be worth your while. But imagine the extreme of aestheticism combined with the extreme of comfort, and you will get a rough notion of our environment. There are broad, open fire places, deep chimney corners, luxurious Turkey rugs, antique chairs and tables, beautiful pictures, interesting books—though we don't read them—and every thing else a fellow's heart could desire. There is no piano—the sea air would make short work of one—but I have hired a guitar from a Portsmouth music dealer, and she accompanies her songs on this.... Our mode of existence has been a perpetual *dolce far niente*, diversified by occasional strolls about the country—to Fort Constitution, a ruin of 1812—to the hotel, where a capital orchestra dispenses music every afternoon—or simply across the meadows, without an objective point. We can sight several light-houses from the tower windows; and a mile out at sea, in everlasting restlessness, floats a deep-voiced, melancholy bell-buoy, which recalls all the weird creeping of the flesh we had in reading the shipwreck in *L'homme qui rit*.. . . Of course we have written a glowing letter of thanks to Mr. Flint. She, I forgot to tell you, could not at first believe her senses—believe that this little earthly paradise was meant for our occupation. When at last the truth was borne in upon her, you ought to have witnessed her delight.... Oh, Julian, old boy, you can't form the least conception of the great, radiant joy that fills my heart. I am really half afraid that it's a dream from which I shall presently wake up. I don't dare to verify it by pinching myself, lest that misfortune might indeed befall me. My happiness is so much in excess of other men's, I don't feel that I deserve it; and sometimes I am tormented by a morbid dread that it may not last. Just think, *she is actually my wife!* Ah, how my heart leaps, when I say that to myself, and realize all that it means!.... I have tried to put business quite out of my mind; but now and then it recurs to me, despite myself. I feel more and more uncomfortable about that advertisement. I have no doubt the woman richly deserves the worst that can happen to her, and all that, but nevertheless I can't get rid of a deucedly unpleasant qualm of conscience, when I think of the trap I have helped to set for her. Between ourselves, I derive some consolation from the thought that the chances are ninety-nine in a hundred that she will decline to nibble at our bait.... Unless I telegraph to the contrary, expect us to breakfast with you to-morrow week—Saturday, August 9th."

Hetzel carried his letter across the street, and gave it to Mrs. Hart. She, not to be outdone, read aloud fragments of one which she had received from Ruth by the same mail. Among the paragraphs in the latter which she suppressed was this:

"I have offered twice to tell him the whole story. I very much want to do so—to have it off my mind. It doesn't seem right that I should keep it secret; and he is so kind and tender, I feel that I could bring myself to tell him every thing. But with characteristic generosity, he declines to listen—bids me keep my secret as a proof of his confidence in me. Perhaps, then, it will be just as well for me to wait till we get back to town. Sooner or later—and the sooner, the better—I shall insist upon his allowing me to speak. A regret grows upon me daily that I did not insist upon that before we were married. Though I know so well that he loves me, my heart stands still when I stop to think, 'How may he feel towards me when he knows it all?' or, 'Suppose before I have explained it to him, he should hear it from somebody else?' Oh, it is not possible that he will cease to care for me, is it? I wish I could go to him this instant, and tell him about it, and then for good and all know my fate. Why did I wait till we were married? I could not bear to have him change in his feelings toward me now. Oh, I wish this miserable secret were off my mind—it tortures me with such terrifying doubts. But perhaps I had best not interrupt the happiness of his holiday by introducing a subject which he appears anxious to avoid. Do you agree with me? I say, I wish I could go, and tell it to him; and yet when the time comes for doing so, I am afraid my tongue will cleave to the roof of my mouth. If it should destroy his love for me! make him despise me! If for a single moment, as I was speaking, he should recoil from me!—withdraw his hand from mine! Oh, God, why can not the past be blotted out? I *must* speak to him before any body else can do so. If some one of his acquaintances should recognize me, and tell him, what might he not do? He *thinks* he would not care. He says *no matter what the past has been, it is totally indifferent to him.* But perhaps he would not feel that way if he really knew it. God bless him and keep him from all pain!"

Saturday morning, surely enough, the truants came home, and took up their quarters at Mrs. Hart's, where for the present they were to remain. They hoped to set up a modest establishment of their own in the spring.

Late Monday forenoon Arthur screwed his courage to the sticking place, and tore himself away from his wife's side. Reading the newspapers on his way down town, he had the satisfaction of seeing himself in print. The Peixada advertisement occupied a conspicuous position. He went straight to his office, where he found a number of letters waiting for him. These he disposed of as speedily as might be; and then he sallied forth to call upon Mr. Flint. He got back at about halfpast two o'clock. Less than five minutes later, his office-boy stuck his head through the doorway, and announced, "A gentleman to see you."

"Show him in."

The gentleman appeared. The gentleman wore the garb of a porter. "I come from Mr. Peixada, sir, with a note," he explained.

Arthur took the note and broke it open. The gum on the envelope was still damp.

The note bore evidence of having been dashed off in haste. Here it is:

"Office of B. Peixada & Co.,

"No.———Reade Street,

"New York, Aug. 11, 1884.

"Dear Sir:

"If you are in town, (and to-day was the day fixed for your return), please come right over here at your earliest convenience. *Mrs. P. is in my private office!* I am keeping her till your arrival.

"Yours truly,

"B. Peixada."

Arthur stood still, his eyes glued upon this sheet of paper, long enough to have read it through a dozen times.

"Any answer?" Mr. Peixada's envoy at last demanded.

"Oh—of course—I'll go along with you at once."

His heart was palpitating. The prospect of a face to face encounter with the redoubtable Mrs. Peixada caused him unwonted trepidation. The tidings conveyed in Peixada's note were so unexpected and of such grave importance, no wonder Arthur's serenity was ruffled. Striding up Broadway at the messenger's heels, he tried to picture to himself the impending scene. The trap had sprung. What manner of creature would the quarry turn out to be? Poor woman! There was a lot of trouble in store for her. But it was not his fault. He had done nothing but that which his duty as an attorney had required of him. He would exert his influence in her behalf—try to smooth things down for her, and make them as comfortable as under the circumstances they could be. Still for all slips of hers, she was one of Eve's family. He felt that he pitied her from the bottom of his soul.

Peixada was nervously pacing back and forth in the show-room.

"Ah," he cried, catching hold of Arthur's hand and wringing it vigorously, "you have come! What luck, eh? I can scarcely believe it is true. I'm quite put about by it, I declare. She walked in here, as large as life, not half an hour ago, and asked to see me. I had no idea the sight of her would upset me so. I told her that my business with her was of a legal nature, and I guessed she'd better wait while I sent round for my attorney. But I was desperately afraid you hadn't got back. She acted just like a lamb. I tell you, that advertisement was a happy thought, wasn't it? Pity we didn't advertise in the first place, and so save all that delay and money. But I'm not complaining—not I. I'd be willing to spend twice the same amount right over again for the same result. Now we'll get a round hundred thousand; and I won't forget you."

"Have you notified Mr. Romer, too?"

"Oh, yes; of course. Sent word for him to come with his officers. She—she's in my private office—there—behind that door. Won't you go in, and tell her about the will, and keep her occupied till they get here?"

"I—I think it would be best to wait," said Arthur, his voice trembling.

"No—no. She'll begin to get impatient. Please go in now. It'll relieve my agitation, anyhow. I'm really surprised to find myself so shaken up. Here—this is the door. Open it, and go ahead in."

"Oh—very well," consented Arthur.

He put his hand upon the knob, fortified himself with a long breath, and entered the room. Peixada, sticking his head in behind him, rattled off, "Here, madam, is the gentleman I spoke to you about. He'll explain what we want you for," and withdrew, slamming the door.

Peixada's private office was scarcely more than a hole in the wall—a small, square closet, lighted by a single grimy window, and destitute of furniture except for a desk and a couple of chairs.

In one of these chairs, with her back toward the door, and engaged apparently in looking out of the window, sat a lady.

Standing still, a yard beyond the threshold, Arthur said, "I beg your pardon, madam—Mrs. Peixada."

The lady rose, turned around, faced him.

The lady was his wife.

A slight, startled smile crossed her face. "Why—Arthur—you—?" she began in atone of surprise, her eyes brightening.

But suddenly a change; a look of perplexity, followed by one of enlightenment, as if a dreadful truth had burst upon her. The blood sank from her cheeks, her lip curled, her breast fluttered—a terrible fire flashed from her eyes. She drew herself up. She was awful, but she was superb.

"Ah," she said, "I see. So you have been prying into my secrets behind my back—you, who were too magnanimous to let me tell them to you! It was for you that Mr. Peixada bade me wait. This is the surprise he spoke of—a surprise of your contriving. You have found out who I am. I hope you are—-"

She broke off. Her voice had been very low, but had vibrated with passion. Now, the flaming, contemptuous eyes with which she covered him, spoke her mind more plainly than her tongue could.

He, upon her first rising and facing him, had started back, gasping, "Good God—you—Ruth!" Since then a chaos of emotions had held him, dumb.

But gradually he recovered himself in some measure.

His face a picture of blank amazement, "For heaven's sake, Ruth, what does this mean?" he cried.

She did not hear him. Her anger of a moment since gave way to a paroxysm of pain.

"Oh, merciful God," she moaned, "how I have been deceived! Oh, to think that he—my—my husband—Oh, it is too much! It is more than I can bear."

She broke down in a torrent of tears and sobs.

An impulse carried him to her side. He put his arm around her waist, drew her to him, bent over her, stammered out broken syllables of love, comfort, entreaty.

His touch rekindled her wrath, and endowed her frame with preternatural strength. She repulsed him—flung him away from her, over against the opposite wall, with as little effort as if he had been a stick in her path. This fragile woman, towering above this stalwart man, her cheeks now burning scarlet, her limbs quivering with strong emotion, cried, "How dare you touch me? How dare you speak to me? How dare you insult me with your presence? Is it not enough what you have *done*, without forcing me to remain in the same room with you? Are you not content to have consorted with Benjamin Peixada—to have listened to the story of your wife's life from that man's lips—without coming here to confront me with it—to compel me to defend myself against his accusations. Wasn't it enough to put that advertisement in the paper? Haven't you sufficiently punished me by decoying me to this place, as you have done? What more do you want? What new humiliation? Though you hate me, now that you know who I am and what I haye done—you, who talked of loving me in spite of every thing—can you not be merciful, and leave me alone? Go—out of my sight—or, at least, stand aside and let me go."

Her words were followed by a prolonged, convulsive shudder.

Exerting his utmost self-control, dazed and bewildered as he was, he began, "Ruth, will you not give me a chance to speak? Will you not listen to me? Can't you see that this is some—some frightful error into which we have fallen—which we can only right by speaking? You are doing me a great wrong, Ruth. You are wronging yourself. I beg of you, subdue your anger—oh, for God's sake, don't look at me like that. Try to be calm, Ruth, and let us talk together. Let me explain to you. Explain to me, for I am as hopelessly in the dark as you can be. Let us have some understanding."

His plea passed totally without effect: I suppose, because his wife was a woman. The tumult and the violence of the shock she had sustained had shattered her good sense. Her perceptive faculties were benumbed. Her entire vitality was absorbed by her pain and her indignation. I doubt whether she had heard what he said. But she caught at the last word, at any rate.

"Understanding? What is there to understand? I understand—I understand quite enough. I understand that you have sought information about me from Benjamin Peixada. I understand that it was you who got me here by false pretenses—by that advertisement. I understand that you—you think I am—that you believe what Benjamin Peixada has told you—and that—that the love you protested so much about, has all—all died away—and you—you shudder to think that I am your wife. Well, you may understand this, that I too shudder. I shudder to think that you are my husband—to think that you could have done this behind my back—that—that you—even when you were pretending to love me most, and telling me that you did not care about my secret—even then, you were fraternizing with Benjamin Peixada! You may understand that, however base you may believe me to be, I believe you to be baser still. Oh, if you would only go away, and never, never intrude yourself upon my sight again!"

Completely undone, he could only press his hands to his temples, and murmur, "Oh my God, my God!"

So they stood: he, hanging his head, deserted by his manhood, crushed as by a blow from out the skies; she, erect, scornful, magnificent, all her womanhood aroused, all her unspeakable fury blazing in her eyes: so they stood, when, the door creaking open, two new personages advanced upon the scene.

He did not recognize them; but an instinct told him who they were. He was petrified. It did not occur to him to interfere.

"Mrs. Peixada, I believe, ma'am?" said one of them, with a smirk.

He had to repeat his query thrice before she deigned to give him her attention.

Then with supreme dignity, bending her neck, "What do you wish with me?" she asked.

"Here, ma'am, is a bench-warrant which I have the honor of serving upon you—matter of the People of the State of New York against Judith Peixada, otherwise known as Judith Karon, charged with murder in the first degree upon the person of Edward Bolen, late of the City, County, and State of New York, deceased. Please come along quiet, ma'am, and make no resistance.—Donnelly, get behind her."

The officer delivered himself rapidly of this address, and thrust his warrant into the prisoner's hand. The man spoken to as Donnelly, took a position behind her, obedient to orders. His superior opened the door, and pointing toward it, said, "Please move along fast, ma'am."

She, flinging one last, brief, scorching glance at her husband, bowed to the officer, and swept out of the room.

For an instant Arthur remained motionless, riveted to the spot where she had left him. All at once his body quivered perceptibly. Then, realizing what had happened, he dashed headlong through the show-room—heedless of

Romer, Peixada, and a score of Peixada's clerks, who stood still and stared—and out into the street, calling, "Ruth, Ruth, come back, come back," at the top of his voice.

On the curbstone, hatless, out of breath, stupefied, he halted and looked up and down the street. Ruth was nowhere to be seen.

Here he was joined by Romer and Peixada.

"What is it—what has happened?" Romer asked.

"What has happened?" he repeated, dully. "Did—didn't you know? *She is my wife!*"

CHAPTER VIII.
"WHAT REST TO-NIGHT?"

PUT yourself in his place. At first, as we have seen, he was simply stunned, bewildered. His breath was taken away, his understanding baffled. His senses were thrown into disorder. It was as if a cannon had gone off under his feet, all was uproar and smoke and confusion. But by degrees the smoke lifted. The outlines of things became distinct.

One stupendous fact stared Arthur in the face. Its magnitude was appalling. Its proportions were out of nature: The sight of it froze his blood, sickened his heart, turned his brain to stone. Judith Peixada, the woman whom he had pursued, insnared, betrayed; the woman whom he had delivered over to the clutches of the law, whom the officers had just dragged away from him, who even at this moment was under lock and key for a capital offense in the Tombs prison; the woman whom he had heretofore regarded as an abandoned murderess, beyond the pale of human pity, but whom he knew now, all appearances, all testimony, to the contrary notwithstanding, now at the eleventh hour, to be somehow as guiltless as the babe unborn: this woman was identical with his wife, with Ruth, with the lady whom he had wooed and married! He had been groping in the dark. He had brought his own house crashing down around his ears.

The vastness of the catastrophe, its apparent hopelessness, its grim, far-reaching corollaries, and the bitter knowledge that he might have prevented it, loomed up before him like a huge, misshaped monster, by which his earthly happiness was irretrievably to be destroyed. Add to this his consciousness of what she thought of him, and the sternest reader must pity his condition. She believed that, surreptitiously, he had been prying into the story of her life—a story which on more than one occasion she had volunteered to tell him, but to which, with feigned magnanimity, he had refused to listen, preferring to gather it covertly from other lips. She believed that, once having discovered her identity, he had ceased to love her, and had entered ruthlessly into a conspiracy whose object it was to lure her within reach of the criminal law. Unnatural, impossible, enormous, as such baseness would be, she nevertheless believed it of him. Ignorant of the circumstances, too indignant to suffer an explanation, she had jumped to the first conclusion that presented itself, and had gone to her prison, convinced that her husband had played her false.

His sensations, of course, were far too complicated, far too turbulent, to be easily disentangled. Senseless hatred of Peixada for having crossed his path; senseless hatred of himself for having accepted Peixada's case; self-reproach, deep and bitter, for having forbidden her to share her secret with him; a wild desire to follow her, see her, speak to her, force her to understand; an intense wish to be doing something that might help to remedy matters, without the remotest notion of what ought to be done; a remorse that bordered upon fury, in thinking of the past; a despair and a terror that bordered upon madness, in thinking of the future; a sense of impotence that lashed him into frenzy, in thinking of the present; these were a few of the emotions fermenting in Arthur's breast. His intelligence was quite unhinged. He had lost his reckoning. He was buffeted hither and thither by the waves of thought and feeling that smote upon him, like a ship without a rudder in a stormy sea. He wandered aimlessly through the streets, neither knowing nor caring whither his steps might lead him: while the people along his route stopped to stare and wonder at this crazy man, who, without a hat, with eyes gleaming vacantly from their sockets, with the pallor of death upon his cheek, hurried straight forward, looking neither to the right nor to the left. His blood coursed like liquid fire through his arteries. There was the hubbub of bedlam in his ears. The sole relief he could obtain came from ceaseless motion.

Toward four o'clock that afternoon Hetzel, who lay prone upon his sofa, glancing lazily at the last issue of his favorite magazine, heard a heavy, unsteady footfall upon the stairs. Next instant the door flew open, and Arthur stood before him, hair awry, clothing disordered, countenance drawn, haggard, and soiled with dust and perspiration. Hetzel jumped up, and was at his side in no time.

"What—what is the matter with you?" he demanded.

Arthur tottered a short distance into the room, and sank upon a chair.

It flashed across Hetzel's mind that his friend might possibly be the worse for drink. He laid hold of an ammonia bottle, and held it to Arthur's nostrils.

"No—no; I don't need that," Arthur said, waving Hetzel away.

"Well, then, speak. Tell me, what is the trouble?"

"Oh, Julian, I am ruined. If—if you knew what I have done!"

Arthur buried his face in his hands.

"Is—has—has something happened to your wife?"

"Oh, my wife, my wife," groaned Arthur, incoherently.

Hetzel was perplexed, puzzled as to what to do or say; so, very sensibly, held his tongue. By and by Arthur began, "My wife—my wife—oh, Hetzel, listen."

Then, brokenly, in half sentences, with frequent pauses, he managed to give Hetzel some account of the day's happening, winding up thus: "You—you see how it is. She had offered to tell me that secret she said she had, but I wouldn't let her. I wanted her to keep it, to show her how much I loved her. At least, that's what I thought. But I—I know now that it was my cowardice. I was afraid to hear it. We were so happy, I didn't want to run any risk of having our happiness lessened by—by thinking about unpleasant things. My ignorance was comfortable—I dreaded enlightenment. I was afraid of what it might be. I preferred to keep it entirely out of my head. God, that was a terrible mistake! If I had only had the courage to let her speak! But I was a coward. I went to work and persuaded myself that I was acting from motives of generosity—that I wanted to spare her the pain of talking about it—that I loved her too much to care about it—and all that. But that wasn't it at all. It was weakness, and downright cowardice, and evasion of my duty. I see it plainly now—now, when worse has come to worst. And she—she thinks—she thinks that I made inquiries behind her back, and found out what it was, and got to be friendly with Peixada in that way, and then went and put that advertisement into the papers just for the sake of—of humiliating her—oh, God!—and she thinks it was I who arranged to have her taken to prison. She actually believes that—believes that I did that! She wouldn't listen to me. Her indignation carried her away. She doesn't see how unreasonable it is. She hates me and despises me, and never will care for me again."

Hetzel himself was staggered. Arthur's tale ended, there befell a long silence.

Finally Arthur broke out petulantly, "Well, why don't you speak? Why don't you tell me what there is to be done?"

"It—I think it is very grave. You must let me consider a little while."

Another long silence. Hetzel, with bent head, was walking up and down the room. At length, coming to a standstill, he began, "Yes, it is very serious. But it is not—can not be—irremediable. There must be a way out of it—of course there must. I—I—by Jove, let's look it squarely in the face. It will merely make matters worse to—to sit still and think about how bad it is."

"What else is there to do?"

"This," answered Hetzel. "We must get her \ out of prison."

"That's very easy to say."

"Well, we'll do it, no matter how difficult it may be. She mustn't be left in the Tombs an hour longer than we can help. After that, it will be time to make her understand your part in the business. But now we must bend every muscle to get her out of prison. Whom do you know who will go bail for her?"

"That's the worst of it. They don't take bail in—in—murder cases,"

"They don't? Are you sure? Is it never done? We must move heaven and earth to induce them to, in this case."

"It's their rule. Romer might depart from it, she being—who she is. But I am afraid not."

"Well, we must try, at any rate, and without dillydallying. Whom can you get to go upon her bond?"

"The only person I know would be Mr. Flint."

"Then we must see Mr. Flint at once. Where does he live? Every minute is precious. We'll ask him to be her bondsman. Then we'll seek out Romer, and persuade him. If he's got a grain of manhood in him, he won't refuse. If we make haste, there's no reason why she shouldn't be free before sundown to-night. Come—let's be about it."

Hetzel's speech really inspired Arthur with a certain degree of hope and confidence. At all events, it was a relief to feel that he was doing something to repair the mischief he had wrought. So, in a hat borrowed from his chum, he led the way to Mr. Flint's residence.

On the way thither he began, "To think that it was I who started the authorities upon her track—I who urged them to prosecute her! And to think how the prosecution may end!"

Hetzel retorted, "End? I wish the end had come. I'm not afraid of the end. I know nothing of the circumstances of the case, but I do know—and you know, and we all know—that she never was guilty of murder. I know that we can prove it, too—establish her innocence beyond a shade of suspicion. We shall only need strength and patience to do that. You needn't worry about the end."

"But the meanwhile, then! Meanwhile, fancy what she thinks of me! Fancy her despair! Meanwhile, she—she may die—or—she may go mad—or kill herself."

"You little know your wife, if you think that. She's altogether too strong a woman to succumb to misfortune like that, altogether too noble a woman to do any thing of that kind. And as for her opinion of you, why, it stands to reason that she'll see the absurdity of it, as soon as the first shock has passed off. Just as soon as she's in a condition to use her mind, and think things over, she'll say to herself that there's something which she doesn't understand, and she'll ask you to explain. Take my word for it."

As they mounted Mr. Flint's steps, Arthur said, "Will—will you do the talking? I don't think I could bear to go over the whole story again."

Mr. Flint had but just got home from down-town. He was now in his bath. He sent word to the callers that he would dress and be with them as quickly as he could. They waited silently in the darkened drawing room, and listened to the ticking of an old-fashioned hall-clock. In about ten minutes Mr. Flint joined them.

Hetzel stated their errand. Of course, Mr. Flint was horrified and amazed. Of course, he agreed eagerly to do every thing in his power to aid them.

"Now then, for Romer," said Hetzel. "Where shall we find him?"

"I don't know," said Arthur. "We must look in the directory."

They stopped at an apothecary's shop, noted Romer's address, and started for the nearest elevated railway station.

Half way there Mr. Flint halted.

"No," he said, "we can't depend upon the cars. We must have a carriage. There's no telling how much traveling we shall have to do, before this business is completed."

They engaged a carriage at a hack-stand hard-by; and in it were jolted over the cobble-stones to Mr. Romer's abode.

Mr. Romer was not at home!

For a moment they gazed blankly into each other's faces. Finally Mr. Flint said, "Where has he gone?"

"I don't know," returned the servant.

"Is there any body in this house who does know?"

"His mother might."

"Well then, we want to see his mother."

The servant left them in the vestibule, and went up-stairs. Presently she returned, accompanied by a corpulent old lady.

"Did you desire to see Mr. Romer upon official business?"' inquired the old lady.

"We did, madam—important official business," said Mr. Flint.

"Then, gentlemen, you can't see him till to-morrow morning at his office. He don't see people officially after office-hours. If he did, he'd get no peace."

Mr. Flint accepted the situation, and was equal to it.

"I understand," he said; "but this is business in which Mr. Romer is personally interested. We *must* see him to-night. To-morrow morning will be too late. If you know where he is, you'd better tell us. Otherwise, I shan't answer for his displeasure."

"Oh, in that case," said the old lady, quite deceived by Mr. Flint's white lie, "in that case, you'll find him dining at the * * * Club. At least, he said he should dine there, when he left the house this morning."

"Thank you, madam," said Mr. Flint. In the carriage, "Bless my soul!" he added. "It couldn't have fallen out better. I'm a member of the * * * Club, myself."

They entered the club-house. Mr. Flint led Arthur and Hetzel into the reception-room, where, for a moment, he left them alone. Shortly returning, "Mr. Romer," he announced, "is in the bowling-alley—hasn't yet gone up to dinner. I've sent him my card."

In due time Romer appeared, his face flushed by recent exercise. Catching sight of Arthur, "What, you—Ripley?" he exclaimed. "I'd fust been telling the fellows down-stairs about—that is—I—well, I—I'm real glad to see you."

"Mr. Romer," said Mr. Flint, plunging *in medias res*, "I have ventured to disturb you in your leisure for the purpose of offering bail in the case of Mrs. Ripley, who, I am informed, was taken in custody to-day by your officers."

"Oh," said Romer, "a question of bail."

"Yes—we want to give bail for the lady at once—in any amount that you may wish—but without delay. She must be out of prison before to-morrow morning."

"Hum," mused Romer, "I don't see how you'll manage it."

"Manage it? What is there to be managed? I offer bail; it only remains for you to take it."

"Oh, excuse me, but I have no authority in the matter—no more than you yourself. Mr. Orson, my chief, is the man for you to see, and he's out of town. We don't take bail generally in murder cases; and *I* can't make an exception of this one—though I'd like to, first rate, for Ripley's sake. Perhaps Mr. Orson might do so—in fact I should advise him to—but, as I've said, he's not on hand. Then, the amount would have to be determined, the papers drawn, the proceedings submitted to a magistrate—and on the whole, it couldn't be arranged inside of a day or two, at the shortest."

"The devil you say!" cried Mr. Flint.

"I'm very sorry, I'm sure. But that's about the size of it," said Romer.

"And is—is there nothing to be done? Is this lady to remain indefinitely in the Tombs—a common prisoner?"

"Until you can bring the question before Mr. Orson, at any rate."

"Well, where is he, Mr. Orson?"

"He's on his vacation—down at Long Branch."

"What hotel?"

"The * * *."

"Good. Will you go with me to Long Branch to-morrow morning?"

"To-morrow morning? No, I can't go to-morrow morning."

"Why not?"

"Because I've got a calendar on my hands."

"When can you go?"

"I might arrange to run down to-morrow night, and come back Wednesday morning."

"For mercy's sake, then, do so. On what train will you start with me to-morrow night?"

"Call at my office at four o'clock in the afternoon, and I'll let you know. You may count, Ripley, upon my doing all I can for you."

Mr. Romer went back to his bowling.

Mr. Flint said, "Well, I don't see that we can go any further to-night."

"I suppose we'll have to reconcile ourselves to waiting and hoping," said Hetzel.

"Good God! Is she to—to pass the night in prison?" cried Arthur.

"Come, come, my dear boy," said Mr. Flint.

"We must make the best of it." Turning to Hetzel. "Where are you going now?" he asked.

"I think—it has just occurred to me—that we ought to see Mrs. Hart," Hetzel returned.

"Well then, set me down at my house on your way up." And Mr. Flint gave the necessary instructions to the driver.

Mrs. Hart was posted on her stoop, peering anxiously up and down the street, as the carriage containing Hetzel and Arthur rumbled into Beekman

Place. When she saw that the carriage had stopped directly in front of her domicile, she made a rush toward it, pulled open the door, and cried, "Ruth, Ruth—at last you have come back! I was so much worried!" Then, discovering her mistake, "Oh, it is not Ruth? Where can she be?"

"She is perfectly safe," said Hetzel. "Come into the house."

"You have seen her?" questioned Mrs. Hart. "She has been gone such a long time! I was frightened half to death. Tell me, why doesn't she come home? What—?"

Mrs. Hart faltered. By this time they had reached the parlor, which was brilliantly lighted up; and at the spectacle of Arthur's face, livid enough at best, but rendered doubly so by the gas-jets, Mrs. Hart faltered.

"Let me reassure you. Mrs. Ripley is perfectly safe," repeated Hetzel.

"But then—then, *why does he look like this?*" pointing to Arthur, and laying a stress upon each syllable.

"Sit down," said Hetzel, "and compose yourself; and he will tell you."

To Arthur, "Now, Arthur, try to command your feelings, and tell Mrs. Hart all about it."

As best he could, he told Mrs. Hart as much as was needful to make her comprehend the state of affairs.

Mrs. Hart was nervous enough at the outset. As Arthur's story proceeded, her nervousness became more and more ungovernable. When she learned that Ruth had been carried off to prison, she cried, "Oh, take me to her at once. I must go to her at once. She must not be left alone there all night."

"It would be impossible to obtain admittance at this hour," said Hetzel.

But saying it did not suffice. Mrs. Hart insisted. "Oh, they would surely let me in. She—she will die if she is left there alone."

Hetzel undertook to comfort her, and to bring her around to reason. Finally she was sufficiently calm to listen to the rest of what Arthur had to say.

His tale complete, Hetzel took up the sequel, explaining how they had tried to have her liberated on bail, how Mr. Flint was to visit Mr. Orson at Long Branch to-morrow night, and going on to express his assurance that in a week's time at the furthest the storm would have blown over, and made way for calm and sunshine.

For a long while Mrs. Hart could only cry and utter inarticulate syllables of grief.

By and by Hetzel asked, "Can you tell us how she came to go down there—to Mr. Peixada's place?"

"Oh, yes," said Mrs. Hart. "It was my fault. I advised her to. You see, this is the way it happened. After Arthur had left the house this morning, Ruth picked up the newspaper. She was just glancing over it—not reading any thing in particular—when all at once, she gave a little scream. I asked her what it was; and she said, 'Look here.' Then she showed me the advertisement that he has spoken of. 'Would you pay any attention to it?' she asked. I read it, and considered, and then asked her what action her impulse prompted her to take. She said that she hardly knew. If there was something they wanted of her, which was right and proper, she supposed she ought to do it; but she hated to have any dealings with Peixada. 'I thought Judith Peixada had been dead two years,' she said; 'but now she comes to life again just when she is least expected.' I suggested that she might write a letter. But on thinking it over she said, 'No. Perhaps the best thing I can do will be to go at once and beard the lion in his den. I shall worry about it otherwise. I may as well know right away what it is. After lunch I'll go downtown and call upon Mr. Peixada; and then I'll surprise Arthur in his office, and bring him home.' Then I—I said I thought that was the best thing she could possibly do," Mrs. Hart interrupted herself to dry her eyes. Presently, "You see, it was my fault," she resumed. "I ought to have suspected that they meant foul play; but instead, I let her walk straight into their pitfall. Right after lunch, at about halfpast one, she started out. She promised to be home again by four o'clock. When she didn't come and didn't come, I began to get more and more anxious about her. I was almost beside myself, when at last you arrived."

Hetzel said, "It is bad enough to think of her being locked up in prison, but that is not the worst. I'm sure we can get her out of prison; and although I don't know the first thing about the case, I'm sure that we can prove her innocence. The trouble now is this. She's suffering all manner of torments, because she totally misconceives her husband's part in the transaction. Our endeavor must be to put her husband's conduct before her in the right light—make her understand that he acted all along in good faith, and without the faintest suspicion that she and Judith Peixada were one and the same. She was so much incensed at him this afternoon, that she wouldn't let him justify himself. We must set this mistake right tomorrow morning. I think that you, Mrs. Hart, had better visit her as early to-morrow as they will admit you, and—"

"Of course I will," interpolated Mrs. Hart.

"—And tell her Arthur's side of the story. When she understands that, she'll feel like another woman. Then he can see her, and talk to her, and find out the facts of the case, and lay them before the authorities. It seems to me that this is the plain course to take."

"And meanwhile, meanwhile!" cried Arthur, wringing his hands.

"Come," said Hetzel, "show your grit. Look at Mrs. Hart. See how bravely she bears up. Do you want to make it harder for every one by your example?"

"Mrs. Hart isn't her husband," Arthur retorted.

Then he bit his lip and kept silence. Mrs. Hart sat bolt upright, staring at vacancy, with brows knitted into a tight frown. Hetzel tugged away at his whiskers, and was evidently thinking hard.

By and by the door-bell rang. A servant entered.

"Here is a note, ma'am, a man just left," she said to Mrs. Hart.

Mrs. Hart read the note and passed it to Hetzel. It was written upon a half sheet of paper, headed in heavy black print, "City Prison." It was brief:—

"My dear, dear Friend:—You must be anxious about me. I have tried hard to get word to you. At last they have found a messenger for me. You see by this letter-heading where I am. The advertisement was a trick. But it was worse, much worse, than you can fancy. If I could only see you! Will you come to me to-morrow morning? I am too heartsick to write, Ruth."

Hetzel was returning the note to Mrs. Hart, when Arthur stretched out his hand for it.

"Am I not to read what my own wife has written?" he demanded fiercely.

He took in its contents at a glance. Even this sheet of common prison paper was sweet with that faint, evanescent perfume that clung to everything Ruth's fingers touched. Letting it drop to the floor, "I can't stand it," he cried in a loud voice, and left the room.

They heard the vestibule door slam behind him.

"He is mad," said Mrs. Hart. "He will do himself an injury."

"No, he won't—not if I can stop him," said Hetzel; and he hurried forth upon Arthur's track.

But he came back in a little while, panting for breath.

"I ran as far as First Avenue," he explained; "but he had succeeded in getting out of sight. Never mind. He'll come home all right. No doubt he needs to be alone."

Once out of doors, Arthur dashed blindly ahead. It was a sultry night. The odor of ailanthus trees hung heavy on the air. Many people were abroad. On the door-steps of most of the houses, the inmates sat, chatting, smoking, dozing, airing themselves. The city had given itself over to rest and recreation. Through open windows escaped bursts of song and laughter and piano playing. Young girls, dressed in white, promenaded on the arms of young men who puffed cigarettes.

Arthur had no fixed destination. He walked, because walking was a counter-irritant. He walked rapidly, and took no notice of the sights and sounds round about him. He remembers dimly that he left the respectable quarters of the city far behind, and entered a maze of crooked, squalid, foul-smelling streets. Then, he remembers that all at once he looked up and wondered where he was. And there, a blot upon the sky, there loomed the prison that held his beloved.

He remained within eyeshot of this dismal structure till daybreak, when at last he went back to Beekman Place.

CHAPTER IX.
AN ORDEAL.

ARTHUR ran up the steps of Mrs. Hart's house, and, opening the door with his latch-key, entered the parlor. The gas was burning at full head. Hetzel was stretched at length in an easy-chair, his hands thrust deep into his trowsers-pockets. At sight of Arthur, he rose and advanced on tip-toe to meet him.

"Hush-sh," he said, putting his finger to his lips. He pointed to the sofa, upon which Mrs. Hart lay, asleep. Then he took Arthur's arm, and led him through the hall into the back room. There they seated themselves.

"I didn't expect to find you up," said Arthur.

"We haven't been abed," said Hetzel.

"I suppose nothing new has happened? You haven't heard from her again?"

"No."

They remained silent for some time.

Hetzel began, "After you left in that abrupt way, Mrs. Hart, who had borne up wonderfully, quite went to pieces. She has been in a half hysterical condition all night. I persuaded her to lie down about an hour ago, and now she's asleep."

Arthur vouchsafed no comment.

"We have had a lot of reporters pestering us, too," Hetzel went on. "Of course I refused to see them, one and all."

At this Arthur started.

"Then I suppose the whole thing is in the papers, curse them!" he cried.

"I am afraid so."

"Haven't you looked to see?"

"It isn't time yet. The papers haven't been delivered yet."

Arthur pulled out his watch.

"Not going—run down," he said; "but of course it's time. It must be seven o'clock."

"Oh, I didn't know it was so late. I'll go see." Hetzel went away. Presently he returned, saying, "Surely enough, here they are."

"Well?" queried Arthur.

Hetzel undid the newspapers, and commenced to look them over.

"Yes, it's all here—a column of it—on the front page," he groaned.

"Let me see," said Arthur, extending his hand.

But the head-lines were as much as he had the heart to read. He threw the sheet angrily to the floor and began to stride back and forth across the room.

"Sit down," said Hetzel, "or you'll wake Mrs. Hart."

"Oh, to be sure," assented Arthur; and did as he was bidden.

By and by, "Do you know at what hours visitors are admitted?" Hetzel asked.

"I—I think between ten and four."

"Well, then, we'll want a carriage here at halfpast nine. I'll send out now to order one."

For a second time Hetzel left the room. When he got back, he said that he had dispatched a servant to the nearest livery stable.

At this juncture Mrs. Hart appeared, very old and gray and pallid. She came in without speaking, and took a chair near the window.

"I hope your nap has refreshed you," Hetzel ventured.

"Oh, yes," she replied dismally, "I suppose it has.—Where have you been, Arthur?"

"Nowhere—only out of doors."

All three held their peace.

Presently the servant returned from her errand, and told Hetzel that the carriage would be on hand at the proper time.

"Bridget," said Mrs. Hart, "you'd better brew some coffee, and serve it up here."

When Bridget had gone, "You have sent for a carriage? At what hour are we to start?" Mrs. Hart inquired.

"At half-past nine."

"Then, if you will excuse me, I'll go up-stairs and get ready."

"Certainly," said Hetzel. "And while you're about it, you'd better put a few things together to take to her, don't you think?"

"Why, she won't need them. She'll be with us again to-day, will she not?"

"You know, Mr. Flint can't see Mr. Orson till this evening. So, it seems to me——-"

"Oh, yes, I had forgotten," said Mrs. Hart, gulping down a sob, and left the room.

During her absence, Bridget brought in the coffee.

"Take a cup up to your mistress," said Hetzel.

Then he poured out a cup for Arthur. He had to use some persuasion to induce him to drink it; but eventually he prevailed. Having swallowed a portion for himself, he lighted a cigarette.

"Better try one," he said, with a woful attempt at cheerfulness, offering the bunch to Arthur. "There's nothing like tobacco to brace a man up."

But Arthur declined.

Half-past nine was leisurely in arriving. At last, however, they heard the grinding of carriage-wheels upon the pavement outside.

They climbed into the carriage. The coachman cracked his whip. Off they drove.

That drive was a purgatory. At its start their hearts were oppressed by a nameless terror. It had intensified into a breathless agony, before their drive was over. Their foreheads were wet with cold perspiration. Their lips were ashen. As they turned from Broadway into Leonard Street, and knew that they were nearing their journey's end, each of them instinctively winced, and gasped, and shuddered. When the carriage finally drew up before the prison entrance, not one of them dared to speak or to stir.

At last Hetzel said, "Well, here we are."

No answer.

After an interval, he went on, "Mrs. Hart, you, of course, will go in first. You must explain to her about Arthur, and induce her to see him. You can send word, or come back, when she's ready to."

With this, he opened the carriage door, dismounted, and helped Mrs. Hart to follow. Arthur remained behind. He closed his eyes for a little, and held his hands to his forehead. His hands were cold and damp. His forehead was now dry and hot; and he could count the pulsations of the arteries in his temples. His throat ached with a great lump. He mechanically watched the people pass on the sidewalk, and wondered whether any of them were as miserably unhappy as he. The myriad noises of the street smote his ears with a strange sharpness, and caused him from time to time to start and turn even paler than he had been. Gradually, however, he began to lose consciousness of outward things, and to think, think, think. He had plenty to think about. Pretty soon, he was fathoms deep in a brown study.

He was aroused by the reappearance of Hetzel and Mrs. Hart. They got into the carriage. The carriage moved.

"What—what is the trouble now?" Arthur asked.

"Damn them for a set of insolent scoundrels!"

Hetzel blurted out, forgetful of Mrs. Hart's sex. "They wouldn't let us in."

"Why not?"

"Oh, they insist on a tangle of red-tape—say we must have passes, and so forth, from the district-attorney."

"Well?"

"Well, we're on our way to procure them now." But at the district-attorney's office there was fresh delay. The clerk whose duty it was to make out the passes, had not yet reached his post; and none of his colleagues seemed anxious to play the lieutenant's part.

Hetzel lost his temper.

"Come, what are you lazy louts paid for, I'd like to know?" he thundered. "Where's your master? Where's Mr. Romer? I'll see whether you're to sit around here in your shirt-sleeves, grinning, or not. I want some one of you to wait on me, or I'll make it hot for the whole pack."

He got his passes.

They drove back to the Tombs. This time Mrs. Hart encountered no obstacles to her entrance.

Hetzel rejoined Arthur in the carriage. A quarter-hour elapsed before either spoke.

Arthur said, "She—she's staying a long while."

"Oh," responded Hetzel, "they've got such a lot to talk about, you know."

At the end of another quarter-hour, more or less, Arthur complained, "What under heaven can be keeping her so long?"

"Be patient," said Hetzel. "It'll do no good to fret."

By and by Arthur started up. "By Jove, I can't wait any longer. I can't endure this waiting. I must go in myself," he cried.

But just at this moment Mrs. Hart issued forth.

Hetzel ran to meet her.

She was paler than ever. Her eyelids were red.

"We may as well drive home," she said. "She won't see him."

"For heaven's sake, why not?" asked Hetzel.

"I'll tell you all about it, as we drive along."

"But how—how shall we break the news to him?"

"You—you'd better speak to him now, before I get in."

Hetzel approached the carriage window.

"Arthur," he began, awkwardly, "try—try to keep quiet, and not—the—the fact is—"

"Is she ill? Is she dead?" cried Arthur, with mad alarm.

"No, no, my dear boy; of course not. Only—only—just now—she—"

"She refuses to see me?"

"Well—"

"I was fully prepared for that. I knew she would."

His head sank upon his breast.

They had covered half the distance between the Tombs and Beekman Place, when at length Arthur said, "Please, Mrs. Hart, please tell me about your visit."

Mrs. Hart shot a glance at Hetzel, as much as to ask, "Shall I?" He nodded affirmatively.

"There isn't much to tell," she began. "They led me down a lot of stone corridors, and through a yard, and up a flight of stairs, and across a long gallery, past numberless little, black, iron doors; and at last we stopped before one of the doors, and the woman who was with me called out,'.eixada, alias Ripley'—only think of the indignity!—and after she had called it out that way two or three times, a little panel in the door flew open, and there—there was Ruth's face—so pale, so sad, and her eyes so large and awful—it made my heart sink. I supposed of course they were going to let me in; but no, they wouldn't. The prison woman said I must stand there, and say what I had to say to the prisoner in her presence."

Mrs. Hart paused, and swallowed a sob.

"Well, I stood there, so frightened at the sight of Ruth's face, that I didn't know what to do; till by and by she said, very softly, 'Aren't you going to kiss me, dear?' Oh, her voice was so sweet and sad, I couldn't help it, but I burst out crying; and she cried, too; and she put her face up close to the open place in the door; and then we kissed each other; and then—then we just cried and cried, and couldn't speak a word."

The memory of her former tears brought fresh tears to Mrs. Hart's eyes. Drying them, she went on, "We were crying like that, and never thinking of any thing else, when the prison woman said, 'If you have any communication to make to the prisoner, you'd better make it right off, because you can't stay here all day, you know.' Then I began about Arthur. I said, 'Ruth, I wanted to tell you that Arthur is down outside, and that he wishes to see you.' Oh, if you could have seen the look that came upon her face! It made me tremble. I thought she was going to faint, or something. But no. She said, very calmly, 'It would do no good for me to see Arthur. It would only pain him and myself. I do not wish to see him. I could not bear to see him. That is what she said."

"Go on, go on," groaned Arthur, as Mrs. Hart paused.

"She said she didn't want to see you, and couldn't bear to. I said, 'But, Ruth, you ought to see him. You and he ought to speak together, and try to understand each other.' She said, 'There is no misunderstanding between us. I understand every thing.'—'Oh, no,' said I, 'no, you don't. There is something which he wants to explain to you—about how he came to be associated with Mr. Peix-ada.'—'I don't care about that,' said she. 'There are some things which he can not explain. I am miserable enough already. I need all my strength. I should break down, if I were to see him.'—But I said, 'Consider, him, Ruth. You can't imagine how unhappy he is. He loves you so much. It is breaking his heart.'—'Loves me?' she said. 'Does he still pretend to love me? Oh, no, he does not love me. He never loved me. If he had loved me, he would never have done what he did. Oh, no, no—I can not see him, I will not see him. You may tell him that I said it would do no good for us to see each other. Every thing is over and past between him and me.' She had said all this very calmly. But then suddenly she began to cry again: and she was crying and sobbing as if her heart would break, and she couldn't speak a word, and all I could do was to try and soothe her a little, when the prison woman said I must come away. I tried to get her to let me stay—offered her money—but she said, 'No. It is dinner time now. No visitors are allowed in the building at dinner time. You must go.'—So, I had to leave Ruth alone."

"It is as I supposed," moaned Arthur. "She hates me. All is over and past between us, she said."

"Nonsense, man," protested Hetzel. "It is merely a question of time. Mrs. Hart simply didn't have time enough. If she had been allowed to stay a half hour longer, your wife would have loved you as much as ever. She does love you as much as ever, now. But her heart is crushed and sore, and all she feels is the pain. It's less than twenty-four hours since the whole thing happened; she hasn't had time enough yet to think it over. We're going to have her home again to-morrow; and if between the three of us we can't undeceive her respecting your relations to Peixada—bring her to hear and comprehend the truth—I'll be mightily surprised."

They drove for some blocks in silence.

"Did you give her her things, Mrs. Hart?" Arthur asked, abruptly.

"No," said Mrs. Hart; "they wouldn't let me. I forgot to tell you that they made me empty my pockets before they led me to her. The prison woman took the things, and said she would examine them, and then give her such as were not against rules."

"And—and it was a regular prison cell in which she was confined?"

"Oh, yes; it was horrible. The walls were whitewashed, and there was only one little bit of a grated window, and the floor was of stone, and the bed was a narrow iron cot, and she had just a wretched, old, wooden stool to sit on, and the air was something frightful."

"Did you tell her of our efforts to get bail for her?" asked Hetzel.

"Dear me, I forgot all about it."

"Perhaps you'd better write her a note, when we get home. I'll send a messenger with it."

"All right, I will," acquiesced Mrs. Hart.

But in Beekman Place she said to Hetzel: "About that note you spoke of—I don't feel that I can trust myself to write. I'm afraid I should say something that—that might—I mean I think I *couldn't* write to her. I should break down, if I tried. Won't you do it, instead?"

"One word from you would comfort her more than a dozen from me."

"But—it is such hard work for me to keep control of myself, as it is—and if I should undertake to write—I—I—"

"Oh, very well," said Hetzel. "Can you let me have pen and paper?"

What he wrote ran thus:—

"My dear Mrs. Ripley: I only want to send you this line or two, to tell you that your friends are hard at work in your behalf, and that before this time to-morrow we mean to have you safe and sound at home. Meanwhile, for Arthur s sake, try to bear up and be of good cheer. The poor boy is breaking his heart about you. All I can do for him is to promise that in a few hours, now, he shall hold you in his arms again. I should like to make clear to you in this note how it was that he seemed to have had a share in the trickery by which you were betrayed; but I am afraid I might make a bungle of it; and after all, it is best that you should hear the tale from his own lips, as you surely will to-morrow morning. I beg and pray that you will strive hard not to let this thing have any grave effect upon your health. That is what I most dread. Of other consequences I have no fear—and you need have none. If you will only exert your strength to bear it a little while longer, and come home to us to-morrow sound and well in health, why, we shall all live to forget that this break in our happiness ever occurred. I think I feel the full pain of your position. I know that it is of a sort to unnerve the staunchest of us. But I know too that you have uncommon powers at your command; and I beg of you, for your own sake, for Arthur's, for Mrs. Hart's, to call upon them now. Weather the storm for one more night, and then I vouch for the coming blue skies.

"God bless you and be with you!

"Julian Hetzel."

"I want to add a postscript," said Arthur, when Hetzel laid down his pen.

"Do you think you'd better?" asked Hetzel, dubiously.

"Let me have it, will you?" cried Arthur, savagely; and held out his hand for the paper.

Hetzel gave it to him. On the blank space that was left he wrote: "Ruth—my darling—for God's sake, overcome your anger against me. Don't judge me before you have heard my defense. Be merciful, Ruth, and wait till you have let me speak and justify myself, before taking for granted that I have been guilty of treachery toward you. Oh, Ruth, how can you condemn me on mere appearances?—me, your husband. Oh, please, Ruth, *please* write me an answer, saying that you have got over the anger you felt for me yesterday and this morning, and that you will suspend judgment of me till I have had a chance to clear myself. I can not write my explanation here, now. I am not calm enough, and it is too long a story. Oh, Ruth, I shall go mad, unless you will promise to wait about condemning me. Write me an answer at once, and send it by the messenger who brings you this. I can not say any thing else except that I love you. Oh, you will kill me, if you go on believing what you told Mrs. Hart—that I do not love you. You must believe that I love you—you know I love you. Say in your answer that you know I love you. I love you as I never loved you—more than I ever loved you before. Oh, little Ruth, please cheer up, and don't be unhappy. If this thing should result seriously for your health, I—I shall die. Dear little Ruth, just try to keep up until to-morrow morning. If you will only come home all right to-morrow morning, then our sufferings will not count. Ruth!"

Hetzel said, "I'll run out to the corner, and find some one to carry this to her."

He went off. Mrs. Hart and Arthur sat silent and motionless in the parlor. In due time Hetzel got back. He too took a seat and kept his peace. So the afternoon wore away. No one spoke. Their minds were busy enough, God knows; but busy with thoughts which they dared not shape in speech. The clock on the mantel-piece ticked with painful distinctness. Street-sounds penetrated the closed windows—children's voices, at their games—the cries of fruit venders—hand-organ music—the noise of wheels on paving stones—and reminded the listeners that the life of the city was going on very much as usual. Now and then a steam-whistle shrieked on the river. Now and then one of our tongue-tied trio drew a deep, audible sigh. Ruth's piano, in the corner, was open. On the rack lay a sheet of music, and with it a tiny white silk handkerchief that she had doubtless thrown down carelessly, and left there, the day before. When Arthur perceived this, he got up, crossed the floor, took possession of it, and tucked it into his pocket.

Towards six o'clock the door-bell rang. All three started violently. The same notion occurred to all three at once.

"It—it is from her. It is her answer," gasped Arthur, and began to breathe quickly.

Hetzel went to the door. After what seemed an eternity to those he had left behind, he returned.

"No," he said, replying to their glances; "not yet. It is only your office-boy, Arthur. He has brought you your day's mail."

Arthur apathetically commenced to look over the envelopes. At last he came to one which he appeared on the point of opening. But then abruptly he seemed to change his mind, and tossed it to Hetzel.

"Read that, will you, and tell me what he says," was his request.

Hetzel read the following:—

"Office of

"B. Peixada & Co.,

"No.—Reade Street,

"New York, Aug. 12, 1884.

"Dear Sir:—In view of the extraordinary occurrence of yesterday morning, I presume it is needless for me to say that your further services as my attorney can be dispensed with. Please have the goodness to transfer my brother's will and all other papers in your keeping, in reference to the case of my late sister-in-law, to Edwin Offenbach, Esq., attorney, No.— Broadway. I don't know if you expect me to pay you any more money; but if you do, please send memorandum to above address, and oblige,

"Respectfully Yours,

"B. Peixada.

"A. Ripley, Esq., attorney, etc."

"He wants you to transfer his papers to another lawyer and render your bill, that's all," said Hetzel.

"Oh, is that all?" Arthur rejoined. "Well, then, let me have his note."

Arthur put Peixada's note into his pocket. The trio relapsed into their former silence.

Again by and by the door-bell rang. Again all three started. Again Hetzel went to the door.

Arthur leaned forward, and strained his ears. He heard Hetzel take down the chain; he heard the door creak open; he heard a boy's voice, rough and lusty, say, "No answer. Here, sign—will you?" And then he sank back in his chair.

Hetzel staid away for some minutes. Coming back, "It was the messenger," he said; "but he had no answer. The prison people told him that there was none."

It was now about seven o'clock. Presently Bridget appeared upon the threshold, and asked to speak with her mistress. Mrs. Hart stepped into the hall, where for a time she and the servant conversed in low tones. Re-entering the parlor, she said, "Dinner.—She came to tell me that dinner is ready. I had forgotten it. Will you come down?"

Hetzel rose. Arthur remained seated.

"Come, Arthur. Didn't you hear what Mrs. Hart said? Dinner is ready," Hetzel began.

"Oh, you don't suppose I want any dinner, do you? You two go down, if you choose. I'll wait for you here."

"Now, be sensible, will you? Come down-stairs with us. Whether you want to, or not, you must eat something. You'll get sick, fasting like this. We've got enough on our hands, as it is, without having a sick man to look after. Come along."

Hetzel took Arthur by the arm, and led him out.

But their attempt at dinner was pretty doleful. Despite their long abstinence from food, none of them was hungry. Hetzel alone contrived to finish his soup. Mrs. Hart and Arthur could swallow no more than a few mouthfuls of bread and wine apiece.

Afterward they went back to the parlor. As before, Arthur sat still and nursed his thoughts. Hetzel picked up an illustrated book from the table, and began to turn the pages. Mrs. Hart said, "If you will excuse me, I think I'll lie down for a little. I have a splitting headache." She lay down on the sofa. Hetzel got a shawl, and covered her with it.

The clock was striking ten, when for a third time the bell rang. For a third time Hetzel started to answer it. Arthur accompanied him.

Hetzel opened the door. A telegraph-boy confronted him.

"Ripley?" the boy demanded.

"Yes—yes," said Arthur, and seized hold of the dispatch that the boy offered.

But his courage forsook him. He turned white, and leaned against the wall for support.

"Some—something has happened to her," he gasped. "Read it for me, Hetz, and let me know the worst."

"No, it isn't from her. It's from Mr. Flint," said Hetzel, after he had read it.

"Oh," sighed Arthur.—"Well, what does he say?"

"Here."

Hetzel put the telegram into Arthur's hands. Its contents were:—

"Victory! Meet me to-morrow morning, 10:30, at district-attorney's office. Every thing satisfactorily arranged. Absolutely nothing to fear.—Arthur Flint."

"There," Hetzel added, "now I hope you'll brace up a little."

"I suppose I ought to," said Arthur. "Anyhow, I'll try."

Mrs. Hart was much relieved. Indeed, her spirits underwent a considerable reaction. Her eyes brightened, and she cried, "Oh, to think! The dear child will be home again by luncheon-time to-morrow!"

"And now," put in Hetzel, "I would counsel both you and Arthur to go to bed. A night's rest will work wonders for you."

"Yes, I think so, too," agreed Mrs. Hart. "But you—you will not leave us? You will sleep in our spare room?"

"Oh, thank you. Yes, perhaps I'd better stay here, so as to be on hand in case any thing should happen."

All three climbed the staircase. Mrs. Hart showed Hetzel to his quarters, and inspected them to satisfy herself that every thing was in proper order for his comfort. Then he escorted her back to her own bed-chamber. Arthur was standing in the hall. Mrs. Hart bade them both good night, and disappeared. Thereupon Hetzel, turning to Arthur, said, "Now, old boy, go straight to bed, and refresh yourself with a sound sleep. Good-by till morning."

But Arthur stopped him. In a voice that betrayed some embarrassment, he began, "I say, Julian, I wonder whether you would very much mind my sleeping with you. You see, I—I haven't been in there"—pointing to a door in front of them—"since—since—" He broke off.

"Oh, of course. You don't feel like being left alone. I understand. Come on," said Hetzel.

"Thanks," said Arthur. "Yes, that's it. I don't feel like being left alone."

The sky was overcast next morning, and a cold wind blew from across the river. Hetzel and Mrs. Hart were up betimes; but Arthur, who had tossed restlessly about for the earlier half of the night, lay abed till late. He did not show his face downstairs till nine o'clock.

"We want to start in about half an hour, Arthur," said Hetzel. "That will give us time to stop at your office, before going to the district-attorney's."

"What do we want to stop at my office for?"

"Why, to attend to the matters that Peixada wrote you about—return the will—and so forth."

"Oh, yes. I had forgotten."

"Then, I suppose, Mrs. Hart, that we shall be back here for luncheon, and bring Ruth with us. But if we shouldn't turn up till somewhat later, you mustn't alarm yourself. There's no telling how long the legal formalities may take."

"You speak as though you were going to leave me behind," said Mrs. Hart.

"Why, I didn't think you would want to go with us. The weather is so threatening, and the district-attorney's office is so unpleasant a place, I took for granted that you would prefer to stay home."

"Oh, no. I should go wild, waiting here alone. You must let me accompany you. I want to be the first—no, the second—to greet Ruth."

Hetzel made no further opposition.

They went straight to Arthur's office. There he did the Peixada documents up in a bundle, directed the same to Mr. Edwin Offenbach, and told his office boy to deliver it to Mr. Offenbach in person. Then they proceeded on foot up Broadway and down Chambers Street to the district-attorney's.

The identical lot of supercilious clerks with whom Hetzel had had it out the day before, were lolling about now in the ante-room. "We wish to see Mr. Romer," Hetzel announced.

Nobody seemed to be much impressed by this piece of intelligence.

"Come, you fellow," Hetzel went on, addressing one young gentleman in particular, who appeared to have no more weighty duty to perform than the trimming of his finger-nails; "just take that card into Mr. Romer—will you?—and look sharp about it."

The young gentleman glanced up languidly, surveyed his interlocutor with a mingling of pity and amusement, at length drawled, "Say, Jim, see what this party's after," and returned to his toilet.

Hetzel's brow contracted.

"What do you want to see Mr. Romer about?" demanded Jim, leisurely lifting himself from the desk atop which he had been seated.

Hetzel's brows contracted a trifle more closely. There was an ugly look in his eyes.

"What do I want to see Mr. Romer about?" he repeated. "I'll explain that to Mr. Romer. What I want you to do is to conduct us to Mr. Romer's office; and I want you to do that at short notice, or, I promise you, I'll find out the reason why."

Hetzel had spoken quietly, but with an inflection that was unmistakable.

"Well, step this way, then, will you?" said Jim, the least bit crestfallen.

They followed him into Mr. Romer's private room.

Romer was seated at his desk. Mr. Flint was seated hard-by at a table, examining some papers. Both rose at the entrance of the visitors.

"Ah, Arthur, my dear boy," Mr. Flint exclaimed, "here you are." He clapped his godson heartily upon the shoulder, and proceeded to pay his compliments to Mrs. Hart and Hetzel.

"How do, Ripley?" said Romer. "Glad to see you."

Thereupon befell a moment of silence. Nobody seemed to know what to say next.

Finally Mr. Flint began. "I think," he said, "I ought to tell you that Mr. Romer is to be thanked for all the good luck that we have met with. Except for his intercession, Mr. Orson would not have considered the bail question for a moment. As it is, Mr. Romer has persuaded him—But perhaps you'd better go on," he added, abruptly turning to Romer.

"Well," said Romer, "the long and short of it is that Mr. Orson agrees to accept bail in twenty-five thousand dollars. You know, Ripley, it's our rule not to take bail at all in cases of this sort; and so he had to fix a large amount to ward off scandal."

"And here are the papers, all ready to be signed," said Mr. Flint.

"But where——" Hetzel began.

"Yes, just so. I was coming to that," Romer interposed. "We've sent for her, and she'll get here before long. But what I was going to say is this: Mr. Orson makes it a condition that before bail is accepted, she be required to—to plead."

"Well?" queried Hetzel.

"Well, you see, she must put in her plea of not guilty in—in open court."

"What!" cried Arthur. "Subject her to that humiliation? Drag her up to the bar of a crowded court-room, and—and—Oh, it will kill her! You might as well kill her outright."

"Is this absolutely necessary?" asked Hetzel.

"Mr. Orson made it a *sine qua non*," replied Romer; "and if you'll listen to me for a moment, I'll tell you why."

He paused, gnawed his mustache for an instant, at length resumed, "You know, Ripley, we never should have gone at this case, at all, except for you. That's so, isn't it? All right. Now, what I want to make plain is that we're, not to blame. You started us, didn't you? Well and good. We unearthed that old indictment, which otherwise might have lain moldering in its pigeon-hole till the day of doom, we unearthed it simply because you urged us to. We never should have moved in the matter, except for you. I want you to confess that this is a true statement of the facts."

"Oh, yes; it's true," groaned Arthur.

"All right, Ripley. That's just what I wanted to bring out. Now I can pass on to point two. Point two is this. I suppose you're very sorry for what's happened. I know we are—at least, I am—awfully sorry. And what's more, I feel—I feel—hang it, I feel uncommonly friendly toward you, Ripley, old boy. Don't you understand? I want to do all I can to get you out of this confounded mess. And so, what I went to work to do with Mr. Orson was not only to induce him to take bail, but also, don't you see, to get him to drop the case. What I urged upon him was this. I said, 'Look here, Mr. Orson, we didn't start this business, did we? Then why the deuce should we press it? The chances of conviction aren't great, and anyhow we've got our hands full enough, without raking up worm-eaten indictments. I say, as long as she has turned out to be who she is, I say, let's leave matters in *statu quo*.' That's what I said to Mr. Orson."

"By Jove, Romer, you—you're a brick," was the most Arthur could respond. There was a frog in his voice.

"Well, sir," Romer continued, "I put it before Mr. Orson in that shape, and I argued with him a long time about it. But what struck him was this. 'What'll the public say?' he asked. 'Now it's got into the papers, there'll be the dickens to pay, if we don't push it.' And you can't deny, Ripley, that that's a pretty serious difficulty. Well, he and I, we talked it over, and considered the pros and cons, and the upshot of it was that he said, 'All right, Romer. I have no desire to carry the matter further than is necessary to set us right before the public. So, what I'll consent to do is to have bail fixed in a large sum—say twenty-five thousand dollars—and then she must plead in open court. That'll satisfy the reporters. Then we'll put the indictment back into the safe, and let it lie. As long as we're solid with the public, I don't care.' That's what Mr. Orson said. So now, you see, she's got to plead in open court, to prevent the newspapers from raising Cain with us, and the bail's got to be pretty considerable for the same reason. But after that's settled, you can take her home, and rest easy. As long as we're in office the charge won't be revived; and by the time we're superseded, it will be an old story and forgotten by all hands."

"You see," Mr. Flint said, "how much we have to thank Mr. Romer for."

"And I hope Mr. Romer will believe that we appreciate his kindness," added Hetzel.

"I—I—God bless you, Romer," blurted out Arthur.

"Well," said Romer, "to come down to particulars, we've got a crowded calendar to-day, and so the court room is likely to be full of people. I wanted to make this pleading business as easy as possible for her, and on that account I've sent an officer after her already. Just as soon as the judge arrives, she can put in her plea. Then we'll all come back here, and have the papers signed; and then you can go home and be happy. Now, if you'll follow me, I'll take you into the court room by the side entrance."

"Oh, we—I don't want to go into the court room. I couldn't stand it. Let us wait here till it's over," whimpered Arthur, through chattering teeth.

Romer looked surprised. "Just as you please," said he; "but prisoners generally like to see a friendly face near them, when they're called up to plead."

"Ripley doesn't know what he's saying," put in Hetzel. "Of course we will follow you into court." In a lower tone, turning to Arthur, "You don't mean that you want her to go through that ordeal alone, do you?" he demanded.

"Oh, I forgot about that," Arthur confessed.

"But—but," asked Mrs. Hart, "can't we see her and speak to her before she has to appear in court?"

"I don't think that could be managed," replied Romer, "without some delay. You know, I want to have her plead the moment she gets here, so as to avoid the crush. It'll only take a few minutes. You'd better come now."

They followed Romer out of his office, down a long, gloomy corridor, along which knots of people stood, chatting and smoking rank cigars, and into the General Sessions court room—the court room that Arthur had visited a few months before, out of idle curiosity to witness the scene of Mrs. Peixada's trial.

There were already about forty persons present: a half dozen lawyers at the counsel-table, busy with books and papers; a larger number of respectable looking citizens, who read newspapers and appeared bored—probably gentlemen of the jury; and a residue of damp, dirty, dismal individuals, including a few tattered women, who were doubtless, like those with whom we are chiefly concerned, come to watch the fate of some unfortunate friend. Every body kept very still, so that the big clock on the wall made itself distinctly heard even to the farthest corner of the room. Its hands marked five minutes to eleven. The suspense was painful. It seemed to Arthur that he had grown a year older in the interval that elapsed before the clock solemnly tolled the hour.

Romer had chairs placed for them within the bar, a little to the right of the clerk's desk, so that they would not be more than six feet distant from the prisoner, when she stood up to speak. Then he left them, saying, "I'll see whether the judge has got down. I want to ask him to go on the bench promptly, as a favor to me."

Soon afterward a loud rapping sounded upon the door that led from the corridor, and the officers who were scattered about the room, simultaneously called, "Hats off."

The judge, with grave and rather self-conscious mien, stalked past our friends, and took his position on the bench. Romer followed at a few paces. He smiled at Arthur, and crossed over to the district-attorney's table.

There was a breathing space of silence. Then the crier rose, and sang out his time-honored admonition, "Hear ye, hear ye, hear ye, all persons having business with this court," etc., to the end.

Another moment of silence.

The clerk untied a bundle of papers, ran them over, got upon his feet, and exchanged a few whispered words with the judge. Eventually he turned around and faced the audience.

Ah, how still Arthur's heart stood, as the clerk cried, in rasping, metallic accents, "Judith Peixada, alias Ruth Ripley, to the bar!"

There were by this time quite seventy-five spectators present. Every one of them leaned forward on his chair, and craned his neck eagerly, to catch a good glimpse of the prisoner. In the distance, somewhere, resounded a harsh click (as of a key turned in a stiff lock), succeeded by a violent clang (as of an iron door opened and slammed to, in haste). Then, up the aisle leading from the rear of the court room, advanced the figure of a lady, dressed in black. She had to run the gauntlet of those seventy-five on-lookers, more than one of whom was bold enough to obtrude himself upon her path, and stare her squarely in the face. She had no veil.

But she marched bravely on, looking fixedly ahead, and at last reached the railing where she had to halt. She was terribly pale. Her features were hard and peaked. Her under-lip was pressed tight beneath her teeth. Her face might have been of marble. It contrasted sharply with the black hair above it, and the black gown underneath. Her eyes were empty of expression, like those of one who is blind. She appeared not to see her friends: at any rate, she gave them no sign of recognition. Yet they were only a few feet away, and almost exactly in front of her. She stood motionless, with both hands resting on the rail.

What must have been Arthur Ripley's feelings at this moment, as he beheld his wife, standing within arm's reach of him, a prisoner in a court of law, prey to a hundred devouring eyes, and recognized his utter helplessness to interfere and shield her!

"Judith Peixada, alias Ruth Ripley," began the clerk, in the same mechanical, metallic voice, "you have been indicted for murder in the first degree upon the person of Edward Bolen, late of the first ward of the City of New York, deceased, and against the peace of the People of the State of New York, and their dignity. How say you, are you guilty or not guilty of the felony as stated?"

The prisoner's hands clutched tightly at the railing. She drew a deep breath. Her pale lips parted. So low that only those within a radius of a yard or two could hear, she said, "I am guilty."

The clerk assumed that he had misunderstood. "Come, speak up louder," he said, roughly. "How do you plead?"

A spasm contracted the prisoner's features, She bit her lip. Her hands shook violently. She repeated, "I plead guilty."

The clerk's face betrayed a small measure of surprise. Speedily controlling it, however, he began to recite the formula, for such case, made and provided: "You answer that you are guilty of the felony as charged in the indictment, and so your plea shall stand record—"

"One moment, Mr. Clerk," the judge at this point interrupted.

Mr. Flint and Hetzel were looking into each other's faces with blank consternation. Arthur's head had dropped forward upon his breast. Mrs. Hart sprang to her feet, ran toward the prisoner, grasped her arm, and cried out, "Oh, it is not true. You don't know what you have said, Ruth. It is not true—she is not guilty, sir," directing the last words at the clerk. The on-lookers shifted in their seats and conversed together. The court-officers hammered with their gavels and commanded, "Order—silence." Mr. Romer stood up, and tried to catch the judge's eye.

"One moment, Mr. Clerk," the judge had said; then addressing himself to the culprit, "The plea that you offer, Judith Peixada, ought not, in the opinion of the court, to be accepted. The penalty for murder in the first degree is fixed by law, and that penalty is hanging. No discretionary alternative is left to the magistrate. Therefore to permit you to enter a plea of guilty of murder in the first degree, would be to permit self-destruction. It has never been the custom of our courts to accept that plea; though, naturally, they have seldom enough had occasion to decline it. If I remember rightly, the Connecticut tribunals have in one or two instances allowed that plea to be recorded; but, unless I am misinformed, the statutes of Connecticut empower the sentencing officer to choose between death and imprisonment for life.

"I can not consistently and conscientiously violate our precedents, and for that reason I must decline to entertain the plea that you have offered. If, however, you are in your heart persuaded of your guilt, and wish to spare the

People the expense and labor of a trial before a jury, I will accept a plea of murder in the second degree, the punishment for which, I must beg you to recollect, is confinement at hard labor in the State Prison for the term of your natural life. The clerk will now put the question to you, Judith Peixada, and you are at full liberty to reply to it as you deem fit."

"If the court please," said Romer, "I should like to make a brief statement, before these proceedings are continued."

"Certainly," said the judge. "You can wait, Mr. Clerk, until we have heard from the district-attorney."

Every man and woman in the court-room, save only two, strained forward to catch each syllable that Romer might pronounce. The two exceptions were the prisoner and her husband. He sat huddled up in his chair, apparently deaf and blind to what was going on around. She leaned heavily upon the railing in front of her, and the expression in her eyes was one of weary indifference.

"Will you kindly see that a chair is furnished the prisoner?" Romer asked of the clerk.

An attendant brought a chair. The prisoner sat down.

"If your honor please," said Romer, "I desire to state that, in case the prisoner be allowed to plead to murder in the second degree, it will be against the protest of the People. The evidence in support of the indictment is of such a nature as to admit of doubt concerning the prisoner's guilt; and, if it were submitted to a jury, I think the chances would be even whether they would acquit her or convict her. The People feel that there is evidence enough to justify a trial, but they are reluctant to—become accessories to what, in their judgment, may be the hasty act of an ill-advised woman. It is the duty of the district-attorney to endeavor to secure a conviction—it would be his duty to consent to a plea—when fully convinced in his own mind of the accused person's legal guilt. But when he is doubtful, or at least not entirely satisfied, of that guilt, as I confess to being in the case at bar, it is his duty to submit the question for arbitration to a jury. That, your honor, is the stand which I am compelled to take in these premises. I entertain grave doubts of the prisoner's guilt—doubts which could only be set at rest by a verdict rendered in the regular way. I protest therefore against the entry of a plea such as your honor has suggested; and, if the court please, I desire that this protest on the part of the People be made a matter of record."

Mr. Flint and Hetzel breathed more freely. Mrs. Hart fanned herself with manifest agitation.

The judge replied: "The clerk will procure a transcript of the district-attorney's remarks from the stenographer, and enter the same in the minutes. In response to those remarks, I feel called upon to say that it is to be presumed that the prisoner at the bar, better than any one else, is competent to decide upon the question of her own guilt or innocence. She certainly can not be in doubt as to whether she committed the felony charged against her. The court has already enlightened her respecting the sentence that will be imposed in the event of her pleading guilty of murder in the second degree. Whatever evidence might be adduced in her behalf at a trial, is certainly not to be weighed against her own voluntary and unconstrained confession. It would be contrary to public policy and to good morals for the court to seal the prisoner's lips, as the district-attorney appears anxious to have it do. The clerk will now put the necessary inquiries to her; and if she elect to offer the plea in debate, the court will feel obliged to accept it." Romer bowed and sat down.

The clerk forthwith proceeded to business. "Judith Peixada, stand up," he ordered. Upon her obeying, he rattled off, "Judith Peixada, do you desire to withdraw your plea of guilty of murder in the first degree, and to substitute for the same a plea of guilty of murder in the second degree, as charged in the second count of the indictment? If so, say, 'I do.'.rdquo;

Mrs. Hart cried, "No, no! She does not. Don't you see that the child is sick? How should she know whether she is guilty or not? Oh, it will be monstrous if you allow her to say that she is guilty."

"Order! Silence!" called the officers. One of them seized Mrs. Hart's arm and pushed her into a chair.

The prisoner's lips moved. "I do," she whispered.

"You answer," went on the clerk, "that you are guilty of the felony of murder in the second degree, as charged in the second count of the indictment; and so your plea shall stand recorded. What have you now to say why sentence should not be pronounced upon you according to law?"

Romer stepped forward.

"If your honor please," he said, "the People are not yet prepared to move for sentence. In the absence of counsel for the prisoner, I must take it upon myself to request that sentence be suspended for at least one week."

"The court suspends sentence till this day week at eleven o'clock in the forenoon," said the judge; "and meanwhile the prisoner is remanded to the city prison."

The prisoner was at once led away.

CHAPTER X.
"SICK OF A FEVER."

ROMER drew near to Mr. Flint.

"I did all I could," he said.

"Things look pretty desperate now, don't they?" Mr. Flint returned.

Hetzel tugged at his beard.

Mrs. Hart started up. "Oh, for mercy's sake, Mr. Romer, you are not going to let them take her back to—to that place, are you?"

"I don't see how I can help it. Bail is out of the question, after what has happened, you know."

"But can't I see her and speak to her just a moment, first?"

"Oh, certainly; you can do that."

Romer stepped aside and spoke to an officer.

"Unfortunately," he said, returning, "they have already carried her off. But you can drive right down behind her.—Hello! What's the matter with Ripley?"

They looked around toward Arthur. A glance showed them that he had fainted.

"When did this happen?" asked Romer.

No one could tell. No one had paid the slightest attention to Arthur, since the prisoner had first appeared in court.

"Well, we must get him out of here right away," said Romer.

Mr. Flint and Hetzel lent a hand apiece; and his three friends carried the unhappy man out of the room, of course thereby creating a new sensation among the spectators. They bore him along the corridor, and into Mr. Romer's office, where they laid him upon a sofa. Romer touched a bell.

"I'll have to send some one to take my place in court," he explained.

To the subordinate who appeared, "Ask Mr. Birdsall to step here," he said.

Mr. Birdsall came, received Romer's orders, departed.

"There, now," said Romer, "I've got that off my hands. Now, let's bring him around. Luckily, I have a flask of brandy in my desk."

He rubbed some brandy upon Arthur's temples, and poured a drop or two between his lips.

"You fan him, will you?" he asked of Hetzel.

Mrs. Hart proffered her fan. Hetzel took it, and fanned Arthur's face vigorously.

Mrs. Hart looked on for a moment in silence. At length she said, "Well, I can't wait here. I am going to the prison."

"Oh, to be sure; I had forgotten," said Romer. "I'll send a man to obtain admittance for you."

"May I also bear you company?" inquired Mr. Flint.

Mrs. Hart replied, "That is very kind of you. I should like very much to have you."

Romer rang his bell for a second time. A negro answered it.

"Robert," said Romer, "go with this lady and gentleman to the Tombs, and tell the warden that they are special friends of mine, and that I shall thank him to show them every courtesy in his power."

Then he returned to the sofa, on which Arthur still lay inanimate.

"No progress?" he demanded of Hetzel.

"None. Can you send for a physician? Is there one near by?"

A third stroke of the bell. Hetzel's acquaintance, Jim, entered.

"Run right over to Chambers Street Hospital, and tell them we want a doctor up here at once," was Romer's behest.

"Our friend's in a pretty bad way," he continued to Hetzel. "And, by Jove, his wife must be a maniac."

"I don't wonder at him," said Hetzel. "I feel rather used up myself, after that strain in court. But her conduct is certainly incomprehensible."

"The idea of pleading guilty, when I had things fixed up so neatly! She must be stark, raving mad. Insanity, by the way, was her defense at the former trial. I guess it was a *bona fide* one."

"No doubt of it. But I suppose it's too late to make that claim now—isn't it?—now that the judge has ordered her plea of guilty to be recorded. Yet—yet it isn't possible that she will really have to go to prison."

"We might have a commission appointed."

"What is that?"

"Why, a commission to inquire into, and report upon, her sanity."

"We might? We will. That's exactly what we'll do. But how? What are the necessary steps to take?"

"Why, when she's brought up for sentence, next week, and asked what she has to say, and so forth, you have an attorney on hand, and let him declare his conviction, based upon affidavits, that she's a lunatic, and then move that sentence be suspended pending the investigation of her sanity by a commission to be appointed by the court—understand? Our side won't oppose, and the judge will grant the motion as a matter of course."

"Ah, yes; I see.—Mercy upon me, I never knew a fainting fit to last so long as this; did you?"

"Well, I'm not much posted on fainting-fits in general, but it' does seem as though this was an uncommonly lengthy one, to be sure."

Arthur's face betrayed no sign of vitality except for the gentle flutter of his nostrils as his breath came and went.

"Poor fellow," mused Romer, "what an infernal pickle he's gone and got himself into! It's the strangest coincidence I ever heard of. There he was, pegging away at that case month after month, and never suspecting that the lady in question was his wife! And she—she never told him. Queer, ain t it? As far as we were concerned, we never should have lifted a finger, only I was anxious to do Ripley a good turn. He's a nice fellow, is Ripley, and I always liked him and his father before him. That's why we took this business up—just for the sake of giving him a lift, you know. As for his client, old Peixada, we'd have seen him hanged before we'd have troubled ourselves about his affairs—except, as I say, for Ripley's sake. And now, this is what comes of it. Well, Ripley never was cut out for a lawyer anyhow. He had too many notions, and didn't take things practically enough. Why, when the question of advertising first came up, he was as squeamish about it, and made as much fuss, as if he'd known all the time who she was."

"Here's the doctor, sir," cried Jim, entering at this point.

Jim was followed by a young gentleman in uniform, who, without waiting to hear the history of the case, at once approached the sofa, and began to exercise his craft. He undid Arthur's cravat, unbuttoned his shirt collar, placed one hand upon his forehead, and with the other hand felt his pulse.

"Open all the windows, please," he said in a quiet, business-like tone.

He laid his ear upon the patient's breast, and listened.

"When did this begin?" he asked at length.

"I should say about half an hour ago," Romer answered, looking at his watch.

"Is—is there any occasion for anxiety?" Hetzel inquired.

The doctor shrugged his shoulders. "Can't tell yet," was his reply.

He drew a leather wallet from his pocket, and unclasping it, disclosed an array of tiny glass phials. One of these he extracted, and holding it up to the light, called for a glass of water. Romer brought the water. The doctor poured a few drops of medicine from his phial into the tumbler. The water thereupon clouded and became opaque. Dipping his finger into it, the doctor proceeded to moisten Arthur's lips.

"Each of you gentlemen please take one of his hands," said the doctor, "and chafe it till it gets warm."

Romer and Hetzel obeyed.

"Want him taken to the hospital?" the doctor inquired presently.

"Oh, no," said Hetzel. "As soon as he is able, we want to take him home."

"Where does he live?"

"In Beekman Place—Fiftieth Street and the East River."

"Hum," muttered the doctor, dubiously; "that's quite a distance."

"To be sure. But after he comes to, and gets rested, he won't mind it."

"Perhaps not."

"Why, do you mean that that he's going to be seriously sick?"

"Unless I'm mistaken, he's going to lie abed for the next six weeks."

"What?"

"Sh-h-h! Not so loud. Yes, I'm afraid he's in for a long illness. As for taking him to Beekman Place, if you're bound to do it, we must have an ambulance."

"I think if he's got to be sick, he'd better be sick at home. What is it necessary to do, to procure an ambulance?"

"I'll send for one.—Can you let me have a messenger?" he asked of Romer.

Romer summoned Jim.

The doctor wrote a few lines on a prescription blank, and instructed Jim to deliver it to the house-surgeon at the hospital. Returning to Arthur's side, "He's beginning to come around," he said; "and now, I think, you gentlemen had better leave the room. He mustn't open his mouth for some time; and if his friends are near him when he recovers consciousness, he might want to talk. So, please leave me alone with him."

"But you won't fail to call us if—if—" Hetzel hesitated.

"Oh, you needn't be afraid. There's no immediate danger."

"You'll find us in the next room," said Romer, and led Hetzel out.

Whom should they run against in the passageway but Mrs. Hart and Mr. Flint?

"What! Back so soon?" Romer exclaimed.

"She refused to see me," said Mrs. Hart.

Romer pushed open a door. "Sit down in here," he said.

"Where is Arthur?" asked Mr. Flint. "How is he getting on?"

Romer explained Arthur's situation.

"Worse and worse," cried Mr. Flint.

"But how was it that she refused to see you?" Hetzel questioned, addressing Mrs. Hart.

"She sent me this," Mrs. Hart replied, holding out a sheet of paper.

Hetzel took it and read:—

"My dear one:—It will seem most ungracious and ungrateful of me to send word that I can not see you just now, and yet that is what I am compelled to do. My only excuse is that I am writing something which demands the utmost concentration and self-possession that I can command; and if I should set eyes upon the face I love so well, I should lose all control of myself. It is very hard to be obliged to say this to you; but what I am writing is of great importance—to me, at least—and the sight of you would agitate me so much that I could not finish it. Oh, my dear, kind friend, will you forgive me? If you could come to see me to-morrow, it would be a great comfort. Then my writing will be done with. I love you with all my heart, and thank you for all your goodness to me.

"Ruth."

"Don't blame her too severely, Mrs. Hart," said Hetzel. "She is probably half-distracted, and scarcely knows what she is doing."

"Oh, I don't blame her," replied Mrs. Hart; "only—only—it was a little hard to be denied."

"Have you any idea what it is that she is writing?"

"Not the remotest."

"Perhaps it is an explanation of her conduct today in court."

"Perhaps,"

Mr. Flint said, "Well, Mr. Romer, the bright plans that we were making last night have been knocked in the head, haven't they? But I won't believe that there isn't some way out of our troubles, in spite of all. It isn't seriously possible that she'll be sentenced to prison, is it?"

"As I was suggesting to Mr. Hetzel, a while ago, her friends might claim that she's insane."

"Well, insane she must be, in point of fact. A lady like Mrs. Ripley—to plead guilty of murder—why, of course, she's insane. It's absurd on its face."

"You don't any of you happen to be posted on the circumstances of the case, do you?" Romer asked. "I mean her side of the story. I'm familiar with the other side myself."

"I know absolutely nothing about it," said Mr. Flint.

"All I know," said Hetzel, "is what Arthur has let drop in conversation, from time to time, during the last few months. But then, you know, he was looking at it from the point of view of the prosecution. I should imagine that if any one would understand the true inwardness of the matter, it would be Mrs. Hart."

Mrs. Hart said, "I know that she is as innocent as the babe at its mother's breast. When she and I first met each other, in England, two years ago, and became friends, she told me all about it; but it was a long and complicated story, and I can't remember it clearly enough to repeat it. You see, I always regarded it as a dark bygone that had best be forgotten. I believe that as far as the mere bodily act went, she did fire off the pistol that killed her husband and that other man. But there were some circumstances that cleared her of all responsibility, though I can't recall exactly what they were. But it wasn't that she was insane. She never was insane. I think she said her lawyers defended her on that plea when she was tried; but she insisted that she was not insane, and explained it in some other way."

"Oh, that don't signify," said Romer. "When defendants really are insane, they invariably fancy that they're not, and get highly indignant at their counsel for maintaining that they are. At any rate, lunacy is what you must fight for now. As I told Mr. Hetzel, you want to retain a lawyer, and have him move for a commission when the case comes up next week. You'll have your motion granted on application, because we shan't oppose."

"And in the event of the commission declaring her to be insane?" queried Mr. Flint.

"Why, then, her plea will be rendered null and void."

"And in case they say that she's of sound mind?"

"There'll be the devil to pay. Sentence will have to be passed."

"And she will—will actually—?"

"I wouldn't worry about that. The chances are that they will report as you wish. And if they shouldn't—if worse came to worst—why, there's the governor, who has power to pardon."

"The ambulance has arrived," said the doctor, coming into the room. "Some one had better run on ahead, and get a bed ready for the patient. Please, also, prepare plenty of chopped ice, and have some towels handy, and a bottle of hot water for his feet. By the way, you didn't give me the number of the house. How's that? No. 46? Thanks. We'll drive slowly, so as not to shake him up; and consequently you'll have time enough to get there first, and make every thing ready."

"Well," said Hetzel, rising, "good-by, Mr. Romer, and I trust that you know how grateful we are to you."

"Oh, that's all right," said Romer. "Don't mention it. Good-by."

In the street Mr. Flint said, "I'll invite myself to go home with you. I want to see how badly off the poor boy is."

In Beekman Place they made the 'arrangements, that the doctor had indicated for Arthur's reception, and then sat down in the drawing-room to await his coming. By and by the ambulance rolled up to the door.

They hurried out upon the stoop. A good many of the neighbors had come to their windows, and there was a small army of inquisitive children bivouacked upon the curbstone. Mrs. Berle ran across from her house, and talked excitedly to Mrs. Hart. Of course, all Beekman Place had read in the newspapers of Judith Peixada's arrest.

The doctor, assisted by the driver, lifted the sick man out. He lay at full length upon a canvas stretcher. His face had assumed a cadaverous, greenish tinge. His big blue eyes, wide open, were fixed upon the empty air above them. To all appearances, he was still unconscious.

They carried him up the stoop; through the hall, and into the room above-stairs to which Mrs. Hart conducted them. There they laid him on the bed.

"Now," said the doctor, "first of all, send for your own physician. I must see him and confer with him, before I go away."

Mrs. Hart left the room, to obey the doctor's injunction.

"You, Jake," the doctor went on, addressing the driver, "needn't wait. Drive back to the hospital, and tell them that I'll come as soon as I can be spared."

"Here, Jake, before you go," said Mr. Flint, producing his purse.

"Oh, thanks. Can't accept any thing, sir," responded Jake, and vanished.

"Now, gentlemen," resumed the doctor, "just lend a hand, and help undress him."

Following the doctor's directions, they got the patient out of his clothes. He seemed to be a mere limp, inert mass of flesh, and displayed no symptoms of realizing what was going on. His extremities were ice-cold. His forehead was hot. His breath was labored.

"A very sick man, I'm afraid, isn't he, doctor?" asked Mr. Flint.

"I'm afraid so."

The doctor covered him with the bed-clothes.

"What do you think is the matter with him?" Mr. Flint pursued.

"Oh, it hasn't developed sufficiently yet to be classified. His mind must have been undergoing a strain for some time, I guess; and now he's broken down beneath it."

"He's quite unconscious, apparently."

"Yes, in a sort of lethargy. That's what makes the case a puzzle. Won't you order a hot-water bottle, somebody?"

Hetzel left the room. In a moment he brought the bottle of hot water. The doctor applied it to Arthur's feet.

"And the chopped ice?" Hetzel inquired.

The doctor placed his hand upon Arthur's brow.

"N—no; we won't use the chopped ice yet a while," he answered.

By and by a bell rang down-stairs. A little later Mrs. Hart came in.

"Our doctor—Dr. Letzup—is here," she announced.

Dr. Letzup entered.

"I suppose you medical men would like to be left alone?" said Mr. Flint.

"Yes, I guess so," said the hospital-doctor.

Mrs. Hart led the way into the adjoining room. There our friends maintained a melancholy silence. Mrs. Hart's cats slept comfortably, one upon the sofa, the other upon the rug before the mantelpiece. The voices of the two physicians, in earnest conversation, were audible through the closed door.

Presently Mr. Hart jumped up.

"What—what now?" Mr. Flint questioned.

"I heard one of them step into the hall. Perhaps they need something."

She hurried to the threshold. There she confronted the hospital-doctor. He had his hand raised, as if on the point of rapping for admittance.

"Ah, I was looking for you," he explained. "I am going now. I don't see that I can be of any further use."

"How is Arthur?"

"About as he was. Dr. Letzup has taken charge of him. Well, good day."

"Oh, you shan't leave us in this way," protested Mrs. Hart. "You must at least wait and let me offer you a glass of wine."

"I'm much obliged," said the doctor; "but they are expecting me in Chambers Street."

Mrs. Hart, flanked by Mr. Flint and Hetzel, accompanied him to the vestibule. All three did their utmost to thank him adequately for the pains he had taken in their behalf. Returning up-stairs, they were joined by Dr. Letzup.

"Well, doctor?" began Mrs. Hart.

"Well, Mrs. Hart," the doctor replied, "our friend in the next room has been exciting himself lately, hasn't he? What he wants now is a trained nurse, soothing medicines, and perfect quiet. The first two I'm going to send around, as soon as I leave the house. For the last, he must depend upon you. That is equivalent to saying that he will have it. Therefore, so far as I can see, you have every reason to be hopeful."

"What do you take his trouble to be, doctor?" asked Hetzel.

"Oh, I don't know of any special name for it," said the doctor. "The poor fellow must have been careless of himself recently—worrying, probably, about something—and then came a shock of one kind or another—collapse of stock he'd been investing in, or what not—and so he went under. We'll fetch him up again, fast enough. The main thing is to steer him clear of brain fever. I think we can do it. If it turns out that we can't—if the fever should develop—then, we'll go to work and pilot him safely through it. Now I must be off. Some one had better stay with him till the nurse comes. Keep him warm—hot water at his feet, you know, and bed-clothes tucked in about his shoulders. When the nurse turns up, she'll give him his medicines. I'll call again after dinner."

Mr. Flint left a little later.

"I suppose I shan't be of any assistance, but merely in the way, by remaining here. So I'll go home. But of course you'll notify me instantly if there should be a change for the worse," was his valedictory.

After dinner the doctor called, pursuant to his promise. Having visited his patient, and held an interview with the nurse, he beckoned Hetzel to one side.

"Don't be frightened," he said, "but I'm afraid it's going to be brain fever, after all. He's a little delirious just now, and his temperature is higher than I should like. The nurse will take perfect care of him. You'd better go to bed early and sleep well, so as to be fresh and able to relieve her in the morning. Good night."

"Good night."

"What did the doctor say to you?" inquired Mrs. Hart.

Hetzel told her.

CHAPTER XI.
"HOW SHE ENDEAVORED TO EXPLAIN HER LIFE."

THURSDAY morning it rained. Hetzel was seated in Mrs. Hart's dining-room, making such an apology for a breakfast as, under the circumstances, could be expected of him, when the waitress announced that Josephine was in the kitchen, and wished to speak with her master.

"All right," said Hetzel; "ask her to step this way."

Josephine presented herself. Not without some embarrassment, she declared that she had heard what rumor had to say of Mrs. Ripley's imprisonment and of Mr. Ripley's sickness, and that she was anxious to learn the very truth of the matter from Hetzel's lips. Hetzel replied good-naturedly to her interrogations; and at length Josephine rose to go her way. But having attained the door, she halted and faced about.

"*Ach Gott!*" she exclaimed. "I was forgetting about these." She drew a bunch of letters from her pocket, and deposited them upon the table beside Hetzel's plate.

Alone, Hetzel picked the letters up, and began to study their superscriptions. One by one, he threw them aside without breaking their seals, till at last "Hello!" he cried, "who has been writing a book for me to read? Half an inch thick, as I'm alive; looks like a lady's hand, too; seems somehow as though I recognized it. Let me see.—Ah! I remember. It must be from *her!*"

Without further preliminary, he pushed back his chair, tore the envelope open, and set out to read the missive through.

"Dear Mr. Hetzel: I received a very kind note from you last night, and I should have answered it at once, only I had so much to say that I thought it would be better to wait till morning, in order to begin and finish it at a sitting. The lights are turned off here at nine o'clock: and therefore if I had begun to write last evening, I should have been interrupted in the midst of it; and that would have rendered doubly difficult what in itself is difficult enough.

"I have much to explain, much to justify, much to ask forgiveness for. I am going to bring myself to say things to you, which, a few days ago, I believed it would be impossible for me to say to any living being, except my husband; and it would have been no easy matter to say them to him. But a great change has happened in the last few days. Now I can not say those things to my husband—never can. Now my wretched failure of a life is nearly ended. I am going to a prison where, I know very well, I shall not survive a great while.

"And something, which there is no need to analyze, impels me to put in writing such an explanation of what I have done and left undone in this world, as I may be able to make. Perhaps I am prompted to this course by pride, or if you choose, by vanity. However that may be, I do feel that in justice to myself as well as to my friends, I ought to try to state the head and front of my offending so as to soften the judgment that people aware only of my outward acts, and ignorant of my inner motives, would be disposed to pass upon me. I have ventured to address myself to you, instead of to Mrs. Hart, out of consideration for her. It would be too hard for her to have to read this writing through. You, having read it, can repeat its upshot to her in such a manner as to make it easier for her to bear. I know that you will be willing to do this, because I know that both she and I have always had a friend in you.

"For my own assistance, let me state clearly beforehand the points upon which I must touch in this letter. First, I must explain why, having a blot upon my life—being, that is to say, who I am—I allowed Arthur Ripley to marry me. Then I must go on to perform that most painful task of all—tell the story of the death of Bernard Peixada and Edward Bolen. Next, I must justify—what you appear to misunderstand, though the grounds of it are really very simple—the deep resentment which I can not help cherishing against your bosom friend, my husband. Finally, I must give the reasons that induced me to plead guilty of murder an hour ago in court.

"But no. I have put things in their wrong order at the outset. It will not be possible for me to explain why I consented to become Arthur's wife, until I have given you the true history of Bernard Peixada's death. I must command my utmost strength to do this. I must forget nothing.

"I must force myself to recount every circumstance, hateful as the whole subject is. I must search my memory, subdue my feelings, and as dispassionately as will be possible, put the entire miserable tale in writing. I pray God to help me.

"I am just twenty-six years old—ten months younger than Arthur. My birthday fell while he and I were at New Castle together—August 4th. How little I guessed then that in ten days every thing would be so altered! It is strange. I trusted him as I trusted myself. I could not conceive the possibility of his deceiving me. He seemed so sincere, so simple-minded, so single-hearted, I could as easily have fancied a toad issuing from his mouth, as a lie. Yet all the time—even while we were alone together there in New Castle—he was lying to me. That whole fortnight—that seemed so wonderfully serene and pure and light—was one dark falsehood. Even then, he was having my career investigated here in New York, behind my back. And I—

I had offered to tell him every thing. Painful as it would have been, I should have told him the whole story; but he would not let me.

"He preferred to hear Benjamin Peixada's—my enemy's—version of it. Even now, when I have—plenty—to remind me of the truth, even now, I can scarcely believe it.

"But I must not deviate. As I was saying, I am twenty-six years old. More than six years ago, when I was nineteen, nearing twenty, my father said to me one day, 'Mr. Peixada has done us the honor to ask for your hand in marriage. We have accepted. So, on the eighth of next August, you will be married to him.'

"You can not realize, Mr. Hetzel, a tithe of the horror I experienced when my father spoke those words to me, until I have gone back further still, and told something of my life up to that time. At this moment, as I recall the occasion of my father's saying that to me, my heart turns to ice, my cheeks burn, my limbs quake, my nature recoils with disgust and loathing. It is painful to have to go over it all again, to have to live through it all again; yet that is what I have started out to do.

"You must know, to begin with, that my father was a watchmaker, and that he kept a shop on Second Avenue, between Sixth and Seventh Streets. He was a man of great intelligence, of uncommon cultivation, and of a most gentle and affectionate disposition; but he was a Jew of the sternest orthodoxy, and he held old-fashioned, orthodox notions of the obedience children owe to their parents. My father in his youth had intended to become a physician; but while he was a student in Berlin, in 1848, the revolution broke out; he took part in it; and as a consequence he had to leave Germany and come to America before he had won his diploma. Here, friendless, penniless, he fell in with a jeweler, named Oppenhym, who offered to teach him his trade. Thus he became an apprentice, then a journeyman, finally a proprietor. I was born in the house on Second Avenue, in the basement of which my father kept his shop. We lived up stairs. Our family consisted only of my father and mother, myself, and my father's intimate friend, Marcus Nathan. Mr. Nathan was a very learned gentleman, who had been a widower and childless for many years, and who acted as *chazzan* in our synagogue. It was to him that my father confided my education. It was he who first taught me to read and write and to care for books and music. How good and loyal a friend he was to me you will learn later on. He died early in 1880.... I did not go to school till I was thirteen years old. Then I was sent to the public school in Twelfth Street, and thence to the Normal College, where I graduated in 1876. I studied the piano at home under the direction of a woman named Emily Millard—an accomplished musician, but unkind and cruel. She used to pull my hair and pinch me, when I made mistakes; and afterward, when they tried me in the court of General Sessions for Bernard Peixada's murder, Miss Millard came and swore that I was bad.

"Bernard Peixada—whom the newspapers described as 'a retired Jewish merchant'—was a pawnbroker. His shop was straight across the street from ours. I never in my life saw another structure of brick and mortar that seemed to frown with such sinister significance, with such ominous suggestiveness, upon the street in front of it as did that house of Bernard Peixada's. It was a brick house; but the bricks were concealed by a coat of dark gray stucco, with blotches here and there that were almost black. The shop, of course, was on the ground floor. Its broad windows were protected, like those of a jail, by heavy iron bars. Within them was exhibited an assortment of such goods and chattels as the pawnbroker had contrived to purchase from distress—musical instruments, household ornaments, kitchen utensils, firearms, tarnished suits of uniform, faded bits of women's finery—*ex voto* offerings at the shrine of Mammon. Behind these, all was darkness, and mystery, and gloom. Over the door, three golden balls—golden they had been once, but were no longer, thanks to the thief, Time, abetted by wind and weather—the pawnbroker's escutcheon, swayed in the breeze. Higher up still—big, white, ghastly letters on a sable background—hung a sign, bearing a legend like this:

B. PEIXADA.

MONEY LENT ON WATCHES, JEWELRY, PRECIOUS STONES, AND ALL VARIETIES OF PERSONAL PROPERTY.

"And on the side door, the door that let into the private hallway of the house, was screwed a solemn brass plate, with 'B. Peixada' engraved in Old English characters upon it. (When Bernard Peixada retired from business, he was succeeded by one B. Peinard. On taking possession, Mr. Peinard, for economy's sake, caused the last four letters of Bernard Peixada's name on the sign to be painted out, and the corresponding letters of his own name to be painted in: so that, to this day, the time-stained PEI stands as it used to stand years ago, and contrasts oddly with the more recent word that follows.) As I have said, the shop windows were defended by an iron grating. The other windows—those of the three upper stories—were hermetically sealed. I, at least, never saw them open. The blinds, once green, doubtless, but blackened by age, were permanently closed; and the stucco beneath them was fantastically frescoed with the dirt that had been washed from them by the rain.

"I think it was partly due to these black blinds, and' to the queer shapes that the dirt had taken on the wall, that the house had that peculiarly sinister aspect that I have spoken of. At all events, you could not glance at its façade without shuddering. As early a recollection as any that I have, is of how I used to sit at our front windows, and gaze over at Bernard Peixada's, and work myself into a very ecstasy of fear by trying to imagine the dark and terrible things that were stored behind them. My worst nightmares used to be that I was a prisoner in Bernard Peixada's house. I never dreamed that some time my most hideous nightmare would be surpassed by the fact.

"But if I used to terrify myself by the sight of Bernard Peixada's dwelling, much keener was the terror with which Bernard Peixada's person inspired me. Picture to yourself a—creature—six feet tall, gaunt as a skeleton, always dressed in black—in black broadcloth, that glistened like a snake's skin—with a head—my pen revolts from an attempt to describe it. Yet I must describe it, so that you may appreciate a little what I endured when my father said that he had chosen Bernard Peixada for my husband. Well, Bernard Peixada's head was thus: a hawk's beak for a nose, a hawk's beak inverted for a chin; lips, two thin, blue, crooked lines across his face, with yellow fangs behind them, that shone horribly when he laughed; eyes, two black, shiny beads, deep-set beneath prominent, black, shaggy brows, with the malevolence of a demon aflame deep down in them; skull, destitute of honest hair, but kept warm by a curling, reddish wig; skin, dry and sallow as old parchment, on which dark wrinkles were traced—a cryptogram, with a meaning, but one which I could not perfectly decipher; these were the elements of Bernard Peixada's physiognomy—fit features for a bird of prey, were they not? Have you ever seen his brother, Benjamin? the friend of Arthur Ripley? Benjamin is corpulent, florid, and on the whole not ill-looking—morally and physically vastly superior to his elder brother. But fancy Benjamin pumped dry of blood, shrunken to the dimensions of a mummy, then bewigged, then caricatured by an enemy, and you will form a tolerably vivid conception of how Bernard Peixada looked. But his looks were not all. His voice, I think, was worse. It was a thin, piercing voice that, when I heard it, used to set my heart palpitating with a hundred horrible emotions. It was a dry, metallic voice that grated like a file. It was a sharp, jerky voice that seemed to chop the air, each word sounding like a blow from an ax. It was a voice which could not be forced to say a kind and human thing. Cruelty and harshness were natural to it. I can hear it ringing in my ears, as I am writing now; and it makes my heart sink and my hand tremble, as it used to do when I indeed heard it, issuing from his foul, cruel mouth. Will you be surprised—will you think I am exaggerating—when I say that Bernard Peixada's hideousness did not end with his voice? I should do his portrait an injustice if I were to omit mention of his hands—his claws, rather, for claws they were shaped like; and, instead of fingers, they were furnished with long, brown, bony talons, terminated by black, untrimmed nails. I do not believe I ever saw Bernard Peixada's hands in repose. They were in perpetual, nervous motion—the talons clutching at the air, if at nothing more substantial—even when he slept. The most painful dreams that I have had, since God delivered me of him, have been those in which I have seen his hands, working, working, the fingers writhing like serpents, as they were wont to do in life. Oh, such a monstrosity! Oh, such a wicked travesty of man! This, Mr. Hetzel, was the person to f-whom my father proposed to marry me. There was no one to plead for me, no one to interfere in my behalf. And I was a young girl, nineteen years old.

"How could my father do it? How could he bring himself to do this thing? It is a long story.

"In the first place, Bernard Peixada was accounted a most estimable member of society. He was rich; he was pious; he was eminently respectable. His ill-looks were ignored. Was he to blame for them? people asked. Did he not close his shop regularly on every holiday? Who was more precise than he in observing the feasts and fasts of the Hebrew calendar? or in attending services at the Synagogue? Was smoke ever to be seen issuing from his chimneys on the Sabbath? Old as he was, did he not abstain from food on the fast of Gedalia, and on that of Tebeth, and on that of Tamuz, as well as on the Ninth of Ab and on Yom Kippur? Had he not, year after year, been elected and re-elected *Parnass* of the congregation? All honor to him, then, for a wise man and an upright man in the way of the law! It was thus that public opinion in our small world treated Bernard Peixada. On the theory that handsome is that handsome does, he got the credit of being quite a paragon of beauty. To be sure, he lacked social qualities—he was scarcely a hail-fellow-well-met. He cared little for wine and tobacco—he abhorred dominoes—he could not be induced to sit down to a game of *penacle*; but all the better! The absence of these frivolous interests proved him to be a man of responsible weight and gravity. It was a pity he had never married. Perhaps it was not yet too late. Lucky the girl upon whom his eye should turn with favor. If he had not youth and bodily grace to offer her, he had, at least, wealth, wisdom, and respectability.

"Bernard Peixada had been the black beast of my childhood. When I would go with my mother to the Synagogue, and sit with her in the women's gallery, I could not keep my eyes off Bernard.. Peixada, who occupied the president's chair downstairs. The sight of him had an uncanny fascination for me. As I grew older, it was still the same. Bernard Peixada personified to me all that was evil in human nature. He was the Ahriman, the Antichrist, of my theology. He made my flesh creep—gave me a sensation similar to that which a snake gives one—only incomparably more intense.

"Well, one evening in the early spring of 1878, I was seated in our little parlor over the shop, striving to entertain a very dull young man—a Mr. Rimo, Bernard Peixada's nephew—when the door opened, and who should come gliding in but Bernard Peixada himself? I had never before seen him at such close quarters, unless my father or mother or Mr. Nathan was present too; and then I had derived a sense of security from realizing that I had a friend near by. But now, here he was in the very room with me, and I all alone, except for this nephew of his, Mr. Rimo. I had to catch for my breath, and my heart grew faint within me.

"Bernard Peixada simply said good evening and sat down. I do not remember that he spoke another word until he rose to go away. But for two hours he sat there opposite me, and not for one instant did he take his eyes from off my face. He sat still, like a toad, and leered at me. His blue lips were curled into a grin, which, no doubt, was intended to be reassuring, but which, in fact, sent cold shivers chasing down my back. He stared at me as he might have stared at some inanimate object that had been offered to him in pawn. Then at last, when he must have learned every line and angle of my face by rote, he got up and went away, leading Mr. Rimo after him.

"I lay awake all that night, wondering what Bernard Peixada's visit meant, hoping that it meant nothing, fearing—but it would take too long for me to tell you all I feared. Suffice it that the next afternoon—I was seated in my bed-room, trying to divert my imagination with a tale of Hawthorne's—the next afternoon my father called me into his office behind the shop, and there in the presence of my mother he corroborated the worst fears that had beset me during the night.

"'Judith,' he said, 'our neighbor, Mr. Peixada, has done us the honor of proposing for your hand. Of course we have accepted. He designates the eighth of August for the wedding-day. That will give you plenty of time to get ready in; and on Sundays you will stay at home to receive congratulations.

"It took a little while, Mr. Hetzel, for the full meaning of my father's speech to penetrate my mind. At first I did not comprehend—I was stupefied, bewildered. My senses were benumbed. Mechanically, I watched my father's canary-bird hop from perch to perch in his cage, and listened to the shrill whistle that he uttered from time to time. I was conscious of a dizziness in my head, of a sickness and a chill over all my body. But then, suddenly, the horror shot through me—pierced my consciousness like a knife. Suddenly my senses became wonderfully clear. I saw the black misery that they had prepared for me, in a quick, vivid tableau before my eyes. I trembled from head to foot. I tried to speak, to cry out, to protest. If I could only have let the pain break forth in an inarticulate moan, it would have been some relief. But my tongue clove to the roof of my mouth. I could not utter a sound. 'Well, Judith,' said my father, 'why don't you speak?'

"His words helped me to find my voice.

"'Speak!' I cried. 'What is there to say? Marry Bernard Peixada? Marry that monster? I will never marry him. I would a thousand times rather die.'

"My mother and father looked at me and at each other in dismay.

"'Judith,' said my father, sternly, 'that is not the language that a daughter should use toward her parents. That is not the way a young lady should feel, either. Of course you will marry Mr. Peixada. Don't make a scene about it. It has all been arranged between us; and your betrothed is coming to claim you in half an hour.'

"'Father,' I answered, very calmly, 'I am sorry to rebel against your authority, but I tell you now, once for all, I will not marry Bernard Peixada.' 'Judith,' rejoined my father, imitating my manner, 'I am sorry to contradict you, but I tell you now, once for all, you will.'

"'Never,' said I.

"'On the eighth of August,' said my father.

"'Time will show,' said I.

"'Time will show,' said he, 'in less than fifteen minutes. Judith, listen.'

"It was an old story that my father now proceeded to tell me—old, and yet as new as it is terrible to the girl who has to listen to it. It does not break the heart in two, like the old, old story of Heine's song: it inflames the heart with a dull, sullen anguish that is the worst pain a woman can be called upon to endure. My father told me how for two years past his pecuniary affairs had been going to the dogs; how he had been getting poor and poorer; how he had become Bernard Peixada's debtor for sums of money that he could never hope to pay; how Bernard Peixada owned not only the wares in our shop, but the very chairs we sat on, the very beds we slept in, the very plates off which we ate; how, indeed, it was Bernard Peixada who paid for the daily bread that kept our bodies and souls together. My father explained all this to me, concluding thus: 'I was in despair, Judith. I thought I should go crazy. I saw nothing but disgrace and the poor-house before your mother and you and me. I could not sleep at night. I could not work during the day. I could do nothing but think, think, think of the desperate pass to which my affairs had come. It was an agony, Judith. It would soon have killed me, or driven me mad. Then, all at once, the darkness of my—sky is lightened by this good man, whom I have already to thank for so much. He calls upon me. He says he will show me a way out of my difficulties.

"I ask what it is. He answers, why not unite our families, accept him as my son-in-law? and adds that between son-in-law and father-in-law there can be no question of indebtedness. In other words, he told me that he loved you, Judith; that he wished to marry you; and that, once married to you, he would consider my debts to him discharged. Try, Judith, to realize his generosity. I—I owe him thousands. But for him we should have starved. But for him, we should starve to-morrow. Ordinary gratitude alone would have been enough to compel me to say yes to his proposition. But by saying yes, did I not also accomplish our own salvation? Now that you have heard the whole story, Judith, now, like a good girl, promise to make no opposition.'

"'So that,' I retorted, indignantly, 'I am to be your ransom—I am to be sacrificed as a hostage. The pawnbroker consents to receive me as an equivalent for the money you owe him. A woman to be literally bought and sold. Oh, father, no, no! There must be some other way. Let me go to work. Have I not already earned money by giving lessons? I will teach from morning to night each day; and every penny that I gain, I will give to you to pay Bernard Peixada with. I will be so industrious! I would rather slave the flesh from my bones—any thing, rather than marry him.'

"'The most you could earn,' my father answered, 'would be no more than a drop in the bucket, Judith.'

"'Well, then,' I went on, 'there is Mr. Nathan. He has money. Borrow from him. He will not refuse. I know that he would gladly give much money to save me from a marriage with Bernard Peixada. I will ask him.'

"Judith, you must not speak of this to Mr. Nathan,' cried my father, hastily. 'He must not know but that your marriage to Mr. Peixada is an act of your own choice. I—to tell you the truth—I have already borrowed from Mr. Nathan as much as I dare to ask for.'

"To cut a long story short, Mr. Hetzel, my father drew for me such a dark picture of his misfortunes, he argued so plausibly that all depended upon my marrying Bernard Peixada, he pleaded so piteously, that in the end I said, 'Well, father, I will do as you wish.'——

"I do not think it is necessary to dwell upon what followed: how my father and mother embraced me, and wept over me, and thanked me, and gave me their benediction; how Bernard Peixada came from his lair across the street, and kissed my hand, and leered at me, and called me 'Judith' in that voice of his; how then, for weeks afterward, my life was one protracted, hopeless horror; how the sun rose morning after morning, and brought neither warmth nor light, but only a reminder that the eighth of August was one day nearer still; how I could speak of it to no one, but had to bear it all alone in silence; how at night my sleep was constantly beset by nightmares, in which I got a bitter foretaste of the future; how evening after evening I had to spend in the parlor with Bernard Peixada, listening to his voice, watching his fingers writhe, feeling the deadly light of his eyes upon me, breathing the air that his presence tainted; how every Sunday I had to receive people's *congratulations!* the good wishes of all our family friends—I need not dwell upon these things. My life was a long heart-ache. I had but one relief—hoping that I might die. I did not think of putting an end to myself; but I did pray that God, in his mercy, would let me die before the eighth of August came. Indeed, my health was very much broken. Our family doctor visited me twice a week. He told my father that marriage would be bad for me. But my father's hands were tied.

"The people here tell me that there is a man confined in this prison under sentence to be hanged. The day fixed for his execution is the first Friday of next month. Well, I think that that man, now, as he looks forward to the first Friday of September, may feel a little as I felt then, when I would look forward to the eighth of August—only he has the mitigation of knowing that afterward he will be dead, whereas I knew that I should have to live and suffer worse things still. As I saw that day steadily creeping nearer and nearer to me, the horror that bound my heart intensified. It was like the old Roman spectacle. I had been flung *ad bestias*. I stood still, defenseless, beyond the reach of rescue, hopeless of escape, and watched the wild beast draw closer and closer to me, and all the while endured the agony of picturing to myself the final moment, when he would spring upon me and suck my blood: only, again there was this difference—the martyr in the arena knew that after that final moment, all would be over; but I knew that the worst would then just be begun. Yet, at last—toward the end—I actually fell to wishing that the final moment would arrive. The torture, long drawn out, of anticipation was so unbearable that I actually wished the wild beast would fall upon me, in order that I might enjoy the relief of change. Nothing, I felt, could be more painful than this waiting, dreading, imagining. The eighth of August could bring no terror that I had not already confronted in imagination.

"Well, this one wish of mine was granted. The eighth of August came. I was married to Bernard Peixada. I stood up in our parlor, decked out in bridal costume, holding Bernard Peixada's hand in mine, and took the vows of matrimony in the presence of a hundred witnesses. The canopy was raised over our heads; the wine was drunken and spilled; the glass was broken. The *chazzan* sang his song; the rabbi said his say; and I, who had gone through the performance in a sort of stupor—dull, half conscious, bewildered—I was suddenly brought to my senses by a clamor of cheerful voices, as the wedding-guests trooped up around us, to felicitate the bridegroom and to kiss the bride. I realized—no, I did not yet realize—but I understood that I was Bernard Peixada's wife—*his wife*, for good and all, for better or for worse! I don't remember that I suffered any new pain. The intense suffering of the last few months had worn out my capacities for suffering. My brain was dazed, my heart deadened.

"The people came and came, and talked and talked—I remember it as I remember the delirium I had when I was sick once with fever. And after the last person had come and talked and gone away, Bernard Peixada offered me his arm, and said, 'We must take our places at the wedding feast.' Then he led me up-stairs, where long tables were laid out for supper.

"A strange sense of unreality possessed me. In a vague, dreamy, far-off way, I saw the guests stand up around the tables; saw the men cover their heads with hats or handkerchiefs; heard the voice of Mr. Nathan raised in prayer; heard the company join lustily in his '*Baruch Adonai,'*. and reverently in his final '*Amen*' saw the head-gear doffed, the people sink into their seats; heard the clatter of knives and forks mingle with the tinkling of glasses, the bubble of pouring wine, the uproar of talk and laughter; was conscious of glaring lights, of moving forms, of the savor of food, mixed with the perfume of flowers and the odor of cologne on the women's handkerchiefs: felt hot, dazzled, suffocated, confused—an oppression upon my breast, a ringing in my ears, a swimming in my head: the world was whirling around and around—I alone, in the center of things, was motionless.

"So on for I knew not how long. In the end I became aware that speeches were being made. The wedding feast, that meant, was nearly over. I did not listen to the speeches. But they reminded me of something that I had forgotten. Now, indeed, my heart stood still. They reminded me that the moment was not far off when Bernard Peixada, when *my husband*, would lead me away with him!

"The speeches were wound up. Mr. Nathan began his last grace. My mother signaled me to be ready to come to her as soon as Mr. Nathan should get through.

"'Judith,' she said, when I had reached her side, 'we had better go up-stairs now, and change your dress.'

"We went up-stairs. When we came down again, we found Bernard Peixada waiting in the hall. Through the open door of the parlor, I could hear music, and see young men and women dancing. Oh, how I envied them! My mother and father kissed me. Bernard Peixada grasped my arm. We left my father's house. We crossed the street. Bernard Peixada kept hold of my arm, as if afraid that I might make a dash for liberty—as, indeed, my impulse urged me to do. With his unoccupied hand, Bernard Peixada drew a key from his pocket, and opened the side door of his own dark abode—the door that bore the brass plate with the Old English letters.

"'Well,' he said, 'come in.'

"With a shudder, I crossed the threshold of that mysterious, sinister house—of that house which had been the terror of my childhood, and was to be—

what? In the midst of my fear and my bewilderment, I could not suppress a certain eagerness to confront my fate and know the worst at once—a certain curiosity to learn the full ghastliness of my doom. In less time than I had bargained for, I had my wish."

Thus far Hetzel had read consecutively. At this point he was interrupted by the entrance of Mrs. Hart.

"Are you busy?" she asked. "Because, if you're not, I think you had better go up-stairs and sit with Arthur. The nurse wants to eat her breakfast and lie down for a while. And I, you know, am expected by Ruth."

"Oh, to be sure," Hetzel replied, with a somewhat abstracted manner. "Oh, yes—I'll do as you wish at once. But it is a pity that you should have to go down-town alone—especially in this weather."

"Oh, I don't mind that. Good-by."

Hetzel gained the sick-room. The nurse said, "You won't have much to do, except sit down and keep quiet."

Arthur lay motionless, for all the world as if asleep, save that his eyes were open. The room was darkened. Hetzel sat down near to the window, and returning to Ruth's letter, read on by the light that stole in through the chinks in the blinds. The wind and rain played a dreary accompaniment.

"To detain you, Mr. Hetzel, with an account of my married life would be superfluous. It was as bad as I had expected it to be, and worse. It bore that relation to my anticipations which pain realized must always bear to pain conjectured. The imagination, in anticipating pleasure, generally goes beyond the reality and paints a too highly colored picture. But in anticipating suffering, it does not go half far enough. It is not powerful enough to foretell suffering in its complete intensity.

"Sweet is never so sweet as we imagine it will be; bitter is always at least a shade bitterer than we are prepared for. Imagination slurs over the little things—and the little things, trifles in themselves, are the things that add to the poignancy of suffering. Bernard Peixada had a copy of Dante's *Inferno*, illustrated by Doré, on his sitting-room table. You may guess what my life was like, when I tell you that I used to turn the pages of that book, and literally envy the poor wretches portrayed there their fire and brimstone. The utmost refinement of torture that Dante and Doré between them could conceive and describe, seemed like child's play when I contrasted it to what I had to put up with everyday. Bernard Peixada was cruel and coarse and false. It did not take him a great while to fathom the disgust that he inspired me with; and then he undertook to avenge his wounded self-love. He contrived mortifications and humiliations for me that I can not bring myself to name, that you would have difficulty in crediting. Besides, this period of my life is not essential to what I have set myself to make plain to you. It was simply a period of mental and moral wretchedness, and of bodily decline. My health, which, I think I have said, had been failing before the eighth of August, now proceeded steadily from bad to worse. It was aggravated by the daily trials I had to endure. Of course I strove to bear up as bravely as I could.

"I did not wish Bernard Peixada to have the satisfaction of seeing how unhappy he had succeeded in making me. I did not wish my poor father and mother to witness the misery I had taken upon myself in obedience to their behests. I said, 'That which is done is done, and can not be undone, therefore let it not appear what the ordeal costs you.' And in the main I think I was successful. Only occasionally, when I was alone, I would give myself the luxury of crying. I had never realized what a relief crying could be till now. But now well, when I would be seized by a paroxysm of grief that I could not control, when amid tears and sobs I would no doubt look most pitiable—it was then that I came nearest to being happy. I remember, on one of these occasions—Bernard Peixada had gone out somewhere—I was surprised by a sanctimonious old woman, a friend of his, if friendship can subsist between such people, a certain Mrs. Washington Shapiro. 'My dear,' said she, 'what are you crying for?' I was in a desperate mood. I did not care what I said; nay, more than this, I enjoyed a certain forlorn pleasure in speaking my true mind 'for once, especially to this *friend* of Bernard Peixada's. 'Oh,' I answered, 'I am crying because I wish Bernard Peixada was dead and buried.' I had to smile through my tears at the horror-stricken countenance Mrs. Shapiro now put on. 'What! You wish Bernard Peixada was dead?' she exclaimed. 'Shame upon you! How can you say such a thing!'—'He is a monster—he makes me unhappy,' I responded. 'In that case,' said Mrs. Shapiro, 'you ought to wish that you yourself were dead, not he. It is you who are monstrous, for thinking and saying such wicked things of that good man.'—'Oh,' I rejoined, 'I am young. I have much to live for. He is an old, bad man. If he should die, it would be better for every body.'—This was, as nearly as I can remember, a month or two before the night of July 30th. As I have told you, it was a piece of self-indulgence.

"I enjoyed speaking my true sentiments; I enjoyed horrifying Mrs. Shapiro. But I was duly punished. She took pains to repeat what I had said to Bernard Peixada. He did not fail to administer an adequate punishment. Afterward, when I was tried for murder, Mrs. Shapiro turned up, and retailed our conversation to the jury, for the purpose of establishing my evil disposition.

"It was in the autumn after my marriage that my father was stricken with paralysis, and died. It was better for him. If he had lived, he could not have: remained ignorant of his daughter's misery; and then he would have had to suffer the pangs of futile self reproach. Of course he left nothing for my mother. The creditors took possession of every thing. Bernard Peixada had been false to his bargain. Instead of canceling my father's indebtedness to him, as he had promised, he had simply j sold his claims. Immediately after my father's death, the creditors swooped down upon his house and shop, and sold the last stick of: furniture over my mother's head. Mr. Nathan generously bought in the things that were most precious as keep-sakes and family relics, and returned them to my mother, after the vultures had flown away. Oddly enough, they did not appear to blame Bernard Preixada—did not hold him accountable.

"They continued to regard him as a paragon of manly virtue. Perhaps he contrived some untruthful explanation, by which they were deceived I had naturally hoped that now my mother would come to live with us. It would have been a great comfort to me, if she had done so. But Bernard Peixada wished otherwise. He cunningly persuaded her that she and I had best dwell apart. So he supplied her with enough money to pay her expenses and sent her to board in the family of a friend of his.

"Well, somehow, that fall and winter dragged away. It is something terrible for me to look back at—that blackest, bleakest winter of my life. I not understand how I managed to live through it without going mad. I was a prisoner in Bernard Peixada's house. My mother and Mr. Nathan came to see me quite frequently; but Bernard was present during their visits and therefore I got but little solace from them.

"The only persons except my mother and Mr. Nathan whom Bernard Peixada permitted me to receive, were his own friends. And they were one and all hateful to me. To my friends he denied admittance, I was physically very weak. My ill health made it impossible for me to forget myself in my books. The effort of reading was too exhausting. I could not sit for more than a quarter of an hour at the piano? either, without all but fainting away. (Mr. Nathan had given me a piano for a wedding-present.) At the time I am referring to—when I was unable to play upon it—Bernard Peixada allowed me the free use of it. But afterward—when I had become stronger, and began to practice regularly—one day I found it locked. Bernard Peixada stood near by, and watched me try to open it. I looked at him, when I saw that I could not open it, and he looked at me. Oh, the contortion of his features, the twisting of his thin blue lips, the glitter of his venomous little eyes, the loathsome gurgle in his throat, as he *laughed!* He laughed at my dismay. Laughter? At least, I know no other word by which to name the hideous spasm that convulsed his voice. The result was, I passed my days moping. He objected to my leaving the house, except in his company. I had therefore to remain within doors. I used to sit at the window, and watch the life below in the street, and look across at our house—now occupied by strangers—and live over the past—my childhood, my girlhood—always stopping at the day and the hour when my father had called me from the reading of that story of Hawthorne's, to announce my doom to me. But I am wasting your time. All this is aside from the point. I did survive that winter. And when the spring came, I began to get better in health, and to become consequently more hopeful in spirit. I said, Why, you are not yet twenty-one years old. He is sixty—and feeble at that. Only try hard to hold out a little longer—a few years at the most—and he must, in the mere course of nature, die. Then you will not yet be an old woman. Life will still be worth something to you. You will have your music, and you will be rid of him.' Wicked? Unwomanly? Perhaps so; but I think it was the way every girl in my position would have felt. However, the consolation that came from thoughts like this, was short-lived. The next moment it would occur to me, 'He may quite possibly live to be ninety!' And my heart would sink at the prospect of thirty years—*thirty years*—more of life as his wife.

"In March, 1879, Bernard Peixada spoke to me as follows: 'Judith, you are not going to be a pawnbroker's wife much longer. I have, made arrangements to sell my business. I have leased a house up-town. We shall move on the 1st of May. After that we shall be a gentleman and lady of leisure.'

"Surely enough, on the 1st of May we moved. The house he had leased was a frame house, standing all alone in the middle of the block, between Eighty-fifth and Eighty-sixth Streets and Ninth and Tenth Avenues. It was a large, substantial, comfortable house, dating from Knickerbocker times. He had caused it to be furnished in a style which he meant to be luxurious, but which was, in truth, the extreme of ugliness. The grounds around it were laid out in a garden. We went to live there punctually on the 1st of May.

"Bernard Peixada now began to spend money with a lavish hand. He bought fine clothes and jewels, in which he required me to array myself. He even went to the length of purchasing a carriage and a pair of horses. Then he would make me go driving at his side through Central Park. He kept a coachman. The coachman was Edward Bolen. (Meanwhile, I must not forget to tell you, Bernard Peixada had quarreled and broken with my mother and Mr. Nathan. Now he allowed neither of them to enter his house.) I was in absolute ignorance concerning them. Once I ventured to ask him for news of them. He scowled. He said, 'You must never mention them in my presence.' And he accompanied this injunction with such a look that I was careful to observe it scrupulously thereafter. I received no letters from them. You may imagine what an addition all this was to my burden.

"But it is of Edward Bolen that I must tell you at present. He was a repulsive looking Irishman. It is needless that I should describe him. Suffice it that at first I was unsuspicious enough to accept him for what he ostensibly was—Bernard Peixada's coachman—but that ere a great while I discovered, that he was something else, besides. I discovered that he and Bernard Peixada had secrets together.

"At night, after the household had gone to bed, he and Bernard Peixada would meet in the parlor, and hold long conversations in low tones. What they talked about, I did not know. But this I did know—it was not about the horses. I concluded that they were mutually interested in some bad business—that they were hatching some villainous plots together—but, I confess, I did not much care what the business was, or what the plots were. Only, the fact that they were upon this footing of confidence with each other, struck me, and abode in my memory.

"One afternoon, about a fortnight before the thirtieth of July, Bernard Peixada had taken me to drive in Central Park. As I was getting out of the carriage, upon our return, I tripped somehow, and fell, and sprained my ankle. This sent me to my room. Dr. Gunther, Bernard Peixada's physician, attended me. He said I should not be able to walk, probably for a month.

"More than a week later, toward sunset, I was lying there on my bed. Bernard Peixada had been absent from the house all day. Now I heard his footfall below in the corridor—then on the stairs—then in the hall outside my door. I took for granted that he was coming to speak with me. I recoiled from the idea of speaking with him just then. So I closed my eyes, and pretended to be asleep.

"He came in. He approached my bedside, kept my eyes shut tight. 'Judith,' he said, did not answer—feigned not to hear. 'Judith,' repeated. Again I did not answer. He placed his hand upon my forehead. I tried not to shudder. I guess she's sound asleep,' he said; 'that's good.' He moved off.

"His words, 'that's good,' Mr. Hetzel, frightened me. Why was it 'good' that I should be asleep? Did he intend to do me a mischief while I slept? I opened my eyes the least bit. I saw him standing sidewise to me, a yard or so away. He drew a number of papers from the inside pocket of his coat. He ran them over. He laid one of them aside, and replaced the others in his pocket. Then he went to the safe—he kept a small safe in our bed-chamber—and opening the door—the door remained unlocked all day; his habit being to lock it at night and unlock it in the morning—he thrust the paper I have mentioned into one of the pigeonholes, pushed the door to, and left the room. I had seen him do all this through half closed eyes. Doubtless this was why it was 'good' for me to be asleep—so that he could do what he had done, unobserved.

"I suppose I was entirely reprehensible—that my conduct admitted of no excuse. However that may be, the fact is that an impulse prompted me to get up from my bed, and to possess myself of the paper that he had put into the safe. I did not stop to question or to combat that impulse. No sooner thought, than I jumped up—and cried out loud! I had forgotten my sprained ankle! For an instant I stood still, faint with pain, terrified lest he might have heard my scream—lest he might return, find me on my feet, divine my intention, and punish me as he knew so well how to do. But while I stood there, undetermined whether to turn back or to pursue my original idea, the terror passed away. I limped across the floor, pulled the safe door open, put in my hand, grasped the paper, drew it out, swung the door back, regained my bed.

"There I had to lie still for a little, and recover my breath. I had miscalculated my strength. The effort had exhausted me. My ankle was aching cruelly—the pains shot far up into my body. But by and by I felt better. I unfolded the paper, smoothed it out, glanced at it.. This was all I had earned by my exertions:—'R. 174.—L. 36s.—R. 222.—L. 30.' This was all that was written upon the paper. And what this meant, how could I tell? I made up my mind, after much puzzling, that it must be a secret writing—a cipher of one sort or another. I was not sorry that I had purloined it, though I was disappointed at its contents. I felt sure that Bernard Peixada could scarcely mean to employ it for good ends. So it was just as well that I should have taken it from him. I was on the point of destroying it, when I decided not to. 'No, I had best not destroy it,' I thought. 'It possibly may be of value. I will hide it where he can not find it.' I hid it beneath the mattress on which I lay.

"How absurd and unreasonable my whole proceeding had been, had it not? Much ado about nothing! With no adequate motive, and at the cost of much suffering to myself, I had committed an unnecessary theft; and the fruit of it was that incomprehensible row of figures. The whim of a sick woman. And yet, though I recognized this aspect of the case with perfect clearness, I could not find it in me to repent what I had done.

"That night Bernard Peixada and Edward Bolen talked together till past midnight, in the parlor.

"I don't know whether you believe in premonitions, in presentiments, Mr. Hetzel. I scarcely know whether I do, myself. But from the moment I woke up, on the morning of July 30th, I was possessed by a strange, vague, yet irresistible foreboding that something was going to happen—something extraordinary, something of importance. At first this was simply a not altogether unpleasant feeling of expectancy. As the day wore on, however, it intensified. It became a fear, then a dread, then a breathless terror. I could ascribe it to no rational cause. I struggled with it—endeavored to shake it off. No use. It clutched at my heart—tightly—more tightly. I sought to reassure myself, by having recourse to a little materialism. I said, 'It is because you are not as well as usual to-day. It is the reaction of body upon mind.' Despite the utmost I could say, the feeling grew and grew upon me, till it was well-nigh insupportable. Yet I could not force it to take a definite shape. Was it that something had happened, or was going to happen, to my mother? to Mr. Nathan? to me? I could not tell—all I knew was that my heart ached, that at every slightest sound it would start into my mouth—then palpitate so madly that I could scarcely catch my breath.

"I had not seen Bernard Peixada at all that day. Whether he was in the house, or absent from it, I had not inquired. But just before dinner-time—at about six o'clock—he entered my room. My heart stood still. Now, I felt, what I had been dreading since early morning, was on the point of accomplishment. I tried to nerve myself for the worst. Probably he would announce some bad news about *my* mother.—But I was mistaken. He said only this: 'After dinner, Judith, you will call the servants to your room, and give them leave of absence for the night. They need not return till to-morrow morning. Do you understand?'

"I understood and yet I did not understand. I understood the bald fact—that the servants were to have leave of absence for the night—but the significance of the fact I did not understand. I knew very well that Bernard Peixada had a motive for granting them this indulgence, that it was not due to a pure and simple impulse of good-nature on his part: but what the motive was, I could not divine. I confess, the fear that had been upon me was augmented. So long as our two honest, kindly Irish girls were in the house, I enjoyed a certain sense of security. How defenseless should I be, with them away! A thousand wild alarms beset my imagination. Perhaps the presentiment that had oppressed me all day, meant that Bernard Peixada was meditating doing me a bodily injury. Perhaps this was why he wished the servants to be absent. Unreasonable? As you please.

"'Is this privilege,' I asked, 'to be extended to the coachman, also?'

"'Who told you to concern yourself about the coachman? I will look after him,' was Bernard Peixada's reply.

"I concluded that the case stood thus:—I was to be left alone with Bernard Peixada and Edward Bolen. The pair of them had something to j accomplish in respect to me—which—well, in the fullness of time I should learn the nature of their j designs. I remembered the paper that I had stolen. Had Bernard Peixada discovered that it was missing, and concealed the discovery from me? Was he now bent upon recovering the paper? and upon chastising me, as, from his point of view, I deserved to be chastised? Again, in the fullness of time I should learn. I strove to possess my soul in patience.

"Bernard Peixada left me. One of our servants brought me my dinner. I told her that she might go out for the night, and asked her to send the other girl to my room. To this latter, also, I delivered the message that Bernard Peixada had charged me with.—When they tried me for murder, Mr. Hetzel, they produced both of these girls as witnesses against me, hoping to show, by their testimony, that I had prearranged to be alone in the house with Bernard Peixada and Edward Bolen, so that I could take their lives at my ease, with no one by to interfere, or to survive and tell the story!

"The long July twilight faded out of the sky. Night fell. I was alone in the house—isolated from the street—beyond hope of rescue—at the mercy of Bernard Peixada and his coachman, Edward Bolen. I lay still in bed, waiting for their onslaught.

"And I waited and waited; and they made no onslaught. I heard the clock strike eight, then nine, then ten, then eleven. No sign from the enemy. Gradually the notion grew upon me—I could not avoid it—that I had been absurdly deluding myself—that my alarms had been groundless. Gradually I became persuaded that my premonition had been the nonsensical fancy of a sick woman. Gradually my anxiety subsided, and I fell asleep.

"How long I slept I do not know. Suddenly I awoke. In fewer seconds than are required for writing it, I leaped from profound slumber to wide wakefulness. My heart was beating violently; my breath was coming in quick, short gasps; my forehead was wet with perspiration.

"I sat up in bed, and looked around. My night-lamp was burning on the table. There was no second person in my room. The hands of the clock marked twenty-five minutes before one.

"I listened. Stillness so deep that I could hear my heart beat.

"What could it be, then, that had awakened me so abruptly?

"I continued to listen. Hark! Did I not hear—yes, certainly, I heard—the sound of voices—of men's voices—in the room below. Bernard Peix-ada and Edward Bolen were holding one of their midnight sessions. That was all. .

"That was all: an every-night occurrence. And yet, for what reason I can not tell, on this particular night that familiar occurrence portended much to me. Ordinarily, I should have lain abed, and left them to talk till their tongues were tired. On this particular night—why, I did not stop to ask myself—swayed by an impulse which I did not stop to analyze—I got straightway out of bed, crept to the open window, and standing there in the chilling atmosphere, played the eavesdropper to the best of my powers. Was it woman's curiosity? In that event, woman's curiosity serves a good end now and then.

"The room in which they were established, was, as I have said, directly beneath my own. Their window was directly beneath my window. Their window, like mine, was open. I heard each syllable that they spoke as distinctly as I could have heard, if they had been only a yard away. Each syllable stenographed itself upon my memory. I believe that I can repeat their conversation word for word.

"Bernard Peixada was saying this: 'You know the number. Here is a plan. The house is a narrow one—only twelve feet wide. There is no vestibule. The street door opens directly into a small reception-room. In the center of this reception-room stands a table. You want to look out for that table, and not knock against it in the dark.'

"'No fear of that,' replied Edward Bolen.

"'Now look said Bernard Peixada; 'here is the door that leads out of the reception-room. It is a sliding door, always kept open. Over it hangs a curtain, which you want to lift up from the bottom: don't shove it aside: the rings would rattle on the rod. Beyond this door there is a short passage-way see here. And right here, where my pencil points, the stairs commence. You go up one flight, and reach the parlors. There are three parlors in a line. From the middle parlor a second staircase mounts to the sleeping rooms. Now, be sure to remember this: the third step—I mark it with a cross the third step *creaks*. Understand? It creaks. So, in climbing this second flight of stairs, you want to skip the third step.'

"'Sure,' was Edward Bolen's rejoinder.

"'Well and good. Now you have finished with the second flight of stairs. At the head you find yourself in a short, narrow hall. Three doors open from this hall. The front door opens into the spare bed-room, now unoccupied. The middle door opens into the bath-room. The last door opens into the room you want to get at. Which of these doors are you to pass through?'

"'The bath-room door.'

"'Precisely. That is the door which your key fits—not the door that leads straight into his room. Well, now observe. Here is the bath-room. You unlock the door from the hall into the bath-room, and—what next?'

"'I lock it again, behind me.'

"'Very well. And then?'

"'Then I open the door from the bath-room into the room I'm after. That'll be unlocked.'

"'Excellent! That will be unlocked. He never locks it. So, finally you are in the room you have been making for. Now, study this room carefully. You see, the bed stands here; the bureau, here; a sofa, here; the safe, here. There are several chairs. You want to look sharp for them."

"'I'll be sure to do that.'

"'All right. But the first thing will be to look after him. He'll probably wake up the instant you open the door from the bath-room. He's like a weasel, for light sleeping. You can't breathe, but he'll wake up. He'll wake up, and most likely call out, "Who's there? Is any one there?" or something of that sort. Don't you answer. Don't you use any threats. You can't scare him. Give him time, and he'll make an outcry. Give him a chance, and he'll fight. So, you don't want to give him either time or chance. The first thing you do, you march straight up to the bed, and catch him by the throat; hold him down on the pillow, and clap the sponge over his face. Press the sponge hard. One breath will finish his voice. Another breath will finish *him*. Then you'll have things all your own way.—Well, do you know what next?'

"'Next, I'm to fasten the sponge tight where it belongs, and pour on more of the stuff.'

"'Just so. And next?'

"'I'm to light the gas.'

"'Right again. And next?'

"'Well, I suppose the job comes next—hey?'

"'Exactly. You have learned your lesson better than I'd have given you credit for doing. The job comes next. Now you've got the gas lit, and him quiet, it'll be plain sailing. The safe stands here. It's a small affair, three, by three, by two and a half. I'll give you the combination by and by. I've got it up stairs. But first, look here. Here's a plan of the inside of the safe. Here's an inside closet, closed by an iron door. No matter about that. Here s a row of pigeon-holes, just above it seven of them—see? Now, the fifth pigeon-hole from the right-hand side—the third from the left—the one marked here with red ink—that's the one that you're interested in. All you'll have to do will be to stick in your hand and take out every thing that pigeonhole contains—every thing, understand? Don't you stop to examine them. Just lay hold of every thing and come away. What I want will be in that pigeon-hole; and if you take every thing you can't miss it. Then, as I say, all you'll have left to do will be to get out of the house and make tracks for home.'

"'And how about him? Shall I loosen the sponge?'

"'No, no. Don't stop to do that. He'll come around all right in time; or, if he shouldn't, why, small loss!'

"'Well, I reckon I understand the job pretty thoroughly now. I suppose I'd better be starting.'

"'Yes. Now wait here a moment. I'll go upstairs and get you the combination.'

"As rapidly as, with my sprained ankle, I could, I returned to my bed. I had scarcely touched my head to the pillow, when Bernard Peixada crossed the threshold. I lay still, feigning sleep. You may imagine the pitch of excitement to which the conversation I had intercepted had worked me up. But as yet I had not had time to think it over and determine how to act. Crime, theft, perhaps murder even, was brewing. I had been forewarned. What could I do to prevent it? Unless I should do something, I should be almost an accomplice—almost as bad as the conspirators themselves.

"Bernard Peixada went at once to the safe, and swung open the heavy door. I lay with my back toward him, and was unable, therefore, to watch his movements. But I could hear his hands busy with rustling papers. And then, all at once, I heard his voice, loud and hoarse, sounding like the infuriated shriek of a madman, 'I have been robbed—*robbed!*'

"Like a lightning flash, it broke upon me. I knew what the paper I had stolen was. I knew what the mysterious figures it bore meant. I had stolen the combination that Bernard Peixada had come in quest of! Without that combination their scheme of midnight crime could not be carried through! It was indispensable to their success. And I had stolen it! I thanked God for the impulse that had prompted me to do so. Then I lay still and waited. My heart was throbbing so violently, I was actually afraid that Bernard Peixada might hear it. I lay still and waited and prayed as I had never prayed before. I prayed for strength to win in the battle which, I knew, would now j shortly have to be fought.

"Bernard Peixada cried out, 'I have been robbed—*robbed!*' Then for a few seconds he was silent. Then he ran to the entrance of the room and shouted, 'Bolen, Bolen, come here.' And when Edward Bolen had obeyed, Bernard Peixada led him to the safe and said—ah, how his harsh voice shook!—said, 'Look! I have been robbed. The combination is gone. I put it in there with my own hands. It is there no longer. It has been stolen. Who stole it? If you did, by God, I'll have you hanged!'

"I had slowly and noiselessly turned over in bed. Now, through half closed eyes, I could watch the two men. Bernard Peixada's body was trembling from head to foot, as if palsy-stricken. His small, black eyes were starting from their sockets. His yellow fangs shone hideously behind his parted lips. His talons writhed, writhed, writhed. Edward Bolen stood next his master, as stolid as an ox. Edward Bolen appeared to be thinking. In a little while Edward Bolen shrugged his massive shoulders, lifted his arm, pointed to my bed, and spoke one word, '*Her.*'

"Bernard Peixada started. 'What—my wife?' he gasped.

"'Ask her,' suggested Edward Bolen.

"Bernard Peixada seemed to hesitate. Finally, approaching my bedside, 'Judith,' he called through chattering teeth..

"I did not answer—but it was not that I meant still to pretend sleep. It was that my courage had deserted me. I had no voice. I clenched my fists and made my utmost effort to command myself.

"'Judith,' Bernard Peixada called a second time.

"'Yes,' I gathered strength to respond.

"'Judith,' Bernard Peixada went on, still all a-tremble, 'have you—have you taken any papers out of my safe?'

"What use could lying serve at this crisis? There was sufficient evil in action now, without my adding answered, 'Yes—I have taken the paper you are looking for.'

"Bernard Peixada had manifestly not expected such an answer. It took him aback. He stood, silent and motionless, glaring at me in astonishment. His mouth gaped open, and the lamplight played with his teeth.

"Edward Bolen muttered, 'Eh! what did I tell you?'

"But Bernard Peixada stood motionless and silent only for a breathing-space. Suddenly flames leaped to his eyes, color to his cheek. I shall not an ineffectual lie to it. I drew a long breath, and transcribe the volley of epithets that I had now to sustain from his foul mouth. His frame was rigid with wrath. His voice mounted from shrill to shriller. He spent himself in a tirade of words. Then he sank into a chair, unable to keep his feet from sheer exhaustion. The veins across his forehead stood out like great, bloated leeches. His long, black finger-nails kept tearing the air.

"Edward Bolen waited.

"So did I.

"But eventually Bernard Peixada recovered his forces. Springing to his feet, looking hard at me, and pronouncing each word with an evident attempt to control his fury, he said, 'We have no time to waste upon you just now, madam. Bolen, here, has business to transact which he must needs be about.

Afterward I shall endeavor to have an understanding with you. At present we will dispose of the matter of prime importance. You don't deny that you have stolen a certain paper from my safe. I wish you at once, without an instant's delay or hesitation, to tell us what you have done with that paper. Where have you put it?'

"I tried to be as calm as he was. 'I will not tell you,' I replied.

"A smile that was ominous contracted his lips.

"'Oh, yes, you will,' he said, mockingly, 'and the sooner you do so, the better—for you.'

"'I have said, I will not,' I repeated.

"The same ominous, sarcastic smile: but suddenly it faded out, and was replaced by an expression of alarm. 'You—you have not destroyed it?' he asked, abruptly.

"It seemed to me that he had suggested a means for terminating the situation. This time, without a qualm, I lied. 'Yes, I have destroyed it.'

"'Good God!' he cried, and stood still, aghast.

"Edward Bolen stepped forward. He tugged at Bernard Peixada's elbow. He pointed toward me. 'Don't you see, she's lying?' he demanded roughly. Bernard Peixada started. The baleful light of his black eyes pierced to the very marrow of my consciousness. He searched me through and through. 'Ah!' he cried, with a great sigh of relief, 'to be sure, she's lying.' His yellow teeth gnawed at his under lip: a symptom of busy thinking. Finally he said, 'You have not destroyed it. I advise you to tell us where it is. I advise you to lose no time. Where is it?'

"'I will not tell you,' I answered.

"'I give you one more chance,' he said; 'where is it?'

"'I'll will not tell you.'

"'Very well. Then we shall be constrained—' He broke off, and whispered a few sentences into Edward Bolen's ear.

"Edward Bolen nodded, and left the room. Bernard Peixada glared at me. I lay still, wondering what the next act was to be, fortifying myself to endure and survive the worst.

"Bernard Peixada said, 'You are going to cause yourself needless pain. You may as well speak now as afterward. You'll be as docile as a lamb, in a minute or two.'

"I held my tongue. Presently Edward Bolen returned. He handed something to Bernard Peix-ada. Bernard Peixada turned to me. 'Which one of your ankles,' he inquired, 'is it that you are having trouble with?'

"I did not speak.

"Bernard Peixada shrugged his shoulders. 'Oh, very well,' he sneered; 'it won't take long to find out.' With that, he seized hold of the bed-clothes that covered me, and with a single motion of his arm tossed them upon the floor.

"I started up—attempted to spring from off the bed. He placed his hands upon my shoulders, and pushed me back, prostrate. I struggled with him. He summoned Edward Bolen to re-enforce him. Edward Bolen was a strong man. Edward Bolen had no difficulty in holding me down, flat upon the mattress. I watched Bernard Peixada.

"Bernard Peixada took the thing that I had seen Edward Bolen give him—it was a piece of thick twine, perhaps twelve inches in length, and attached at each end to a transverse wooden handle—he took it, and wound it about my ankle—the ankle that was sprained. Then, by means of the two wooden handles, he began to twist it around and around—and at every revolution, the twine cut deeper and deeper into my flesh—and at last they pain became more horrible than I could bear—oh, such pain, such fearful pain!—and I cried out for quarter.

"'I will tell you any thing you wish to know,' I said.

"'As I anticipated,' was Bernard Peixada's comment. 'Well, where shall we find the paper that you stole?'

"'Loosen that cord, and I will tell you—I will give it to you,' I said.

"'No,' he returned. 'Give it to me, or tell me where it is, and then I will loosen the cord.'

"'It is not here—it—it is down-stairs,' I replied, inspired by a sudden hope. If I could only get down-stairs, I thought, I might contrive to reach the door that let out of the house. Then, lame though I was, and weak and sick, I might, by a supreme effort, elude my persecutors—attain the street—summon help—and thus, not only escape myself, but defeat the criminal enterprise that they were bent upon. It was a crazy notion. At another moment I should have scouted it. But at that moment it struck me as wholly rational—as, at any rate, well worth venturing. I did not give myself time to consider it very carefully. It made haste from my mind to my lips. 'The paper,' I said, 'is down-stairs.'

"'Down-stairs?' queried Bernard Peixada, tightening the cord a little; 'where down-stairs?'

"'In—in the parlor—in the book-case—shut up in a book,' I answered.

"'In what book?'

"'I can not tell you. But I could put my hand upon it, if I were there. After I took it from the safe—you were absent from the house—I—oh, for mercy's sake, don't, don't tighten that—I crawled down-stairs—ah, that is better; loosen it a little——I crawled down to the parlor—and—and shut it up in a book. I don't remember what book. But I could find it for you if I were there.' In the last quarter hour, Mr. Hetzel, I, who had recoiled from lying at the outset, had become somewhat of an adept at that art, as you perceive.

"Bernard Peixada exchanged a glance with Edward Bolen; then said to me, 'All right. Come down-stairs with us.'

"He removed the instrument of torture. A wave of pain more sickening than any I had yet endured, swept through my body, as the ligature was relaxed, and the blood flowed throbbing back into my disabled foot. I got up and hobbled as best I could across the floor, out through the hall, down the stairs. Edward Bolen preceded me. Bernard Peixada followed.

"At the bottom of the stairs I had to halt and lean against the bannister for support. I was weak and faint.

"'Go light the gas in the parlor, Bolen,' said Bernard Peixada.

"Bolen went off. Now, I thought, my opportunity had come. The hall-door, the door that opened upon the grounds, was in a straight line, not more than twenty feet distant from me. I looked at Bernard Peixada. He was standing a yard or so to my right, in manifest unconcern. I drew one deep breath, mustered my utmost courage, prayed to God for strength, made a dash forward, reached the door, despite my lameness, and had my hand upon the knob, before Bernard Peixada appeared to realize what had occurred. But then—when he did realize—then in two bounds he attained my side. The next thing I knew, he had grasped my arm with one hand, and had twined the fingers of the other hand around my throat. I could feel the sharp nails cutting into my flesh.

"'Ah!' he cried—a loud, piercing cry, half of surprise, half of triumph. 'Ah!' And then he swore a brutal oath.

"At his touch, Mr. Hetzel, I ceased to be a woman; I became a wild beast. It was like a wild beast, that I now fought. Insensible to pain, aware only of a fury that was no longer controllable in my breast, I fought there with Bernard Peixada in battle royal. Needless to detail our maneuvers. I fought with him to such good purpose that ere a great while he had to plead for quarter, as I had had to plead up-stairs a few moments ago. Quarter I gave him. I flung him away from me. He tottered and fell upon the floor.

"Now I looked around. This was how things stood: Bernard Peixada lay—half lay, half sat—upon the floor, preparing to get up. Edward Bolen, his dull countenance a picture of amazement and stupefaction, was advancing toward us from the lower end of the hall. And—and—on a chair—directly in front of me—not two feet away—together with a hat, a pair of overshoes, a bunch of keys, a lantern—I descried my deliverance—a pistol!

"Quick as thought, I sprang forward. Next moment the pistol was mine. Again I looked around. The situation was still much the same. Clasping the butt of the pistol firmly in my hand, and gathering what assurance I could from the feeling of it, I set out once more to open the door and gain the outside of the house.

"I thought I was victress now—indisputably victress. But it transpired that I had my claims yet to assert. I slid back the bolts of the door, unhindered, it is true; but before I had managed to turn the knob and pull the door open, Edward Bolen and Bernard Peixada sprang upon me.

"There was a struggle. How long it lasted, I do not know. I heard the pistol go off—a sharp, crashing, deafening report—once, twice: who pulled the trigger, I scarcely knew. Who was wounded, I did not know. All was confusion and pain and noise, blood and fire and smoke, horror and sickness and bewilderment. I saw nothing—knew nothing—understood nothing. I was beside myself. It was a delirium. I was helpless—irresponsible.

"In the end, somehow, I got that door open. Through it all, that idea had clung in my mind—to get the door open, somehow, at any cost. Well, I got it open. I felt the fresh air upon my cheek, the perfume of the garden in my nostrils. The breeze swept in, and cut a path through the smoke, and made the gas jets flicker. Then I saw—I saw that I was free. I saw that my persecutors were no longer to be feared. I saw Edward Bolen and Bernard Peixada lying prone and bleeding upon the marble pavement at my feet.

"I have explained to you, Mr. Hetzel, the circumstances of Bernard Peixada's death. It is not necessary for me to dwell upon its consequences. At least, I need merely outline them. I need merely tell you that in due order I was taken prisoner, tried for Bernard Peixada's murder, and acquitted.

"I was taken prisoner that very night. Next morning they brought me here—to the same prison that I am again confined in now. Here I was visited by Mr. Nathan. I had sent for him, addressing him in care of the sexton of our synagogue; and he came.

"I told him what I have told you. He said I must have a lawyer—that he would engage a lawyer for me. He engaged two lawyers—Mr. Short and Mr. Sondheim. I repeated my story to them. They listened. When I had done, they laughed. I asked them why they laughed. They replied that, though my story was unquestionably true, no jury would believe it. They said the lawyer for the prosecution would mix me upon cross-examination, and turn my defense to ridicule. They said I should have to plead lunacy. I need not detain you with a rehearsal of the dispute I had with Messrs. Short and Sondheim. Eventually—in deference chiefly to the urging of Mr. Nathan—I consented to let them take their own course. So I was led to court, and tried, and acquitted. It would be useless for me to go over my trial again now in this letter. I shall say enough when I say that it was conducted in the same room that I had to plead in this morning—that the room was crowded—that I had to sit there all day long, for two mortal days, and listen to the lawyers, and the witnesses, and the judge, and support the gaze of a multitude of people. If it had not been for Mr. Nathan, I don't know how I should have lived through the ordeal. But he sat by me from beginning to end, and held my hand, and inspired me with strength and hope. My mother, meantime, I had not seen. Mr. Nathan said she was away from the city, visiting with friends, whom he named; and added that it would be kinder not to let her know what was going on. After my release, Mr. Nathan confessed that, thinking I had already enough to bear, he had deceived me. My mother had been sick; while my trial was in progress, she had died. Well, at last the trial was over, and the jury had declared me not guilty, and the prison people let me go. Mr. Nathan and I went together to an apartment he had rented in Sixty-third Street. Thither came Messrs. Short and Sondheim, and made me sign numberless papers—the nature of which I did not inquire into—and after a while I understood that I had inherited a great deal of money from Bernard Peixada—more than a hundred thousand dollars. This money I asked Mr. Nathan to dispose of, so that it might do some good. He invested it, and made arrangements to have the income divided between a hospital, an orphan asylum, a home for working women, an industrial school, and a society for the protection of children who are treated cruelly by their parents. (I have just now received a paper with a red seal on it, from which I learn that Bernard Peixada left a will, and that the money I have spoken of will have to be paid over to his brother.)

"That winter—the winter of 1879-80—Mr. Nathan and I spent alone together. For the first time since the day on which my father had told me I must marry Bernard Peixada, for the first time, I began to have a feeling of peace, and repose, and security. Mr. Nathan was so good to me—oh, such a good, kind, tender friend, Mr. Hetzel—that I became almost happy. It was almost a happiness just to spend my time near to Mr. Nathan—he was so gentle, so strong; he made me feel so safe, so far away from the storm and the darkness of the past. Was I not tormented by remorse? Did I not repent having taken two human lives? Not for one instant. I held myself wholly irresponsible. If Bernard Peixada and Edward Bolen had died by my hand, it was their own fault, their own doing. No, I did not suffer the faintest pang of remorse. Only, now and then I would remember—now and then the night of July 30th would re enact itself in my memory—and then I would shudder and grow sick at heart; but that was not remorse. It was disgust and horror. Of course I do not mean that I was happy in a positive sense, this winter. Real happiness I never knew until I met Arthur. But I was less unhappy than I had been for a long, long while.

"But in the early spring Mr. Nathan died. The last person I had left to care for, the last person who cared for me, the man who had stood as a rock of strength for me to lean upon, to whom I had perhaps been too much of a burden, but whom I had loved as a woman in my relation to him must needs have loved him—this man died. I was absolutely alone in the world. That was a dreary, desolate spring.

"Soon after his death, I received a paper something like this paper with the red seal that I have received to-day. I found that he had made a will and left me all his money. My doctor said I needed a change. I went to Europe. I traveled alone in Europe for some months, trying to forget myself in sight-seeing—in constant motion. At last I settled down in Vienna, and devoted myself to studying music. I staid about a year in Vienna. Then a spirit of restlessness seized upon me. I left Vienna and went to London.

"In London I met Mrs. Hart. We became friends at once. She was about to make a short trip on the Continent, before returning to America. She asked me to accompany her. I said I would go to the Continent with her, but that I could not return to America. She wanted to know why. I answered by telling her a little something of my recent history. I said, 'In America I am Judith Peixada—the notorious woman who killed her husband. Here I am unknown. So I will remain here.' She asked, 'How old are you?' I said, 'Twenty-three, nearing twenty-four.' She said, 'You are a child. You have a long life before you. You are wasting it, moping about in this aimless way here in Europe. Come home with me. Nobody shall recognize you for Judith Peixada. I will give you a new name. You shall be Ruth Lehmyl. Ruth Lehmyl was the name of my daughter who is dead. You may guess how dearly I love you, when I ask you to take my daughter's name. Come home and live with me, Ruth, and make me happy.'—As you know, I was prevailed upon. After a month or two spent at Aix-les-Bains, we came back to America. We dwelt for a while in an apartment on Fifty-ninth Street. Last April we moved into Beekman Place.

"This brings me to the second point. Why, with that dark stain upon my past—why, being Judith Peixada, for all my change of name—why did I consent to become Arthur Ripley's wife? Oh, Mr. Hetzel, it was because I loved him. I was a woman, and I loved him, and I was weak. He said that he loved me, that it would break his heart if I should refuse him; and I could not help it. I tried hard. I tried to act against my heart. I told him that my life had not been what he might wish it to be. I begged him to go away. But he said that he cared nothing for the past, and he urged me and pleaded with me, and I—I loved him so the temptation was so strong—it was as if he had opened the gates of heaven and invited me to enter—I caught a glimpse of the great joy—of the great sorrow, too, of the sorrow that would follow to him and to me if I sent him away—and my strength was insufficient—and we were married.

"I am very tired, Mr. Hetzel. I have been writing for so long a time that my fingers are cramped, and my back aches from bending over, and my body has become chilled through by sitting still in this damp place, and my head is thick and heavy. Yet I have some things still left to say. You must pardon me if I am stupid and roundabout in coming to the point. And if I do not succeed in making what I have on my mind very clear to you, you must excuse me on the ground that I am quite worn out.

"As I have said, I was frank with Arthur Ripley. I warned him that my past life had been darkened by sin. I said, 'If you knew about it, you would not care to marry me.' He retorted, The past is dead. You and I have just been born.' It did indeed seem so to me—as though I had just been born. I allowed myself to be persuaded. We were married. But then, Mr. Hetzel, as soon as I had yielded, I said to Arthur, 'It is not right that I, your betrothed, should keep a secret from you. I will tell you the whole story.' I said this to him on more than one occasion before we were married. And I repeated it again and again afterward. But every time that I broached the subject, he put it aside. He answered, 'No. Keep your secret as a reminder of my unwavering confidence and perfect love.' I supposed that he was sincere. I marveled at his generosity, and loved him all the better, because of it. Yet what was the truth? The truth was that in his inmost heart? he could not help wishing to know what his wife's secret was. But he played the hypocrite. He forbade me to tell it to him—forbade me to unseal my lips—and so got the credit for great magnanimity. Then, behind my back, he associated with Benjamin Peixada, and learned from his lips—not my secret—no, but the false, distorted version of it, which Bernard Peixada's brother would delight to give. What Benjamin Peixada told him, he believed; and it was worse than he had bargained for. When he understood that his wife had committed *murder*, that his wife had stood, a common criminal, at the bar of the court of General Sessions, lo! all the love that he had boasted, died an instant death. And then—this is what is most infamous—then he contrived a cruel method of letting me know that he knew. Instead of coming to me, and telling me in a straightforward way, he put that advertisement into the paper. That, I do think, was infamous. And all the time, he was pretending that he loved me, and I was believing him, and treating him as a wife treats her husband. I read that advertisement, and was completely deceived by it. I went to Benjamin Peixada's place. 'What do you wish with me?' I asked. He answered, 'Wait a little while, and the gentleman who wrote that advertisement will come and explain to you. Wait a little while, and I promise you a considerable surprise.' I waited. The gentleman came. The gentleman was Arthur. Not content with having decoyed me to that place in that way, he—he called me by that name—he called me Mrs. Peixada! The surprise was considerable, I confess. And yet, you and Mrs. Hart wonder that I am indignant.

"Oh, of course, I understand that Arthur had no share in causing my arrest. I understand that all he intended was to confront me there in Benjamin Peixada's office, and inform me that he knew who I was, and denounce me, and repudiate me. But Benjamin Peixada had a little plan of his own to carry through. When Arthur saw what it was—when he saw that Benjamin Peixada had set a trap for me, and that I was to be taken away to prison—then he was shocked and pained, and felt sorry for what he had helped to do. You don't need to explain that to me. That is not why I feel the deep resentment toward him which, I admit, I do feel. The bare fact that he pried into my secrets behind my back, and went on pretending to love me at the same time, shows me that he never truly loved me. You speak of my seeing him. It would be useless for me to see him. He could not undo what he has done. All the explanations and excuses that he could make, would not alter the fact that he went to work without my knowledge, and found out what I had again and again volunteered to tell him. If he suffers from supposing that I think he had a share in causing my imprisonment, you may tell him that I think no such thing. Tell him that I understand perfectly every thing that he could say. Tell him that a meeting between us would only be productive of fresh pain for each.

"Mr. Hetzel, if you were a woman, and if you had ever gone through the agony of a public trial for murder in a crowded court-room, and if all at once you beheld before you the prospect of going through that agony for a second time, I am sure you would grasp eagerly at any means within your reach by which to escape it. That is the case with me. I am a woman. I have been tried for murder once—publicly tried, in a crowded court-room. I would rather spend all the rest of my life in prison, than be tried again. That is why I pleaded guilty this morning. If there were any future to look forward to—if Arthur had acted differently—if things were not as they are—then, perhaps—but it is useless to say perhaps. I have nothing to live for—nothing worth purchasing at the price of another trial.

"Does any thing remain for me to say? I do not think of any thing. I hope I have made what I had to say clear enough. I beg that you will forgive me, if I have trespassed beyond the limits of friendship, in writing at such length.

"Yours sincerely,

"Ruth Ripley.

"Mr. Julian Hetzel, 43 Beekman Place."

CHAPTER XII.
"THE FINAL STATE O' THE STORY."

ON Thursday, August 14th, at about half, past one in the afternoon, Assistant-district-attorney Romer was seated in his office, poring over a huge law-book', and smoking a huge cigar, when the door suddenly flew open, and in came, or more accurately, in burst Mr. Julian Hetzel. In one hand Hetzel carried a dripping umbrella; the other hand was thrust deep into the breast of its owner's coat. Hetzel's face wore an expression of intense excitement.

Romer lifted his eyes from off his law-book, removed his cigar from between his lips, and ejaculated, "Hello! What's up now?"

Hetzel hurried straight ahead, till he had reached the edge of Romer's desk. Then, extracting a ponderous envelope from the inner pocket of his coat, he threw it emphatically down upon Romer's blotting pad, and cried, "Read that—will you?—and tell me what you think of it."

Romer picked the envelope up, looked inquiringly at its superscription, inserted thumb, and forefinger, drew out its contents, unfolded the same, turned to the beginning, scanned perhaps the first dozen lines, stopped, ran the pages rapidly over to the end, found the signature, then glanced up, and asked, "Are you in a hurry? Have you plenty of time to spare? Because it's a pretty serious undertaking—to read this through."

"Here—give it to me," returned Hetzel. "I've been over it once, and got familiar with the handwriting. I'll read it to you."

Hetzel read Ruth Ripley's letter aloud to Romer. The reading consumed rather more than an hour. Not once did Romer interrupt, or Hetzel pause. At the end, the two men looked at each other in silence. By and by Romer's lips opened.

"By—by God!" was all he said.

Then he began to pace uneasily to and fro across the room.

"Well," asked Hetzel, "do you think that that's the sort of a woman to be left locked up in the Tombs prison?"

"Heavens and earth!" cried Romer; and continued his promenade.

"But the question is," said Hetzel, "whether she's to be left there in the Tombs. In view of what she has written down in those papers, can't we get her out? I want to take her home before nightfall to-day. It seems to me, it's an outrage upon humanity for her to remain locked up an hour longer.

You're acquainted with the practical side of this kind of thing. Now, give me your opinion."

Romer knitted his brows, and kept on moving back and forth, up and down the room, Gradually, pendulum-fashion, the space covered at each turn shortened somewhat; until finally coming to a standstill, Romer said, "Yes, by Jove! You're right. She sha'n'. spend another night in that place if I can help it; and I think I can."

"Good and the less time lost, the better."

"What I mean to do," said Romer, "is this. I mean to take a pretty big responsibility upon my shoulders, but I guess I'm safe in doing so. I'm sure Mr. Orson would approve, if he were here; and as long as he isn't here, I'm going to act on that assumption, and run the chances of getting his approval after the fact. The homicide that that woman committed—why, it was a clear case of self-defense. And what I'm going to take the responsibility of doing is this. I shall send down to the Tombs and have her brought up here—to my office—without a moment's delay. While the officers are gone after her, I'll run into court and speak privately to the judge. I'll lay these facts before him, and tell him that we, the People, are convinced that it was a plain case of justifiable homicide; and I'll ask him to let her withdraw her plea of guilty, and enter one of not guilty, right away. He can't refuse, if I put it on that ground. I'll ask him, moreover, as a personal favor to me, to have the court-room cleared of people, so that she? won't be obliged to face the music again to-day, as she was yesterday. I can't promise that he'll agree to this; but it isn't at all impossible. Well and good. I'll make these arrangements before she arrives. When she does arrive, I'll talk to her. You leave me to do the talking. Then we'll go with her into the judge's presence, and have her do what's necessary there. And then, in your sight and in hers, so that all doubt on that score will be cleared away for good and all, I'll *nolle* the indictment! That is to say, I'll render the indictment null and void by indorsing upon it a *nol. pros.*, together with a memorandum to the effect that the district-attorney is persuaded of the defendant's innocence. Do you understand?"

"Yes," said Hetzel, "I think I understand. And if you can only succeed in doing this, we—we'll—" Hetzel's voice broke. Before he was able to recover it, Romer had left the room.

Half an hour, or thereabouts, elapsed. Hetzel waited as patiently as he could—which is not saying much. Every five minutes, he had out his watch. It was nearly half past three when at last Romer reappeared.

"Well?" Hetzel made haste to inquire.

"Well," said Romer, "congratulate me! The judge agrees to do every thing, just as I wished. At first he was disposed to hesitate. Then I read him that part where she describes the application of the torture. That finished him. They're just winding up a larceny case at this moment. He's on the point of sentencing the prisoner. After that's over, he'll have the court-room emptied, and be ready for us. She ought to get here any minute now, and—" Romer paused; for, at this moment, the door of his office opened, and Mrs. Ripley entered the room.

She halted just across the threshold, looked from Romer to Hetzel, bowed slightly to the latter, and then stood still in passive attendance.

Romer advanced toward her, and said, very gently, "I beg of you, Mrs. Ripley, to come in and sit down. I have something to say, and I shall thank you very much if you will listen. Sit down here in this easy-chair.—There.—Now, when you are ready, I'll speak."

"I am ready," she said. Her voice was faint and weak. She leaned back in her chair, as though feeble and exhausted. Her face was intensely white—snow-white beneath its coronet of raven hair. There were large, dark circles under her eyes.

"Mrs. Ripley," began Romer—then hesitated—then began anew, "Mrs. Ripley, I—that is, Mr. Hetzel—Mr. Hetzel has given me the letter you wrote him yesterday, and I have read it. I dare not trust myself to—to say what—to say any thing about it, more than this, that we—the district-attorney's office—that we are sorry, very, very sorry for all that has happened—for all that you have been made to suffer these last few days, and that—that we are anxious to do every thing in our power to make amends. Of course I know we never can make amends in full. I know that. We can't undo what has been done—can't cure the pain that you've already had to bear. But—but we can spare you—we can save you from having to suffer any more pain, and—and then, you know, being ignorant of the real truth, as we were, it wasn't altogether our fault, was it? No; the original fault lay with your lawyers, Short and Sondheim, when you were first tried, years ago. They—they ought to have been strung and quartered, because, if they had had you tell your story to the district-attorney then, and if you had told it in its completeness, as you have in this letter, why—why, nobody would have doubted your innocence for a moment, and you would have been spared no end of trouble and sorrow and mortification. But that's neither here nor there. It's too late to complain of Short and Sondheim. They have an inborn antipathy to the truth, and always fight as shy of it as they can. There's no use raking up bygones. The point is now that we want to set you at liberty as quickly as possible. That's the most we can do. We mean to *nolle* the indictment against you—which will be as complete an exoneration as an acquittal by a jury and an honorable discharge by a judge would be. That's what we intend to do. But first—before we can do that—first, you know, you will have to untie our hands by withdrawing the plea that you put in yesterday, and by entering in place of it a plea of not guilty. Then you'll be a free woman. Then you can go home with Mr. Hetzel, here, and rest assured that you'll never be troubled any more about the matter."

Ruth sat perfectly still in her chair. Her great, melancholy eyes were fixed upon the wall in front of her. She made no answer.

"Now," Romer said, after having waited in vain for her to speak, "now, if you will be so good, I should like to have you come with me into the court room, in order, you know, to do what I have said."

At this, Ruth winced perceptibly. "Oh," she said, very low, "must—must I go into court again?"

"Oh, this time," explained Romer, "it will not be as hard for you as it was before. There'll be, no spectators and no red tape. You'll tell the judge that you withdraw your plea of guilty, and plead not guilty, and he'll say all right; and then you'll see me *nolle* the indictment; and then it will all be over for good; and, as I've said, you'll go home with Mr. Hetzel."

Ruth rose, bowed to Romer, and said, "I am ready to follow you."

"Is there any objection to my accompanying you?" Hetzel asked.

"Oh, no; come along," said Romer.

Every thing befell substantially as Romer had predicted. They found the judge presiding over an empty court-room. His honor came down informally from the bench, bade Mrs. Ripley be seated, said laughingly, "I'll act as clerk and judge both," went to the clerk's desk, possessed himself of pen, ink, and paper, rattled off *sotto voce,* "You, Judith Peixada, do hereby"—mumble, mumble, mumble—"and enter in lieu of the same"—mumble, mumble—"upon the indictment;" threw down his pen, got up, added in a loud, hearty voice, "That's all, madam: good day," bowed, and left the room.

A few minutes later Ruth was seated at Hetzel's side in a carriage; and the carriage was making at top-speed for Beekman Place. After they had driven for half a dozen blocks in silence, Hetzel began, "Mrs. Ripley, I am sorry to disturb you. I suppose you are so tired that you would rather not be talked to. But there is something which you must hear before we reach home; and I must beg of you to give me permission to say it now—at once."

"Say any thing you wish. I will listen to any thing you wish to say." Her voice was that of a woman whose spirit has been quite broken and subdued.

"Well, then, the upshot of what I have to say is just this. Don't for a moment imagine that I mean to reproach you. Under the circumstances—considering the shock and the pain of your situation last Monday—you weren't to be blamed for jumping to a false conclusion. But now, at last, you are in a position to see things as they truly are. What I want to say is what Mrs. Hart wanted to say when she visited you on Tuesday. It is that Arthur—that your husband—had no more idea, when he put that advertisement into the papers, that you were Judith Peixada, than I had, or than the most indifferent person in the world had. When you fancy that he had been trying to find out your secrets behind your back, you do him a—a tremendous injustice. He never would be capable of such a thing. Arthur is the frankest, honestest fellow that ever lived. He doesn't know what deception means. The amount of the matter was simply this. He had been retained by Mr. Peixada to hunt up his brother's widow. In order to accomplish this, he resorted to a device which, I suppose, precedents seemed to justify, though it strikes me as a pretty shabby one, notwithstanding—he advertised. And when he went to meet Mrs. Peixada in his client's office, and found that she and you were one and the same person, why, he was as much astonished as—as I was when he came home and told me about it. There's the long and short of the story in a nutshell. The detail of it you'll learn when you talk it over with him."

Hetzel waited, expecting Ruth to speak. But she did not speak for a long while. She sat rigid in her corner, with pale face and downcast eyes. At last, however, her lips opened. In a whisper, "Will—will he ever forgive me?" she asked.

"Forgive you?" repeated Hetzel. "He doesn't feel that he has any thing to forgive you for. On the other hand, he hopes for your forgiveness—hopes you will forgive him for having refused to let you speak. It was a coincidence and a mistake. He loves you. When that is said, every thing is said."

For another long while Ruth kept silence. As the carriage turned into Fiftieth Street, she straightened up, and drew a deep, tremulous breath. After a brief moment of hesitation, she said, "I—I suppose he is waiting for us—yes?"

"Well," Hetzel answered, "that reminds me. You—you see, the fact is—"

And thereupon the poor fellow had to break the news of Arthur's illness to her, as best he could. Beginning with that hour, the trained nurse had an indefatigable companion in her vigils.

One morning Ruth said to Hetzel, "To-day is the day fixed for the probate of Bernard Peixada's will. Do you think it is necessary that I should go to the court?"

"I don't know," replied Hetzel, "and I don't care. You sha'n'. do so. I'll be your proxy."

He went to the surrogate's office. When he returned home, he said, "Well, Mrs. Ripley, the enemy has had his Waterloo! The orphan asylum and the home for working-girls will continue to enjoy Bernard Peixada's wealth."

"Why, how is that?" Ruth questioned.

"The will fell through."

"Fell through? Was it a forgery? Or what?"

"No, it wasn't a forgery, but it was a holograph. That is to say, the testator was rash enough to draw it himself—without the assistance of a lawyer; and so he contrived to make a fatal blunder. It seems that the law requires a person, upon signing his will, to explain explicitly to the witnesses the nature of the document—that it *is* a will, and not a deed, or a contract, or what not. And that is precisely what Mr. Peixada fortunately omitted to do. The witnesses swore that he had said nothing whatever concerning the character of the instrument—that he had simply requested them to attest his signature, and then had folded the paper up, and put it into his pocket. The lawyer—Arthur's successor—pressed them pretty hard, but they weren't to be shaken; and the clerk thereupon declared that the will was void and valueless; and then there was a lot of excitement; and I came away; and that's how the case stands at present."

"And so the money will remain where it is?"

"Precisely; though I should think the man to whom it once belonged would turn in his grave, at the thought of the good it's doing. This is the sort of thing that helps one to believe in an avenging angel, isn't it?"

One Sunday afternoon, toward the middle of September, Ruth was very happy. The crisis of Arthur's illness, Dr. Letzup vouched, had passed. His delirium had subsided. He had fallen into a placid slumber. With proper care and vigilant guarding against a relapse, the doctor thought, he ought to be upon his feet within a month.

So, it was natural that Ruth's heart should sing.

But, especially when one is a songstress by birth and training, a singing heart is apt to induce sympathetic action on the part of the voice. Ruth was seated at the window in the room adjoining Arthur's, listening to her heart's song, when, most likely without her being conscious of it, a soft, sweet strain of melody began to flow from her lips. It was very low and gentle, and yet, as the event proved, it was loud enough to arouse the invalid from his much needed sleep. The nurse came bustling in from the sick room, with finger raised in warning, and exclaimed in a whisper, "Hush—hush—sh—sh! You've gone and waked him up!"

Was it possible that she had so far forgotten herself? Oh, dear, dear! Her regret bordered upon despair. Yet, with the impetuosity that is characteristic of her sex, she could not stop there, and let bad enough alone, but must needs be guilty of still further imprudence, and march bodily into the sick man's presence, and up close to his bedside.

He lay with open eyes looking straight ceiling-ward. But at the moment of her entrance he turned his gaze full upon her, and a happy smile lighted up his wan, wasted face. He did not attempt to speak. Neither did she. But she bent over him, and kissed him once upon the forehead, and rewarded his smile with a glance of infinite tenderness.

Then his lips moved. "Was—was it all a dream—my meeting you in Peixada's office, and all the rest?" he whispered.

"Yes—all a dream?" she answered.

He closed his eyes and went to sleep again. When Dr. Letzup called that evening, "Better and better!" he cried. "What panacea have you been administering during my absence?"

On Saturday, October 18th, the steamship Alcibiades, Captain Gialsamino, of the Florio line, sailed from its berth in Brooklyn, and pointed its prow towards Naples. Inscribed on the passenger-list were the names: "M. and Mme. A. Ripli." Monsieur and Madame Ripley were bent upon wintering in Italy. They have remained abroad ever since. Arthur talks in his letters of coming home next spring, though what he will do when he gets here, I don't know, for he has registered a solemn vow never again to practice law.

THE END.

Milton Keynes UK
Ingram Content Group UK Ltd.
UKHW011141220424
441551UK00007B/735